LOVING BEATRICE

MARYANNE FANTALIS

CITY OWL
PRESS

LOVING BEATRICE
Shakespeare's Women Speak, Book 2

CITY OWL PRESS
www.cityowlpress.com

Cover Design by Mibl Art. All stock photos licensed appropriately.

Edited by Tee Tate.

For information on subsidiary rights, please contact the publisher at info@cityowlpress.com.

Print Edition ISBN: 978-1-949090-51-2

Digital Edition ISBN: 978-1-949090-52-9

Printed in the United States of America

To my beloved Aunt Lydia,
my godmother Aunt Elaine,
and
Aunt Helene,
wise and witty women
who could teach Beatrice a thing or two.

PRAISE FOR MARYANNE FANTALIS

"Full of familiar characters and new insights, Finding Kate is a smart and subtle retelling, rich in Shakespearean references and vivid historical details."
- YA Historical Fiction Author, Katherine Longshore

"An amazing book about partnership and knowing someone better than they know themselves and sacrificing something in yourself to help someone else find themselves. Beautifully written!"
- Bookworm100

"I love the idea of taking Shakespeare's plays and rewriting them from the heroine's point of view. Brilliant."
- Contemporary Author, Jessie Gussman

"The period elements are well done and the writing is beautiful. Perfect for a Sunday afternoon read."
– Examiner's Women in Horror Recommended Author, Danielle DeVor

"A new perspective on Shakespeare's The Taming of the Shrew...Ms. Fantalis's period detail shines."
- Historical Fiction Author, Brodie Curtis

CHAPTER 1

We had gathered in the great hall of Ashley House to hear my Aunt Ursula's plans for the annual harvest masque, soon to be upon us. I stood with my cousins, Eleanor, Mary, and Grace, as Aunt Ursula described her rapturous vision of the hall as an autumnal forest, with indoor trees and a night sky of glittering candles overhead, sweeping her arms in wide arcs to demonstrate where each secret glen, each fountain of wine, would be placed.

My aunt did quite love a good party.

I stood arm in arm with my cousin Grace, Aunt Ursula's only daughter, wondering just how much of this work was going to be shunted off onto me, when my attention was caught by a door opening at the rear of the hall. Hoping for an interruption, I turned that way, pulling Grace along with me, motioning at the door, when she began to complain. Her father, my Uncle Lionel, came stumping in, a parchment clutched in his hand. Uncle Lionel, owing to a long-ago injury, had a heavy limp and used a cane, the thick wood striking the stone flags firmly and echoing to the high rafters. Nevertheless, Aunt Ursula seemed not to note his presence.

I cleared my throat to gain her attention. She went on talking.

Uncle Lionel came closer. The parchment fluttered in his grasp as he lofted it before him like a torch in a dark place.

"Mother," Grace said, her voice pitched to break through the flowing stream of Aunt Ursula's inspiration. Yet Aunt Ursula turned away from us, explaining how the cleared area for dancing would—perhaps, if she could arrange it—be made to appear as a clear, still pond.

Uncle Lionel neared, a dusty, exhausted-looking fellow trailing in his wake. "My lady," he called.

At last, she turned toward her husband. She drew her brows together and tiny lines of annoyance formed above her nose. Truly, Aunt Ursula lived for her parties. "Yes, my lord, what is it?"

Uncle Lionel hauled himself to a stop beside his wife, thrusting the letter out before him. The travel-weary lad now stood a short distance away, twisting his cap between his hands. Aunt Ursula looked him over, her expression shifting to apprehension. Given the discord in our kingdom in recent years, the arrival of messengers with urgent commissions had long been a reason for dread. As it was only a few weeks since there had been a battle in the west of England that ended with the old king dead and a new king crowned, we all had cause for concern, for our household had sent many a young man to the fight.

"What news, husband?" Aunt Ursula asked.

"I learn in this letter that his majesty the king comes this day to our home," he crowed, waving the parchment over his head yet again.

Mary squealed and clapped a hand over her mouth. Grace tightened her arm through mine, squeezing me against her. "The king?" she whispered, though no one could hear her save me.

Aunt Ursula stiffened. "His majesty the king?"

The rider stepped forward. Now I could see the fine green and white doublet and green hose beneath the layer of road dust. Green and white, the colors of our new king. "I am sent before his majesty King Henry to alert Lord Ashley's household that the royal party will be here anon. They were not three leagues off when I left them."

Aunt Ursula began to quiver with the desire—nay, the *need*—to move. Much as she loved to organize a celebration, unexpectedly hosting a king and his party in one's home was an entirely different sort of task. Something on the order of planning a military campaign, one might imagine.

"And how large a party is it?" I inquired, attempting to sound merely curious, not at all concerned.

"King Henry himself comes and brings the Princess Elizabeth, his 'trothed bride, as well as his lady mother and some small number of ladies and gentlemen of their court. Mainly gentlemen who fought with him in the recent ended battle wherein the usurper fell."

The victor decides who is the usurper, I thought but did not say.

Uncle Lionel added, "And you will be glad to know that the king informs me in this letter that the men of Ashley House acquitted themselves proudly in his service, and that none were lost, and only a few at all wounded."

Aunt Ursula hurried to cross herself but would not be diverted. "Thanks be to God," she said, "but what are we to feed them, husband?" She huffed out a deep breath and turned to the steward, who had also followed Uncle Lionel in. "Banks," she said, "see to it that this man is rested and clean before his majesty arrives. Thank you, sirrah, for your message."

Both men bowed and turned to leave.

As Aunt Ursula dragged Uncle Lionel off to issue orders to the servants, and as Mary gushed about the imminent arrival of dozens, perhaps hundreds, of eligible gentlemen, I took a few steps after the messenger.

"I say, good fellow," I called out to him.

The rider, eager for refreshment, did not stop walking, but he turned his face toward me. "Aye, milady?"

In retrospect, I should have asked him straight if he had any news of the men who had left here to fight with the king. It was not a difficult question, after all. But if I asked outright, my cousins might think... Mary especially would never let me free from her teasing... So in the moment, I blurted, "Tell me, good fellow, is my lord Quintain among the king's party?"

He gave me a puzzled look. "I—that is an odd name, lady. I know of no lord by that name."

My younger cousins giggled behind my back. Grace, most like a sister and yet ignorant of the reason behind my question, tugged at my arm, under her breath scolding me for impertinence. When I did not elaborate, and the messenger began to walk away, Grace took a step forward, forcing herself to speak despite her shyness. "My cousin means one Edmund Benedict. He was a member of our household here and a dear friend of the family, and so she wonders if he has returned with the king."

"Oh, aye," the fellow said, still peering at me and shifting his feet in his eagerness to be on his way. "There is such a gentleman among the king's men. *Sir* Edmund he is, since the battle, and high in the king's favor for his loyalty and deeds of bravery."

Sir Edmund. I was stunned into silence, and the messenger took the moment to make his escape. Grace took a firm hold of my arms, turning me to look at her. "Beatrice," she said. "Lord Quintain? Why did you mock our dear Benedict to the messenger?"

"*Sir* Edmund now," I corrected her, still struggling to absorb this change in his fortunes. "Don't imagine that he'll be 'our dear Benedict' any longer, now that he stands so 'high in the king's favor.'" I found myself struggling to breathe. It seemed my heart had taken up residence in my very throat and was pounding like a hammer on an anvil. "'Deeds of bravery'," I said, surprised at how bitter my voice sounded. "How many soldiers do you suppose he killed since he left? For I promised him I would eat all of his killing." Among other fierce and hurtful words.

Grace stared at me. She might have questioned me further, but Uncle Lionel returned just at that moment, leaning far more on his cane now. "Mary, Eleanor," he called as he entered, "pull me up a chair, will you?"

Together, the girls dragged one of the heavy armchairs from the side of the room closer to where we all stood, so that they, the chair, and he all arrived at the same moment. He sighed and eased himself into the chair, rubbing at the old wound in his thigh. "Now, my girls, gather round and heed me."

The younger ones, Mary and Eleanor, settled on the floor at his feet. Grace and I stood close by. He looked at us each in turn, his gaze like the warm touch of his hand in blessing. Grace, his only child and heir, and by far the most beautiful of us, with rich dark hair and eyes to match. Mary, already a lush woman at sixteen. Eleanor, a fey and simple child who, it seemed, might never truly grow up. And last of all, me, untamed in every way—unruly hair, sharp-angled features, wayward will, shrewd tongue. Of all of us, mayhap I was the only one who knew whereof he would speak and was ready with a reply.

"My girls," he said. "I have loved you and raised you all together with no regard for whether you were my daughters or not. In my heart, and my wife's, you are all our children. Today, with the king's arrival, you have a chance that will never come to you again. Thus, I trust you will heed me as your father in this moment."

I tried not to hide my face in my hand.

"Among the king's party, there will be gentlemen of title and rank who have braved hardship alongside the king these last few years and fought alongside him at Bosworth last month, helping to ensure his place on the throne. Even our own young Benedict has achieved good fortune in so doing, being knighted on the very field of battle."

Eleanor clapped her hands for him, and I had to breathe against the fluttering of my heart at the simple mention of his name.

What did his return bode?

I could not keep silent. "And in addition to lands and titles and gold, the king wishes to give them the one remaining gift they need to secure their good fortune."

Uncle Lionel gave me a sour look. "Why such anger in your tone, niece? It does not cheapen you or your cousins to speak in this way. You are indeed worthy prizes that need to be earned, true rewards for worthy men. So should you think of yourselves."

Eleanor looked confused. "Prizes? Where? Are there prizes for us?"

My uncle stroked her hair. "Never you mind, sweet thing. I shall find you a gift when the king comes. Would you like that?"

"Oooh, yes, please Uncle!" Eleanor clapped again. At least, it seemed, Uncle planned to keep her safe from the predations of men.

Grace leaned over and took my hand in hers. "Father," she said, "surely you will not offer us like calves at the spring market."

"Of course not," he said. "You will meet the gentlemen when they arrive, and you will have opportunity to speak with them, get to know them, and they you. But in the end, this is a decision for those older and wiser than you, and you will be guided by us."

"Uncle," I said, as my cousins nodded, "if I may be permitted to speak..."

"My dear Beatrice," he said with an indulgent smile, "when have we ever been able to silence you?"

I smiled back. "Uncle, I think we would all agree that cousin Mary is full ready for marriage. Indeed, one can scarce stop her from throwing herself in the path of any man she sees." I pulled my leg aside to avoid her backward-thrown elbow. "Further, I think we all agree that Eleanor is yet young and innocent and should be protected from such as would be required of her in marriage. At least for a time." My uncle nodded, and I continued. "Grace, as your child and heir, is the greatest prize among us." I squeezed her hand to show I meant no disrespect with the word. "She will be greatly sought after as a bride. Yet her temperament is shy and reserved, and she is uncomfortable speaking with strange men. Permit me to remove myself from the hazard so that I may spend my time with her, helping her to be wooed and to prepare herself to be a bride."

Now my uncle frowned. "Beatrice, you are an heiress in your own right.

Many men would overlook your sharp tongue for your fortune and your fair face."

I sighed. Was that meant to make me feel good about myself? "So you say, Uncle, and so it may be, but you do not consider that mayhap I do not wish them to do so."

If possible, my uncle's look grew darker. "Are you saying that you do not wish to marry?" All my cousins, too, looked at me, incredulous. "I know you have said this from time to time since you were younger than Eleanor, but your aunt and I always thought it was a game you were playing, a jest born of your high spirits and agile wit." The cloud forming on his brow grew ever more fearsome. "Are you saying now that you have no intention of heeding me?"

Careful, Beatrice. "I intend no disrespect, Uncle. But consider that you and Aunt Ursula will need someone to care for you in your age and infirmity..."

He scoffed and waved a hand at me. "Let not my weakness be an excuse for you to reject a proper suitor. I have been infirm half my life and have never needed anyone to care for me."

"Except for Mother," Grace teased with a gentle smile.

"And you shall take her place when I am old and feeble, will you not, my dear girl?"

"Of course, Father," she replied, inclining her head.

"There, you see?" Uncle said, turning his gaze back to me. "My daughter will care for me, so you have no excuse for your foolish saying."

"I suspect there is some other reason Beatrice does not want to share, Father," Grace said, still gripping my hand with hers. She was right, of course, though she did not know quite what it was.

"Well, I urge you to converse with yourself roundly and talk yourself out of it," he said, pushing himself out of his chair. "By the time the king departs, I intend to have only one child unmarried under this roof."

We scrambled to our feet, Eleanor whispering in Mary's ear, "Which one?" as we curtsied to him.

Mary whispered a quick explanation in her sister's ear, then whirled on me. "What on earth are you about, Beatrice?" she demanded. "You cannot mean to remain unmarried."

Just the word "unmarried" set my teeth on edge, for I could only hear it as we had spoken it two years ago, Benedict and me, before he left to join King Henry in France. Before King Henry was King Henry, when he was still merely the Earl of Richmond living in exile. Said with anger and bitterness and hurt.

"So you will depart unmarried then, and leave me thus, with no promise, no hope?"

"Aye, I will. Beatrice, you know I must."

"Then go, and God's blessings on you. I hope never to see you again."

In reply to Mary, I could only toss my head and say, "I may marry or not, for certes not in a fortnight. Uncle Lionel will not frighten me into it. I have not met a man who could tempt me to surrender myself and my freedom." Which, of course, was not true. I had met him, and he had left.

"But what will you do with your life if you do not marry?" Mary was incredulous. Indeed, what else was there for a woman of wealth and title?

I sighed. "I am sure, if Uncle grows tired of keeping me and my sharp tongue in his house, I can find a place among the good sisters over in Woking."

Grace blinked. "Surely you do not mean to enter the church? Beatrice, you would make a terrible nun."

I laughed. "Aye, you are right. I could not be a nun. A Mother Superior, mayhap. I do so enjoy telling people what to do." My cousins laughed with me. "Or do you suppose I might go to sea and become a pirate?"

Grace groaned. "Oh, Beatrice, will you not be serious?"

"Nay, not till a hot January."

The sudden scurrying of servants toward the front of the house alerted us to the arrival of the royal party. Mary and Eleanor looked at each other, eyes wide, and hurried out of the hall, while Grace and I followed at a slower pace, arm in arm. I persuaded myself that our stateliness was natural to our greater age and dignity, but in fact it was simply a combination of Grace's shyness tilting toward abject fear with my reluctance to face what awaited me in the courtyard: seeing Benedict again—*Sir Edmund* now. Why could I not cease repeating that to myself, like rubbing lemon juice into a cut? How would he seem? What would he say? What should *I* say?

Out in the packed dirt yard, horses stamped and paced, stirring up little whirlwinds under their hooves. Their earthy scent lingered in the air. Stable boys scurried to hold their headstalls and place wooden blocks for riders to dismount. Porters lugged trunks, baskets, and boxes into the house, suggesting this was more than a pleasant afternoon's visit. On the other side of the yard, three servants helped an older woman in head-to-toe black out of an elaborate litter. Uncle Lionel and Aunt Ursula stood with my cousins at the bottom of the steps, speaking with a well-dressed, serious-looking man wearing a gold circlet about his brows. I might have more courage than Grace, but even I missed a step. That could only be King Henry.

"Deep breath," I whispered, squeezing her arm as we descended the steps. "And pluck up your courage."

We descended the stairs to join the group there. For a few moments, at least, I could observe our new sovereign unnoticed. Because he had claimed his throne by conquest and defeated King Richard III in battle, I had imagined a strong and gallant knight, a man accustomed to feats of arms and days in the saddle. Someone physically imposing, charismatic, and charming.

That was not this king.

King Henry was entirely ordinary, like someone had scrounged in the basement of a church and found a likely clerk or not-yet-professed monk and dragged him up into the daylight, swapped his habit for finery, and put a circlet on his head. His hair was the color of dirty dish-water and hung arrow straight to his shoulders. His eyes were pale—perhaps blue, perhaps grey—as he squinted in the sun, and he was neither tall nor imposing. In fact, he looked suspicious, as though he could scarce believe this was happening, as though he suspected someone was lurking with a knife ready for his back, or a posse was about to toss him into the Thames.

Then the king, noticing our movement, fixed us with a sharp gaze, and suddenly I was a mouse in the shadow of a hawk. He offered a pleasant smile, though, and said to my uncle, "Lord Ashley, I believe this is your daughter come."

Beside me, I could feel Grace shrinking in on herself. How she hated to be called upon to be polite, to exchange cordial greetings. We both curtsied deeply, Grace keeping her head bowed to shield her blushes from view.

"Her mother has many times told me so," Uncle Lionel said, trying to set Grace at ease with a familiar jest.

"Were you in doubt, sir, that you did ask her?" The king's tone was so serious, I glanced up, but a faint smile tugged at his lips.

"Nay, your majesty, of course not," Uncle Lionel said, joining the laughter at the king's remark. Aunt Ursula forced a laugh, seeming rather weary of the jest after all these years, and excused herself, setting off across the yard to welcome the ladies of the royal party. Eleanor and Mary trailed after her. Uncertain whether to accompany her, having just arrived, Grace and I stayed.

"There can be no doubt," the king said, taking Grace's hand to help her rise and gesturing me to do the same. "One can clearly see the stamp of her father on her face."

Poor Grace shot a glance at me, begging for help without words. She knew she was supposed to make some witty remark in reply, but she was ever tongue-tangled in the presence of strangers, especially men. Especially men of rank. Ordinarily, I would reply in her stead, but this was the king. Even I must forbear...

"Oh, heaven forbid!" Uncle Lionel said. "No woman should be so cursed as this." He waved a hand at his visage, which could not, in truth, be called handsome.

"Nevertheless, be happy, Lady Grace," the king said. "For you are like your honorable father."

Grace fumbled for something to say. "Well, then, I must be happy, for your majesty commands it, and it is good to be honorable."

Not witty, I thought, but at least to the point.

My gaze, following my aunt, wandered over the yard, though my attention remained with Grace. Most of the horses had been moved off into the stables, and the baggage had been ported into the house, so individual people were easier to see. My aunt spoke with the woman in black and a young woman swathed in a shimmering veil of golden silk, as though the sun itself had descended to wrap itself about her. A small group of women in elegant clothes waited nearby. This must be the princess and the ladies of her household. Men stood in knots, chatting and laughing nearby, awaiting their summons to enter the house. Some I knew, neighboring lords or old friends of my father who were now allies of the king, while others were strangers here. My eyes, traitors that they were, sought even a glimpse of him whom I did not want to see. Did not want? Nay, longed to see.

"Shall we go in, your majesty?" Uncle Lionel said, gesturing to the king to precede him up the stairs.

"Nay, my lord, we will go in together."

My uncle bowed, sensible of the honor, and walked up the stairs beside our sovereign. The king slowed his progress, placing two feet on each step and conversing with my uncle about the history of Ashley House so that my uncle's limp became a thing of little consequence.

My respect for this king grew.

Grace began to follow them in, and before I fell in behind her, I looked back over the yard to see if we should wait for my aunt and the other ladies. Amidst the general buzz of voices commenting upon the size and condition of my uncle's house and property—my *home!*—I could not help straining against the noise to try to discern that one voice, that one note in the symphony.

And then I saw him.

He stood with a group of gentlemen in company with the Duke of Surrey, to whom my uncle owed fealty. The duke had led the men of his duchy in support of King Henry against the former king, and I could suppose that Benedict, who had joined King Henry in his exile in France, must have reunited with the duke upon their return to England. Benedict had his arm around another man's shoulders, leaning close and saying something in his ear. The young fellow, darkly handsome, put his fingers to his lips to squelch his laughter. The two of them were clearly bosom friends.

The courtyard fell silent, and my vision narrowed to Benedict alone. My body went rigid, and I seemed unable to recall how to breathe.

Sir Edmund now, and in such exalted company. Would we be expected to bow before him?

My ears filled with a strange susurration, an echo of my heart, pounding an erratic lament in my chest. Drawing a deep breath, I tried to force calm into my body. But I had not seen him in two years, almost to the day. How could I be calm when he had returned to our home, when he was laughing and talking in our courtyard as though he had never left? No, not that, because we all were the same but he was entirely different. He was broader than before, wider in the chest and shoulders, thicker in the arms. He wore a beard now, rich and coppery in color, a shade or so darker than his hair. And there was a white, L-shaped scar below his left eye. How had that come to be?

My eyes were like minnows, darting to him and away.

As my aunt reached the stairs with the other women and it became clear that no introductions would be made at this moment, I slipped into place behind her, alongside my cousins. We continued up the stairs, and all the while I fought the desire to look back at the yard, to see if the men were following, to see if Benedict had noted me or not, to know what he thought upon seeing me.

It was all I could do not to run to him.

It was all I could do not to slap his face with all my strength.

As I was mounting the stairs and fighting this battle within myself, I found myself walking beside a young woman clad all in black, her raven hair covered by a black lace veil, her pale face unsmiling. I roused myself from my absorption in my own thoughts.

"Are you well, my lady?" I asked.

She shot me a glance, her eyes a soft shade of grey that belied the wicked intelligence I could see there. "Quite well, I thank you," she replied. "Why do you ask?"

"You seem..." I tipped my head, considering. "Out of step with the rest of the ladies who accompany the princess."

She focused on the steps beneath her feet for a moment, then said, "I am nothing like those other ladies."

Her tone, more than her words, stung, and I should have left her to her thoughts, as I could tell she preferred. "From your dress, I suppose that you are in mourning?"

Another pointed glance came my way and I was thankful that her eyes could not launch arrows lest I end in an early grave. "Aye, I do mourn. And yet, I am dragged about the land to make merry in the homes of strangers until the king is pleased to release me."

At my perplexed look, she sighed and explained, "I am the king's ward, upon the death of my brother in the recent battle. My father died less than two years ago, so I had scarce given over mourning him when my dear brother died. I am utterly alone in the world now." She paused and swallowed hard. "I know not if I ever will be happy again."

I bowed my head. "Forgive my impertinence in inquiring. My mouth ever runs ahead of propriety and good sense."

That coaxed a ghost of a smile from her lips. "Indeed," she said. "My brother always chided me that I did not speak enough when I should, so mayhap you will teach me boldness while I am here, howsoever long that may last."

We had reached the top of the stairs. I placed a hand on her arm. "I shall endeavor to help you in whatever way I may."

"For that sentiment, I thank you."

As we passed beneath the great archway of the doors, I noted—how could I not?—Benedict walking with his fellows into the hall as well. They were noisy, boisterous, openly eyeing us women, nudging and elbowing each other. I caught the exact moment Benedict spotted me. He halted in mid-stride, head turning, gaze drawn seemingly against his own will.

Our gazes locked with all the force of lightning striking the ground. I could not breathe. Could he?

With slow, languid movements, he leaned closer to the dark-haired gentleman beside him, saying something in his ear again. The fellow laughed and shoved his shoulder. My brows drew down, my whole being curled in. What were they saying about me?

The lady beside me sniffed. "What do you suppose they see?"

"He is stunned by our beauty, of course," I said, loud enough to be heard, intending to be heard. She laughed, a bold, musical sound, catching the attention of all the men.

All the men except Benedict, who still had not shifted his gaze from me. He leaned toward his fellow again, about to speak.

Words boiled up within me and spilled out, unbidden. "Can it be that you are still speaking, *Sir* Edmund? Nobody cares to hear you."

"Well, well," he said, shaking his head slowly. "My dear Lady Disdain! Are you yet living?"

Oh, aye, I deserved that. Still, it stung.

I scoffed. "Is it possible that Disdain should die while she has such good meat to feed on as you, sir?" I dipped a little curtsy, mocking his new title. "Courtesy herself must convert to disdain when in your presence."

He acknowledged my curtsy with a stiff bow of his own, and replied, "Then Courtesy is a turncoat and a traitor. But all my friends here may attest that I am well-loved among the ladies of France, not that you would know." A dagger's thrust, and meant to wound. Yet I would not show him how I bled. The gentlemen were chuckling, encouraging him, and he was not done. "Would that I could find it in my heart to change my heart, for the truth is that I love no woman." He put the subtlest emphasis on the word love, again, intending to wound.

"A dear happiness to women, lest they be troubled with an unwanted suitor. Except perhaps in France." More laughter, all around us. Yet could I bear to think about what that meant. *Well-loved among the ladies in France...* Everyone else was so amused, but they could not see the truth beneath the jests. I turned toward the lady at my side. "I thank God that I have cold blood as he does. I would rather hear a dog bark at a crow than hear a man such as this swear he loves me."

Did he flinch? I could not tell.

"May God keep you in that mind," he said, "lest some poor gentleman suffer a scratched face."

"Scratching could not make it worse, if it were such a face as yours."

Noting his new scar, I flinched inwardly. Perhaps that was too far. However, that comment drew appreciative hoots from his friends. I felt quite satisfied at having scored such a mark, but ashamed too.

"I wish my horse had the speed of your tongue. But enough, I'm done." He held up his hands with a smile, a good-natured gesture of surrender, and backed away with a bow of his head.

Making me look the fool for attacking him so fiercely.

But mayhap not, for everyone was smiling and laughing. They all thought it was a fine jest to see two old friends sparring again.

No one could see my hands shaking.

Only the lady beside me seemed to sense something untoward. She linked her arm through mine and said, "My lady, shall we continue on together?"

My cousin Mary hurried over to us, excitement pouring off her in palpable waves. "Father says the king will stay at least a se'n'night!" she announced with delight.

"What do you mean, the king will stay?" I asked. "Does not his lady mother have a home in Woking? That is only a short distance from here. Why would they not ride on?"

"No one has said, but what does it matter?" she said. At my side, the lady in mourning sighed. I looked over Mary's shoulder to where my uncle stood with the king. Our other guests were spread out through the hall in small clusters, though my aunt had already led the princess and the older woman away. Thus, those who remained in the hall were a fairly large group of men...and therein, of course, lay the answer. Time was required for the men to choose their brides—their prizes—and negotiate the terms of marriage.

With any luck, we prizes would have something to say about that.

CHAPTER 2

"My lady the king's mother" was what she must be called. One important person to whom we had not been introduced earlier in the great hall was the oft-married, oft-widowed Lady Margaret Beaufort de la Pole Tudor Stafford Stanley, she who must be called "my lady the king's mother." The herald in neat green-and-white Tudor livery who barred entry to the chambers assigned to her —to my surprise, she had been given Aunt Ursula's own chambers for her use—was very precise in his instruction before he admitted us to her presence.

I chewed over this instruction in my mind as I waited, alongside Grace and our cousins, kept kneeling before two large chairs set on a makeshift dais on the unadorned stone floor of Aunt's outer chamber, the eternal chill of the stone seeping up through our layers of skirts and into our bones. Nay, I was literally chewing on the words, for my teeth ground against themselves and my neck strained against the requirement of staying bowed.

It was worse than church on Maundy Thursday. It was as though we awaited the arrival of the Savior himself.

I could scarce contain my fury.

This was *our* home, she was *our* guest, and yet she could keep us waiting on our knees until such time as it was her pleasure to receive us.

I was ready to rise up, storm out of the chamber, and never look back, king's mother though she might be. Yet, every time I so much as wiggled my toes, Grace steadied me with a glance. Sweet, patient Grace. Saving me from myself.

The door to Aunt Ursula's bedchamber opened, and I lifted my head just enough to peek. The herald returned, followed by two sturdy fellows in Tudor colors with the rattle of armor muffled by their surcoats. Swords knocked against their boots as they walked. Behind them came a tiny woman swathed in a gown of a green so deep it was almost black, her headdress so severe it might as well have been a nun's wimple. This, the woman I'd seen emerging from the litter in the courtyard, must be my-lady-the-king's-mother. At her side glided the princess. She had changed from her traveling clothes, and now her golden hair gleamed under a sheer veil studded with pearls, her lustrous gown of scarlet silk seeming to float around her. My-lady-the-king's-mother would have looked grim next to anyone, but beside Princess Elizabeth, she was a blown milkweed beside a lily in the first heady rush of spring.

The herald retired to the door behind us while the yeomen guards escorted the ladies into the room. They took up positions on either side of the dais, human pillars, while the ladies took their places on the two seats, one large and richly carved and adorned with a thick purple cushion, the other smaller and plainer with no cushion. I watched sidelong as my-lady-the-king's-mother took the throne-like, cushioned chair. I had to stop my mouth from objecting. Should not the princess, destined soon to be our queen, have the honor? And the cushion?

My-lady-the-king's-mother swept us with dark eyes like an eagle about to feed. "You are the children of Lord Ashley, do I understand this aright?" she demanded. I was bold enough to unbow my head, though the other girls continued to cower. My anger blazed anew at the unfairness of such treatment.

"One child, my lady," I replied, my words tasting tart as lemons. "And assorted nieces."

My-lady-the-king's-mother frowned, further pinching her already unwelcoming face. "Are you making mock, young lady?"

Careful, Beatrice. I could almost hear Grace whispering in my ear. "Of course not, my lady," I said, putting all the innocence and respect I could muster into my tone. I gestured to my cousin, kneeling beside me. "This is Lady Grace, the only daughter and heir to Lord Ashley, who is my uncle, being my late mother's brother. And these are Mary and Eleanor, the daughters of my uncle the late Sir Anthony Tindall, Lord Ashley's brother." Looking up at my-lady-the-king's-mother's narrowed, suspicious eyes, I spread my hands to encompass all of us. "Thus, as I said, assorted nieces." I did my best to make a curtsy while trapped on my knees.

Though the old woman was not amused, Princess Elizabeth raised a hand to her lips as though to conceal a smile. I dared to shift my eyes as high as that, meeting her bright gaze with my own.

"And what," demanded my-lady-the-king's-mother, "are we supposed to do with all of you?"

I glanced down the line at the other girls. Poor, simple Eleanor was staring, open-mouthed, while genial Mary looked shocked to be so spoken to in her own home. Grace appeared on the verge of tears. None of them knew the answer, for of course, no one had invited these women here.

"That is for your highness to decide, of course," I replied as calmly as I could, inclining my head toward the princess, for, once again, I could not curtsy while being confined to my knees.

"I asked to come along with his majesty," the princess said, "to come to this house in particular of all houses, precisely because of you ladies." She glanced sidelong at her soon-to-be mother-in-law and I saw something there—impatience? irritation?—and dared to hope that perhaps we would all get along better than the old woman's attitude might suggest. "As queen, I will need ladies around me. Ladies of good reputation and breeding. Ladies of wit and good humor whom I can trust with my concerns. I hoped that here, with so many young ladies in one place, I might find one or two who would suit."

My-lady-the-king's-mother appeared less than pleased with this more than pleasant response. She sniffed audibly and said, "And since I am responsible for your person until the day of your marriage, you would impose these young women upon me for the duration as well, Elizabeth? For how long? Until they all find husbands, I suppose? Quite a fine arrangement for you all, isn't it?"

The fire that had been simmering in my gut flared and surged, boiling up my throat and demanding release. "That is not—"

Grace's hand flew out and gripped my arm. In the same moment, the princess leaned closer to her future mother-in-law and said, "Henry brought me along to visit these young ladies because I asked him to."

My-lady-the-king's-mother twisted in her seat to face the princess, staring straight into her eyes. I watched, fascinated, as they remained locked this way for the space of a drawn breath until the older woman gave a dissatisfied grunt and turned her gaze back to us, the unworthy, unwelcome girls who had been so unsatisfactorily imposed upon her. I almost smiled at her but caught myself in time.

"Fine," she said, smearing us all with her scornful gaze one final time. "If this is what Henry desires, I will keep watch over you while you serve the princess, should you be so fortunate to be selected. But I expect you observe proper decorum while you wait upon her highness. You will comport yourselves as good Christian women. Church every day, confession regularly, fasting on fasting days, and above all, no flirtations. If Lord Ashley arranges a match for you and the king approves, well, God's blessings upon you, but until then, you will keep yourselves chaste and above reproach. Is that clear?"

How dare she suppose that we would not? But I must acquiesce and be meek, so, "More than clear," I replied, my voice rising above the intimidated murmurs of assent from my cousins. That eagle's gaze pierced me again and I widened my eyes to seem as innocent as possible, a trick I had learned long ago from my cousin Mary. It did seem to work with young men; with this woman, I was not so sure.

My-lady-the-king's-mother rose, followed by Princess Elizabeth who said, "I look forward to speaking further with all of you at supper this evening." Her gaze swept over us, but unlike the old woman's, it felt warm and friendly.

Yet even as we were assenting to her kind condescension, my-lady-the-king's-mother snarled, "After which, I expect to see you all at evening prayers."

I could scarce contain my groan, but what could we do but agree?

Amid a flurry of curtsies, the princess followed the king's mother and the two yeomen out of the room. At last, I released a breath that held much of my fury. "Such thoughtlessness reflects a lack of nobility, to my mind," I said, and Grace's hand shot out to restrain me.

"Hush!" she said, "lest someone hear you and tell Lady Stanley."

"You mean 'my-lady-the-king's-mother,' Grace," I said but she did not smile.

"Beatrice, I fear we must please her if we are to stay in the princess' good graces, and the king's," she chided.

"And her pleasure is not to feel pleasure," I replied but I shook my head when she would have remonstrated with me further. "No, I understand. We have been ill treated by her here, but we must keep her happy to ensure our own future happiness. And so..." I straightened up. "Church. Confession. Fasting." I looked at the other girls who were beginning to look horrified at the prospect of such a life. "Best make sure to eat well tonight at supper."

* * *

With the formalities out of the way, we were introduced to the ladies who had accompanied the princess from Westminster. She seemed to favor women named Katherine, but thankfully, they each went by different names. The lady in mourning I had met earlier was Lady Katherine Hardinge, known as Viola for the lavender hints in her grey eyes. A chestnut-haired, high-spirited lady, Kathryn, the Countess of Howarth, was called Kate. And the princess' oldest friend, Katherine Howard, being from an ancient and respected family was, of course, always Katherine. Lady Viola's father had died fighting for King Henry's cause in the autumn of 1483, during the Duke of Buckingham's failed rebellion. That same rebellion had spurred many young men of this household to go join Henry, then the Earl of Richmond, in France, including Benedict. Lady Viola's brother, it seemed, had died either at Bosworth, the recent battle where the king had gained his throne, or soon thereafter. She was reticent to speak of the matter, for which one could hardly blame her. In contrast, Lady Kate's husband had been elevated from knight to baron whilst kneeling in the muck and blood of the battlefield. The spoils of war took many forms.

My cousins and I spent several pleasant hours in the princess' chambers—the best guest chambers, just down the hall from my aunt and uncle's suite of rooms—helping her supervise her maids doing the unpacking and getting to know her and her ladies. At one point, the princess rose and drifted over to the door, glancing out into the corridor as if waiting for someone to arrive. I watched her for a few moments, then extricated myself from the knot of my cousins and joined her.

"May help you with anything, your highness?"

She glanced back at me with a distracted smile. "Oh, I am merely curious about your home and the arrangements your aunt has made for the guests." Even to have her bestow half of her attention upon me was like standing too close to a fire: terribly warm, all encompassing, a bit uncomfortable. Her eyes, I could see now that I was up close, were a hazel so warm and flecked with color as to be nearly golden, as dazzling as the rest of her. I had never met anyone so beautiful in my life. It was hard to frame words in her presence, much less keep one's wits about one.

She had asked about the arrangements. The rooms. I could not fathom a reason for such a curiosity, but I could—I must—answer. "My aunt has given you the finest of the guest chambers, your highness," I replied, "and if you look to the left, there..." I pointed down the corridor to where it intersected with another hall in a T. "Those doors are my uncle's and my aunt's chambers, which have been given over to the king and his mother."

Her mouth twisted in a sour expression and I hurried to add, "Naturally, were you and his majesty married, my aunt's chambers would have been yours, but under the circumstances, that was impossible."

She touched my shoulder and my spirits lifted. It was as if she were an angel in truth, or possessed of miraculous powers. I quashed the heretical thoughts and focused on her words. "Naturally. The king and I will marry in due time." An edge in her voice suggested that the exact timing of their marriage was point of contention between them, but I could not ask. "It is only right that my lady the king's mother should have the finest accommodations." Again, a shading of tone, not quite there, suggested far more than her words said.

I was renowned for speaking far too plainly. How much could I learn from this princess, trained since birth in saying much without saying anything. "Of course," I murmured.

"My own mother wanted to come along as my chaperone, but she and my lady the king's mother do not get along."

I almost laughed. Biting the inside of my cheek to stop it, I made a sound conveying polite interest. Her gaze slid sideways at me and she grinned. "I think I shall enjoy your company whilst we are here, my lady Beatrice," she said. "And perhaps you will consider joining us at court in Westminster when we return thence."

I bowed my head. "Your highness is too kind."

She turned, leaning her back against the door frame and crossing her arms, a decidedly un-princess-like gesture. "I see you are not coy or shy, Lady Beatrice, so let us not mince our words. The Duke of Surrey was most interested in joining the king on this journey, and I do not believe the king's mother's house in Woking holds any particular claim on his heart. Is there aught I should know about the ladies of this house, any prior attachments to the men of the king's company of which the king should be aware?"

Prior attachments. My mouth was so dry of a sudden, I could scarce force words out. "There has ever been a hope—" I paused, shoving aside memories of Benedict and swallowing hard. "My uncle and the duke's father were friends long ago, and so the duke has ever been welcome in this house since he was a boy, and I... I do believe my uncle hopes, and the duke may as well..."

The princess raised her eyebrows. "But is there an understanding? Anything spoken between them?"

I opened my mouth to deny it but was suddenly—again—unable to speak. Just then, voices drifted toward us from the direction of my aunt and uncle's rooms, diverting the princess' attention from my silence. One of them, I noted, was Benedict's.

"And what do you think of her?" a man's voice said.

"I try not to," was Benedict's reply, "but then, I have known her since she was in swaddling bands."

The princess' eyes widened and she pulled me close to her, fading back into the doorway so that we would not be immediately noticed by anyone walking along the corridor. "Who do you suppose they speak of?" she whispered in my ear.

I shook my head. It could be any of us, as Benedict had lived here at Ashley House since he was a young child.

"Nay, but tell me," the other man insisted. "Is she a modest lady?"

Dare I ask a question of my future queen? I considered. She had put her arm around me to engage in spying on these men, and she had as good as invited me to be one of her ladies-in-waiting. I ventured to dare. "Who is that man who speaks?"

"Thomas, Lord Keighton," she said. "My lord puts much faith in him, and he is oft in the company of one Sir Edmund Benedict. Do you know him?"

I sighed. "Indeed, I do. Ben—Sir Edmund was raised here in Ashley House."

She raised her eyebrows. "Ah. So they are speaking of one of you ladies."

I nodded.

Benedict had been answering his friend while the princess and I whispered behind our hands. "...too low for a high praise," he said, "too brown for a fair praise, but were she other than she is, she were unhandsome..."

The princess' mouth twitched. "That is ungenerous."

"Indeed," I agreed, attempting to discern from his words which of my cousins they were discussing.

The princess gave me a measuring look. "You are too tall and not dark enough for them to be speaking of you," she said, and laughed when I gasped. "I think we know it must be your lovely cousin Grace."

"If it be Grace, to call her 'not unhandsome' is paltry praise."

The princess tilted her head back and forth. "Well, Sir Edmund is known for his resistance to female beauty."

"Truly?" I asked but was unable to question her further because I was distracted by his voice again. Even his voice had changed. It was deeper, rougher somehow, than when he left.

"Would you buy her, that you inquire after her?" he said.

"Could all the wealth in the world buy such a jewel?" Lord Thomas sighed.

"Aye, and a case to put it in," Benedict said, a laugh in his voice. My heart melted. That was the Benedict I remembered.

Their voices seemed just outside the door and the princess jerked me back into the room. We half-fell over an empty chest that had been pushed aside, and suddenly there were arms everywhere, trying to catch us. Laughter exploded and as I struggled to keep my feet, I caught a glimpse of Benedict and his friend strolling past the door, their faces turned toward our chamber with surprise at the commotion within. Lord Thomas was clearly wealthy, his clothes the very height of fashion: a doublet in a rich wine-colored velvet with full sleeves slashed to allow glimpses of his pale pink shirt through, hose to match his shirt, and long-toed shoes to match his doublet. But he was handsome as well, with thick, dark hair, sharp cheekbones, and full lips.

Beside me, Grace sucked in her breath.

Benedict caught my eye and his lips twitched. "There, you see, is her cousin, who exceeds her in beauty as the first of May does the last of December."

My cheeks burned at his words, and at the teasing whoops of the women in the room around me. Lord Thomas looked at me, then at Benedict, seeming perplexed by the comparison, for surely no one would call me fairer than Grace. I rolled my eyes at the fellow. "Now it is your place to dispute his saying, my lord," I called through the door, to the delight of the ladies around me. I was pleased to see him blush, all the way to the tips of his ears. It set off the wine-and-pink of his wardrobe very nicely.

"Ah," he stammered, "this cannot be, for surely my lady is an angel descended from heaven."

The ladies applauded while Benedict shook his head. He put an arm around his friend. "Your speech needs work, my lord, for what man has not compared his lady to an angel?" He raised his voice to a mocking tone. "'An angel is like you, my dear, and you are like an angel.'" Then, shaking his head, he went on, "But despite your flaws, we must acknowledge the most beautiful lady of all, our gracious princess, and be on our way."

Both men bowed elegantly, good courtiers that they were, and though I laughed and applauded with the other women, a frisson shot through me because I realized that this was not the Benedict I had known. Courtly, comfortable with lords and princes, probably wealthy too... This Sir Edmund was not the same man who had left here two years ago.

He had accomplished all he had set out to, while I had remained here. In that moment, I understood what I had not acknowledged before: I had been awaiting his return, but it seemed now that he had always had greater things in mind. Little wonder then that he had left me with no promises.

* * *

We suffered through evening prayers as ordered, and as a dubious reward we were allowed to join the gentlemen in the solar, a spacious, circular room at the end of the south wing where, on warm days, Aunt Ursula liked to sit and do her sewing, owing to the windows that let in light and air. Now, nearing harvest time, there was a chill in the air at night and the heavy curtains had been drawn across, lending the room a cozy charm. Thankfully, my-lady-the-king's-mother retired to her chamber—my uncle's chamber—and did not join us.

The gentlemen were sprawled out across the furniture but sprang to their feet as we arrived and rearranged themselves so that the princess could have the best seat on the settle beside the king, right next to the fire. He draped a blanket across her lap, though the night was scarce cold enough for such courtesy, and she smiled at his gesture. The rest of us found places around the room, scrambling with as much grace as we could for the few chairs and more abundant cushions on the floor. The challenge, of course, was determining whose birth had earned them a spot near the fire and the royals.

I waited, watching, as men offered the best places to my cousin Grace and she, flushed with embarrassment, tried to decide what to do. I nudged her toward the Duke of Surrey, who held the highest rank in the room aside from the king, and whose attentions she should not scorn, once offered. Casting me a look that begged me to stay with her, she took his hand and allowed him to seat her beside him on a pillow near the fire. I made my way to that side of the room as well, though no duke offered me his hand.

From his seat on the other side of the fire from the king, my Uncle Lionel said, "I hope everything has been to your liking thus far, your majesty, your highness."

The king inclined his head and raised his goblet in acknowledgement. "You have been more than kind," he replied.

"Nay, your majesty, you do us honor by giving us the opportunity to show our love and loyalty to the crown."

"Your family has shown ample loyalty already, my lord."

Uncle Lionel kept his eyes cast down to show modesty. Although owing to his leg injury he had not been able to fight for the king, he had sent a great number of men and horses to the recent battle as well as allowing young men of the household, like Benedict, to join King Henry in his exile. If the king was not going to give Uncle Lionel a more elevated title or more lands, there was in fact only one reward left to be bestowed: a good marriage for his daughter to a close ally of the king. Such as, perhaps, the wealthy and handsome duke of Surrey.

"Never fear, my lord," the duke said. "I'm sure there are gentlemen here who are willing to help the king show his gratitude for your loyalty."

Although his comment inspired general amusement, I was vexed. "All know, your grace," I replied, "the gratitude whereof you speak." I looked directly at the duke as I said it, to ensure he knew I meant to challenge him. "We ladies know that you gentlemen are seeking to further extend the spoils of your victory."

A few people laughed uncomfortably. Thankfully, my cousin Eleanor broke the tension. Looking puzzled, she said, "What's gone spoiled?"

"Spoils, Eleanor," her sister Mary corrected her. "Prizes. Winnings."

She brightened. "Oh, like gifts?" Everyone laughed and the mood lightened, my challenge thus translated into a jest.

"My cousin is not a prize for the victor," I muttered.

"Majesty," said a new voice, "I pray you will pardon me, but I have no wish to be part of this." I closed my eyes for a long moment, hoping no one would note my reaction. I did not even have to search for him, for I had searched him out—against my will—as soon as I walked in the room. Benedict lounged on his side near the king, one arm draped over his bent knee, taking up far too much space.

"Part of what?" the princess asked. The look on her face was pure innocence, but there was a note in her voice that said she knew exactly what she asked.

"Yes, Sir Edmund," the king said. "Part of what?"

Benedict waved a hand in a lazy circle. "The spoils. I for one have been more than amply rewarded by your majesty and seek nothing more."

"More than you deserve, mayhap," his handsome friend Lord Thomas said, seated close beside him. They seemed inseparable, like they'd caught a plague and could not shake it. How much would it cost to cure the Benedict once one had caught it? Had I enough treasure saved?

"Go to, Sir Edmund," the king said at nearly the same moment. He kicked Benedict's foot, knocking his leg down so he lost his easy pose. "You talk and talk, but surely you want a wife, the same as any other man."

Everyone except me laughed as Benedict attempted to recover his composure, shifting into a sitting position with his legs tucked under him. I hoped he felt the sharp sting of my gaze upon him. I hoped it burned him like fire, like ice.

Yes, Benedict, tell the king how you could have had a wife. Tell him how you could have had an heiress but rejected her because it was too difficult. Her uncle would object because you were a bastard, a nobody, and you were too honorable to defy him.

I put every word of these thoughts into my gaze, but he showed no sign that he noted me at all.

"Nay, your majesty," the duke said. "He is a notorious bachelor. Throughout France, there are many unhappy women, grieving that he will not marry them."

Amidst the laughter, Benedict ducked his head, but he was smiling. "You mock me, my lord."

The duke's grin gleamed amidst his dark beard. "Indeed I do, Sir Edmund."

"But why? Why must a man marry?" Benedict countered, and his tone was earnest.

"Scripture tells us it is better to marry than to burn, but I believe Sir Edmund has found a way around that particular admonition," the king said, half teasing, half chiding.

I frowned and though I wanted not to care, these words stabbed at my heart. I could all too easily imagine what he meant.

"But your majesty, I say again, why must I marry?" Benedict insisted. "A woman may be beautiful..." He trailed off long enough to bow his head to the princess and she, smiling, inclined her head to him in return. "Yet I do not wish to marry her."

"Best not," someone muttered, and Benedict chuckled, leaping to his feet and sweeping a bow to the king. I rolled my eyes, recognizing Benedict performing for a crowd. "Another woman may be wise and yet I can admire her without feeling the pull of the altar..." He surveyed the room and, spying the quiet Lady Viola, he made her a courtly bow. She executed a graceful curtsy in return while the crowd laughed.

Benedict turned away, scanning the room for his next target. "Another may be virtuous..." He looked and looked, seeming not to find anyone to light on, and the men roared with laughter. At last, he seized my cousin Grace's hand and kissed it while she blushed a fetching pink. "And yet," he said, releasing her, "I feel no need to marry. A woman," he said, turning to face the king, "may possess all the grace, beauty, and gifts that God may bestow, and yet I remain unmoved. I am happy as I am."

The princess shook her head, a smile on her lips. "Oh, surely not, Sir Edmund."

"That my mother bore me, I thank her," he replied. "That she brought me up, I likewise give her most humble thanks. But the idea that I will put my head willingly into the yoke like an ox... I thank you, your highness, but I prefer to live a bachelor."

I bit my lips against protest. I would not, could not, reveal myself.

"But this is all nonsense, sir," the princess said. "Surely there is something, some combination of virtues that could exist in one woman that would induce you to matrimony."

I wished she would let the subject die, but of course the princess didn't know. No one knew, not even Grace, which was as it should be. To them, this was all a jest, an amusing way to pass the evening. What was *he* thinking, though? He was too good, now, at hiding his feelings.

I could hear the smile in his voice as he said, "She'd have to be rich, naturally, or else why would anyone marry?" The company, men and women alike, laughed. *Naturally*, they said to each other. *Naturally. Oh, Sir Edmund, so wickedly funny.*

"And wise, for certes."

"Wiser than you!" someone called, and he nodded, acknowledging the taunt.

"Virtuous, or I won't cheapen her..."

"We'd never allow it," the duke said.

"And beautiful, or I'll never look upon her..."

"Of course," Lord Thomas said, with a glance in Grace's direction.

My stomach tied itself in knots. It was unbearable, listening to him, watching him perform for the king and court. Once, he had me—perhaps I was not as beautiful as Grace, or as rich, but he'd had the love of a good woman—and he put me aside. His choice, not mine! This charade was intolerable.

Benedict was still speaking, though I could scarce hear him through the blood pounding furiously in my ears, and every new trait he listed provoked a new gale of laughter. "Mild of temper," he was saying, "or God help me, come not near me. Of good family, of course..."

The princess was giggling helplessly into her fist. The king waved his hand, encouraging him. "What more? What more?"

"Ah, of good discourse and excellent wit, a good musician, well-educated and well-read... Oh let me see..."

"But what of her hair? Her eyes?" the princess demanded through her laughter.

He froze as though the thought had never occurred to him. "They may be of what color it please God."

"With such demands, it is no wonder you claim that no one woman is enough for you," the king said.

"Or perhaps you have not yet found the right woman," the princess said, touching the king's arm playfully.

"With respect, your highness, there is no such woman." And with another sweeping bow, he collapsed back to the floor.

The court's thunderous applause matched the furious thunder of my blood in my veins. *Oh, no. He didn't get to perform like that unanswered.*

Though my legs were stiff and wooden, my hands clenched into fists in my skirts, I rose to my feet, determined to show Benedict that I was unbroken by him.

"I entirely agree with you, Sir Edmund," I said, moving closer to the group around the king.

He shifted to face me. Though there was no change in his casual posture, I thought I noticed a tightening in his jaw as I approached. That, at least, was a small victory.

"Oh dear," said the princess, struggling to appear serious, "Have we in our midst another dissenter from the ranks?"

"Indeed, your highness," I said, "and I believe I have Scripture on my side."

"Scripture?" she said, startled.

"Yes," I said, and I heard my uncle stifle a groan, for my family had heard this discourse many times before. Grace reached out for me, her hand tugging at my skirts, whispering, "Beatrice, please!" I shot her a grin but remained focused on my royal audience.

"Do tell us," the princess said, leaning forward. "I am quite eager to know how Holy Scripture advocates against marriage rather than for it."

"It's quite simple, your highness. The Bible tells us that God fashioned Adam from clay, and then Eve was made from his rib, yes?"

"Well, yes," she said.

"And we are all their children, is it not so?"

"Of course."

"Thus, it follows that if we are all the children of Adam and Eve, every man is my brother, and therefore, I must never marry for it would be a great sin to marry with my brother."

While the group dissolved in laughter once again, I curtsied, but while my head was bowed, I shot Benedict a glance that said, "You see? You are not the only one who can amuse them."

"Oh dear," the princess said, laughing. "I do believe, by your reckoning, we are all living in the greatest sin."

"It is worse than that, your highness," I said. "If Adam was made of clay and all men are his heirs, how can a woman not grieve to be lorded over by a jumped-up bit of dust?"

My quip was greeted by a sudden silence.

It came to me that I said that to the king.

I called the king himself a jumped-up bit of dust.

A few people chuckled but it was clear I had gone too far.

Even I recognized that I had gone too far, but it was too late to take it back, and my mind went utterly blank and I could not think of a way to laugh it away.

The princess herself saved me. "A woman of wit may think she is not fashioned for marriage," she said, "but it may be that a marriage may be found to suit her."

CHAPTER 3

When at last the princess announced she was ready to retire, the rest of us women left the solar along with her. Some of the princess' high-ranking ladies had been offered the family bedchambers rather than the smaller guest chambers, requiring a shuffling of rooms that had landed Grace and me in a tiny room at the far end of the guest corridor and—much to our amusement and their consternation—had shunted Eleanor and Mary back into the nursery. The men, of course, were lodged a hall and a floor away, with a locked door between us and them, with the exception of the king who had my uncle's bedchamber. Even my uncle had moved down with the bachelor knights for the duration of the royal visit.

Grace and I were greeted in our temporary bedchamber by our shared maid, Margaret. Ordinarily an easy-going person, she looked harried and tired, having spent all day moving our belongings into this temporary room in between helping settle the royal party. Grace sank onto a cushioned bench, waiting for Margaret to help her prepare for bed, while I poked about in the chests and boxes scattered about the room to see what Margaret had deemed important enough to transfer.

"And how many days are they like to stay?" Margaret complained as she began yanking the pins out of Grace's hair. "That's what I'd like to know. Turning our lives topsy-turvy for who knows how long?"

"Never fear, Margaret," I said, lifting a chemise I did not recognize out of a chest. She must have been in quite a dither when she packed for us. "I am sure there will be diversions enough to make their time with us enjoyable." I tossed the chemise at her, and it draped over her shoulders and hair like a veil. "Mayhap there will be a handsome husband in the bunch for you as well."

Margaret blushed, a pretty pink highlighting her cheeks and even coloring the tips of her ears, and I laughed out loud. "Margaret," I exclaimed, crossing the room to her side, "I do believe you have yourself a man."

Margaret laughed and pulled the chemise off her head, tossing it back at me. "Fie, my lady, to speak so."

"Who is he?" Holding both ends of the chemise, I looped it around her, catching her. "Do we know him? Is he of good character, of good family? Is he from here? Tell, tell."

Still blushing, she said, "All I will say is that his name is Hugh, my lady."

I glanced at Grace, who was hiding a grin behind her hands and shaking her head at my antics. "Hugh," I said, considering. "A good name, a solid name. I approve. Only, take care, Margaret, that the *hue* of your cheek does not give you away in his presence."

Both of them groaned at my pun, and Margaret pulled the chemise from my hands. "Have done, my lady, and let me do my job."

"Yes, Beatrice, let her do her job," Grace repeated.

"Ah well, if you are both against me," I conceded, going to sit on the bed.

At that moment, there came a sharp rapping on the door to our bedchamber. We all looked at each other, the same thought in our minds: who could be knocking after we had retired? "It must be Mother," Grace said, but she did not sound certain.

Margaret went to the door and demanded in a sharp tone who was there at such a late hour. She cracked the door open, spoke a few soft words, then shut the door again. Turning to us, her back against the door, she looked puzzled as she said, "Her highness requests the pleasure of Lady Grace's presence to keep her company before she falls asleep."

Grace and I looked at each other. "I suppose this is a good thing?" Grace said.

"I suppose," I said. "I'll wait up for you."

She shook her head. "There's no way of knowing how late she'll keep me. No need for both of us to be sleepy tomorrow."

"Very well," I said. "You must tell me everything in the morning."

"Never fear," she said. "Though I doubt I will have much to tell."

* * *

The candle I left burning had long since guttered and the room was full dark, save for the glow of the banked fire, when I awoke to the sounds of Grace's return. She moved with unaccustomed clumsiness, bumping into things in the dark and stifling giggles as she navigated the unfamiliar room. Most surprising of all, there was a distinct odor of wine about her. Curious, I sat up in bed, propping a pillow behind me. "Grace? What is wrong?"

"Oh, thank goodness you are awake," she said and went to the hearth to light a taper. As she moved more confidently back to the bed, I noted that her color was high, her eyes bright with more than mirth.

"Have you been drinking wine so late?"

She pressed the back of a hand to her cheek. "Some," she admitted as she sank down onto the bed. "I'm glad you're awake," she added. "Margaret's asleep, and I can't get out of my clothes without help." This must have struck her as rather funny, because she tipped backwards toward me laughing, and I had to push her back upright.

"Heavens, Grace, just how much wine is 'some'?" I asked as I started to unlace her kirtle.

"I don't know," she said. "Lord Keighton kept refilling my cup..."

"Lord Keighton?" The handsome, dark-haired gentleman who was Benedict's good friend, whom the princess and I had overheard talking with Benedict about Grace? "What was he doing in the princess' chamber?"

"Oh, he wasn't. Well, not at first. That is, when I arrived, it was only the princess and me, but then the king arrived with Thomas, and we talked and drank wine for some time, and then Thomas asked me to step out into the antechamber with him..."

Suspicion pricked at me. She was calling him *Thomas*... "To what end?"

She glanced at me over her shoulder. "To keep watch over them, to keep them from harm."

I pulled on her shoulder until she turned her body and looked me in the eye. Her eyes were bright, her breath sour with wine, her words tumbling out of her. This was not my cousin. "Grace," I said, "the king and the princess both have their yeomen. Remember them? All those strapping young men in green and white livery roaming through our home? They do not need you and some stripling of a baron to keep them from harm."

She frowned at me. "But that's what he told me, and I believed him. What other end?"

I sighed. "Grace. Did you leave the king and the princess alone in her bedchamber?"

"Well, yes."

I waited. She considered.

"Oh!" She gasped and leapt up from the bed, her half-laced kirtle drooping around her shoulders. "Beatrice, what have I done?"

I pushed back the covers, rising reluctantly from the warm bed to take her hands and calm her distress. "Fear not, Grace. You have done nothing wrong. Your innocence protects you." I pulled her back down to sit on the bed, for she was swaying on her feet. Heavens, how much wine had Lord Keighton plied her with? "If the king and the princess are simply talking with friends late into the night, no one can reproach them. And if you are asked, you were with them tonight, do you understand? The whole time. At all costs, Lady Stanley, the king's mother, must never know." I shook her hands as though I could shake sense into her with them. "Do you hear me, Grace? You must say so, for the princess' sake as well as for your own."

She nodded and shrugged out of her kirtle. When she began to crumple it into a mangled mess, I helped her to fold it and place it in one of the trunks Margaret had brought in for our clothes. "I don't like this feeling," she said as she climbed into bed beside me.

I did not like it either, that they had taken advantage of my sister's innocence and my family's hospitality in this manner. But they were royal and could do as they pleased.

"I know," I said, and blew out the candle.

* * *

In the morning, Grace was subdued all through the church services that my-lady-the-king's-mother forced us to attend and remained quiet while we broke our fast. The men had gone out hunting before dawn, cleverly riding out before they could be dragged into chapel, so we ladies were alone for the morning. After Princess Elizabeth inquired of Aunt Ursula where the most pleasant spot for sewing would be, Aunt Ursula led us back to her solar where we had spent the previous evening.

Taking the room's most comfortable seat by the fire, my-lady-the-king's-mother eyed Aunt Ursula as if daring her to dispute her claim. Not a timid woman, Aunt Ursula nevertheless settled in another chair as if that had been her plan all along. I gritted my teeth. The pride of this ostentatiously Christian woman. The princess glided to the chair opposite her future mother-in-law with a serene expression. I marveled at her everlasting composure. How did she manage it?

We all found places around the room, much as we had the night before, but this time without having to displace the men. My-lady-the-king's-mother glanced around the room from under lowered lids, seeming displeased with all she saw. Aunt Ursula lifted her sewing from out of the basket next to her chair—the chair Lady Stanley was sitting in—without a word and set to work.

"Do you and your daughters do good works?" the old woman said, frowning at the shirt of fine linen on which Aunt Ursula worked. The fabric and ornamental stitching of it proclaimed that she made it for Uncle Lionel.

Aunt Ursula did not glance up as she found her place in the stitching. "Naturally, as Christian women."

My-lady-the-king's-mother sniffed. "By my question, I mean do you ever do needlecrafts for the poor? The Princess Elizabeth has begun to sew a shirt for a peasant every time she makes one for my son, the king."

Princess Elizabeth, working away on a shirt of coarse stuff clearly intended for the self-same peasant, did not even look up.

"For certes, my lady," Aunt Ursula said, her tone carrying just a hint of annoyance. "We pray, and fast, and do good works, as do all good Christian souls."

"Oh yes, we do everything proper," my cousin Eleanor said, cheerfully plying her needle to a bedsheet, the only project anyone would ever trust her with (and still we had to pick out and redo her seams). "No good Christian soul would seek to be condemned into everlasting redemption."

We who knew her chuckled or smiled, for Eleanor was always saying such things, mixing up words as she had the night before. My-lady-the-king's-mother, who had not been with us then, looked repelled by her and seemed on the verge of chiding the poor girl. The princess looked up from her meticulous work, glancing first at Eleanor and then at her ladies, and I watched as a silent communication flowed between them. Lady Katherine Howard shot a quick look my way.

"My lady Beatrice," she said, "what do you think of the gentlemen who have accompanied us here to your home?"

The princess bowed her head once more, looking satisfied. I realized that with no words necessary, the women had designed a way of bringing an end to Lady Stanley's badgering, so I answered as quickly as I could.

"Some of the gentlemen were known to me of old, as they were men of this household before they left to join his majesty in exile. Sir Edmund, for instance."

"Aye, and we learned what you think of him last night," the princess said drily, to the amusement of the other ladies. My-lady-the-king's-mother scowled, although she could have not known precisely what the princess referred to.

I inclined my head, acknowledging the jibe, and went on. "The other men of the court, I know not, and I have not had the chance to speak with them."

"And now they are afraid to speak to you," the princess said.

"Indeed," I said with a smile.

"But what think you of John Lord Beymond?" the princess asked, letting her needlework fall into her lap. "Did you note him at all?"

An oddly specific question, I thought. "I looked upon him, but did I note him?" I made a noncommittal gesture. "He seems a goodly gentleman, but as I said, I have not spoken to him at all. He is not unhandsome." I hoped she would remember the reference.

"It seems to me odd that he is permitted so close to the king's person," Grace said. "For I understand that he was in the court of King Richard and is newly reconciled to his majesty."

I froze in the middle of placing a stitch. Grace was guileless and meant nothing more than to speak the truth, but now, in this room and with these people, it was dangerous to bring up the past—and not so long past, either—when there had been another king and an entirely different possible future for every one of us. Including, and perhaps most especially, for this princess.

The merest suggestion of a furrow between pale brows darkened the princess' expression and flew away, replaced by a smile for Grace. "For certes, he was a member of my uncle's court," she said, "but he has given good assurance of his loyalty, and we have evidence of his good character. Is that not so, my lady mother?"

My-lady-the-king's-mother did not even glance up from her work, just grunted what could have been an affirmation or rejection of the princess' words. The princess pressed her lips for a moment, then continued to speak. "I only mention him because I believe he would do well to find a wife, and soon. Poor Lord John lost his wife not a year since, which has triggered a deep melancholy in him." The princess looked directly at me, challenging. "But then, you have determined never to marry, Lady Beatrice, is that not so?"

My cousins tittered behind their hands. I forced myself to smile and incline my head. "As I have said, your highness."

My-lady-the-king's-mother clucked her tongue and shifted in her chair. "Preposterous."

"Repastrous," Eleanor said, enjoying the sound of this new word. "Purpasteros. Pater-noster-ous."

Mary placed a hand on Eleanor's arm and whispered in her ear, but to no avail. "Will no one silence that idiot child?" my-lady-the-king's-mother snapped. Aunt Ursula surged to her feet, flinging her needlework to the floor. All of us—her daughter and nieces—stood with her, trying to prevent her from saying something that would irreparably damage her relationship with this woman who was, after all, the king's mother. But she restrained herself, biting her lip, and took Eleanor by the hand.

"Come along, child," she said to Eleanor, her voice shaking with the effort of remaining calm. "Let us walk in the garden and see if there are any flowers to gather."

When they had gone, we all resumed our seats, one after the other. I was the last to sit, and my whole body trembled with anger.

"How old is she?" Princess Elizabeth inquired when they had gone.

"Eleanor is two years younger than me," Mary replied, "and not yet sixteen."

"Ah." The princess looked thoughtful as she placed a few stitches. "Perhaps she is not...ready to accompany me to court."

"There are so very many daughters of this house," Lady Stanley said, and she did not mean it as a compliment. I bristled on Aunt Ursula's behalf. She was the one woman now living who was responsible for all the 'many daughters' since Uncle Lionel's brother and sister—Mary's father and my mother—had died years ago. Mayhap my-lady-the-king's-oh-so-self-important-mother thought the mere fact of her son's birth gave her something to lord over other women who had merely delivered girls. As though she were to be congratulated on producing a male child. To the contrary, I had read that some learned men believed that it was the responsibility of husbands to ensure their wife's pleasure in the marriage bed to make the birth of a son more likely. I was opening my mouth to say as much when Lady Stanley's sharp gaze lit upon me again. "And who was it that sired the impertinent Lady Beatrice? Perhaps a father's firm hand would have kept her tongue in check."

Now even the princess looked uncomfortable. "Are we—" she began, but my ire was up. I must respond. Sired, indeed.

"My mother was the sister of Lord Ashley, my lady," I said. To speak over the princess showed unpardonable disrespect, but she did not even glance at me in rebuke. "My father was Baron Welles, who died at—"

"Losecoat Field, yes, of course." My-lady-the-king's-mother peered at me with her dark, criticizing eyes. My father had been a rebel then, and been executed for it. If he had not lost, if things had gone another way... well, her son might not today be king. I smiled at her, tight and thin. "I was not quite five years of age at the time, my lady, and my mother never got over the loss. Although I suppose you could say that she had never been a strong woman, given that none of her babies survived childbirth, save me. Save only a daughter. So perhaps she may be forgiven for weeping at my birth. A disappointing girl, and not a longed-for son."

The room was utterly silent. My hands, clenched in fists in my lap, were trembling. Perhaps I should not have revealed so much. For certes, I should not have spoken so to the royal family.

Beside me, one of the princess' Ladies Katherine drew a breath. "I do believe we began by speaking of Lord John Beymond."

"Yes, my lady," the princess said, looking up from her needlework with relief on her face. "My lord the king agrees with me that marriage would have a steadying influence on Lord Beymond."

"As it does on all men," my-lady-the-king's-mother said.

"Steadying?" Mary said with a snort. "He's already as dull as a bag of rocks."

"Mary," I snapped. She twisted in her seat to look at me, but all protest died when she saw my face.

"I beg your pardon, your highness, my lady," she mumbled, bending closer over her needlework.

I was wondering how much worse this morning could possibly get when the door creaked open behind me. Everyone looked up, grateful for the interruption. It was the Duke of Surrey, looking handsomely apologetic and yet not sorry at all.

"Your highness, I beg your pardon for interrupting, but the king and his attendants, including myself, have returned from our morning ride, and the king was hoping that you might be persuaded to leave aside your womanly pursuits in favor of some entertainment with the gentlemen." He paused, his dark eyes flicking to my-lady-the-king's-mother, who was glaring at him as if she could set him ablaze with the force of her will. "Wholesome entertainment," he added. "Of course."

He had scarce finished speaking before the princess stood, her needlework rolled up neatly in the basket at her feet. "We would be delighted. You will spare us until dinner, will you not, my lady mother?"

Lady Stanley lifted her beady eyes from her needlework to peer up at the princess. Pursing her lips in distaste, she wrapped thin fingers around her needlework like an owl clutching a rabbit in its talons. Every instinct, every desire in her, all of us could see, wanted to refuse. And yet it seemed that the countervailing pull to deny her son nothing he desired was too powerful, and so she said nothing, simply nodded with a grim, tight countenance, and returned to her sewing.

As we followed the princess out of the room, I fell in beside Grace. Slipping my arm through hers, I said in her ear, "Will she spend the rest of the morning on her knees in chapel, do you think?"

Grace giggled, scandalized. "Hush," she whispered.

Lady Viola, appearing at my other elbow, murmured, "Since your poor aunt would have to accompany her, let us hope not."

CHAPTER 4

O ur mood much lightened by escaping from my-lady-the-king's-mother, we were glad to join the duke in the corridor and follow him down to the great hall where all the young gentlemen were assembled. The king was, naturally, the center of the group, and stood with his arms crossed over his chest, looking—to my mind—a bit uncomfortable with this whole idea of entertainment.

"For the princess' sake, I hope he is not as gloomy as his mother," I whispered to Grace as we descended.

"I wonder," she mused, "with all the difficulties he has faced in his life, all the threats of assassination, if perhaps his majesty is just unhappy in a crowd." I looked at my innocent cousin, marveling at her insight, and then wondered if perhaps the handsome Lord Thomas had dropped some stories in her ear last night. But before I could ask her to elaborate, we arrived in the main hall, the ladies creating a circle around the gentlemen, who greeted us with smiles.

The duke, satisfied that his little flock had followed him quite obediently, pressed through the men, all of whom parted before his noble rank and his outsize presence. Reaching the king, he swept a courteous bow and turned to face the crowd, a broad grin stretching his lips. He raised his hands over his head for attention.

"Come, come closer, friends, and listen," he called. "While out hunting this morning, I was struck with a thought that was surely inspired by heaven. There we were, mighty astride our horses and armed with our weapons sharp and deadly, and riding in pursuit of prey delicate and fair, but each equipped with weapons of their own. Size. Speed. Agility. Grace. Wits. A pelt that masks its appearance from all but the sharpest eyes." As he spoke, the duke's voice and hand motions wove a spell over his listeners, dropping a blanket of silence over the group. "How apt, I thought, to the hunt we undertake inside the four walls of Lord Ashley's home, where the men seem to have all the advantages, yet the ladies have weapons of their own."

Thankfully, none but the ladies closest to me heard my derisive snort at his use of the word "hunt."

"Thus," he went on, "I have proposed a game of pursuit for our entertainment, one that will keep us merry until it is time to dine." He reached into his belt pouch and held up a fistful of colorful ribbons. "Each lady here will hide herself away, using all her skills." He paused, bestowing his bright smile over the lot of us. "All of her sharp wits, her small stature, her lithe grace, and her ability to conceal that which she does not wish to show. We gentlemen shall remain here a *paternoster*-while and then go forth in pursuit, each with a ribbon with which to bind our prey when—if —we are so fortunate to capture her."

All around me, ladies were giggling and smiling at each other, nudging each other, eyeing the men. Already deciding, it seemed, whom they wanted to be captured by.

No one, I decided. I would not be caught.

"Each gentleman can claim credit for only one lady," the duke continued, "and he will take care to bind her gently around the wrists so as not to harm her. My lady, if I may..." He gestured to Grace, standing nearby. She blushed quite pink as he drew her forward and turned her to face the group, making her put her hands out in front of her so he could tie a long yellow ribbon around her wrists. I noted that he selected a color that complemented her green kirtle quite nicely. "Thus, a gentleman may claim his victory in the hunt. After he has discovered her and bound her thus, he will convey her gallantly back to this spot where they will enjoy refreshments until all of the ladies have been discovered." Behind him, along the walls, servants were setting up long tables, covering them with clean cloths, beginning preparations for the refreshments. "Are there any questions?"

"The rules, Surrey," one of the gentlemen called out.

"Oh, yes, a few rules, ladies. The hunt will be confined to the main part of the house. No going into bedchambers or down into the kitchens. Stay out of privy closets, if you please." A few people laughed or made false gagging noises at that. "And finally, keep out of locked rooms."

"How does one hide in a locked room, your grace, if one does not have the key?" someone asked, to general laughter.

"Yes, well, good point, sir, so no forcing locks or using keys if you have them, and more to the point, it would be unsporting to lock a door behind you once you have entered. Agreed?"

Murmurs of assent went up from the crowd and the duke went on, "One last thing, if you please. Only one lady to a hiding place, and no moving once you have selected your spot. Are we ready to begin?"

As the duke unbound Grace's hands—the poor girl was trembling with embarrassment and with the proximity to a strange male—I moved closer to them and asked, "What if a lady eludes all of the gentlemen?"

He looked up, startled, his fingers fumbling the knot. "I had not even pondered the possibility, Lady Beatrice."

"Not all of us will prove easy prey," I said.

He grinned, slipping the ribbon from Grace's wrists. "That sounds like a challenge, my lady."

I shook my head. "Do not take it so, your grace."

"Prey that eludes the hunter gets to live another day. Any woman who eludes all the men would clearly be the victor, do you not think?" He raised the clutch of ribbons over his head and raised his voice. "Gentlemen, come get your snares."

The gentlemen all pressed forward to retrieve their ribbons from him, and the ladies scattered in small groups to the fringes of the room, voices rising in excited chattering and laughing, ready to flee. I pulled Grace with me out from the center. "Is everyone ready to begin?" the duke asked.

"How long do we have to hide?" one of the ladies asked.

"Did you not hear? The space of a *paternoster*," a man said.

"I did. I just didn't think it was that kind of game," the lady replied.

"Go!" shouted the duke, and with a collective squeal, the ladies set off running. I looked the duke in the eye, facing down his broad, challenging grin with a defiant glare, but when Grace tugged at my hand, I followed her without complaint. As we departed, I could hear his supple, musical voice leading the men in an irreverent chant: "*Pater noster, qui es in cœlis...*"

We did not have long to conceal ourselves.

It was hard to decide if this game was exhilarating or ridiculous, charging along the corridors of our home with family and a handful of strangers, flinging open doors, diving behind an arras or inside a cupboard for concealment, yelling at each other as a better place was found. For the space of two or three breaths—"...*adveniat regnum tuum*..."—I seriously contemplated withdrawing my hand from Grace's and returning to the sewing room. Could the company of that bitter old woman really be worse than this? But Grace was flushed with sudden eagerness. How could I leave her to be captured alone?

"Here," I said, tugging her into the steward's office near the front of the house. To my dismay, I discovered few places to hide in that room. There was no time to find another, though, as the men were winding down their impious prayer. "Go, Grace," I said, pushing her toward the arras on the far wall. It was more than decorative, bulky, and draped so as to keep out the chill of the exterior walls, and therefore able to conceal her slight body.

From afar, I could hear pounding boots as the gentlemen began to disperse in their search. I had to hide, and quickly. After all my brash words to the duke, I did not want to be caught, and helping Grace had hampered my ability to conceal myself well. All that remained of potential hiding places in the study was a rack for storing scrolls, accounting books, and other documents which would not conceal me, a chest too small to hold me, and the space under the massive oak desk, as obvious a hiding place as one could imagine.

I sighed and squeezed underneath the desk, dragging the heavy chair in close. At least I'd have that much concealment.

The sound of distant screeches and laughter drifted down the corridor as the first protesting women were discovered and bound in colored ribbons. "Do you think anyone will come here?" Grace whispered, her voice muffled by the thick arras.

"Shush!" I hissed. "If we talk, someone will hear."

No sooner had the words left my lips than boot heels rang out in the corridor just outside the still-open door. Cursing myself inwardly, I held my breath, listening. The footsteps came to the doorway, paused, and stood. I imagined a person standing, breath held, poised to listen just as I was. Would he leave? No, that was too much to hope for, not without at least a cursory search of the room. Putting action to my thoughts, the boots thudded again, stepping from the stone flags near the doorway onto the thick carpet at the center of the room. *Ugh, Beatrice, stop thinking! This man is taking the thoughts right out of your head!*

Now that he was on the carpet, I could no longer hear him moving about. I had no idea where he was. Was he near the desk or no? Was he peeking behind the arras or behind the hearth screen?

A loud shriek answered my inner queries and I flinched, banging my head on the underside of the desk. "I beg your pardon, lady!" a man's voice exclaimed. I leaned forward, peering through the legs of the chair and rubbing at the top of my head, straining to see who had found Grace.

Grace fought her way out of the hangings, covering her face with one hand in embarrassment. A dark-haired man knelt before her, his head bowed. "Forgive me, please. I had no idea..."

Grace fanned her face with her hands as if to cool it. "No, of course you did not. Rise, sir. Do not trouble yourself."

The man stood, his back still to me. Grace looked, if possible, more embarrassed. She drew in her breath and collected herself. "Lord Beymond," she said, dipping a curtsy that lacked her usual poise. In fact, she wobbled as though she had imbibed too much wine.

Lord Beymond gave her a deep bow, practically falling back to his knees. "Lady Grace. Once again, permit me to apologize. I had no idea..."

"Please." Grace held out a hand to stop him. "Let us never speak of it again."

Suddenly, I understood. Wrapped in the arras as she had been, Grace must have been subjected to some unwelcome contact as Lord Beymond had run his hands through the fabric.

"Yes. Of course. Well, then. If you will permit me...?" He was holding out a pale pink ribbon.

Grace shot a glance at the door, as though hoping someone else would arrive. "Yes, I suppose you have caught me."

He cocked his head, picking up on her hesitation. "...or if you prefer, I could..." He gestured toward the door, the ribbon hanging, sad and limp, from his fingers.

"No," Grace said in a flat tone after another glance at the door. She was waiting for Lord Keighton—*Thomas*—to rescue her. "You have won. I acquiesce."

I rubbed my still-aching head as Grace stuck her hands out in front of her, her eyes averted as Lord Beymond looped the ribbon loosely around her wrists and tied it in a pretty bow. He paused as they both stared at her hands.

"My lady, I am a simple man," he said. "I eat when I am hungry. I sleep when I am drowsy. I laugh when I am merry, which is not often since my

wife's passing. It cannot be said I am a flattering man, unlike some. Lord
Keighton, for instance..."

"Yes," Grace said, breathing the word.

"Yes," Lord John repeated, his tone sour in light of her response. "He is
skilled in flattery, as I am not. He is handsome, as I am not. Yet I must be
what I am, a plain-dealing man."

Goodness. I was starting to feel bad for him.

Even Grace seemed to soften. "You must not be so hard on yourself,
sir," she said.

He waved a hand in the air, dismissing. "I ask only for a chance to be
heard. The same as any man."

Grace drew a breath. "All right."

Lord John took her hands in his, seeming satisfied with her noncommittal commitment. "My lady," he said, "if you please." Grace said no more
as he guided her out of the room.

I hesitated, wondering what to do. Ought I surrender myself and go
after my cousin, or should I remain where I was and play out the game? In
the corridor, jovial voices called out to them as they passed, teasing Grace
for getting caught and inquiring of Lord Beymond where he had found
her. The voices came closer, and I squeezed back under the desk, instinct
making the decision for me. Someone came into the room, made a half-
hearted circuit with shuffling feet, and went out again, talking all the
while of the womanly attributes of my cousin Mary with another man
who remained outside. Silently, I seethed. I remembered Benedict's
teasing yesterday about a gentleman ending with a scratched face if he
spoke to me of love. Well, this fellow deserved it, the way he spoke of
Mary.

After they left, it fell quiet for some time, not just in the room but in
the corridor as well. I wondered if I had missed some signal, if perhaps the
game had finished. Perhaps I had won after all.

I pushed the chair away and clambered out from under the desk.

Benedict was leaning in the doorway, one leg bent and propped against
the wall, arms crossed on his chest. He was looking right at the desk,
watching me scramble like a child.

He had known where I was hidden.

Not so surprising, surely, that I would be hidden near to Grace.

But that he should be the one to capture me.

He raised one hand, slow as the Thames running backward. From his
slender fingers dangled a length of yellow ribbon.

"If you think—" I began, leaning my hands on the desk, ready to quarrel.

"If I think, what?" he asked, cutting me off. "If I expect to take you in? I do, for I have found you."

"Not at all. You happened to be standing there when I emerged from my hiding place. That scarce counts—"

"Of course it does. I knew exactly where to look for you, and I knew that you could not resist revealing yourself. I know you of old, Beatrice."

That he did. But it did not follow that he knew me still. I moved around the desk and crossed the room. I was pleased that my aspect was alarming enough that he abandoned his relaxed pose, dropping his foot to the floor and edging his hands out in front of him, as if to ward me off. I halted only when my skirts swallowed up his boots and was surprised when I had to tilt my head quite high to look up at him. Had I forgotten how much taller he was than I, or had he grown so much in the two years he was gone? Had we truly been so young that he had had so much growing still to do? I shook my head against such thoughts. *Stop it.*

"I care not," I said at last. "It means naught. It is merely a game."

"Your distemper suggests otherwise."

I gave him a sour look and thrust out my hands in tight fists, stopping just short of striking him in the stomach. He flattened himself backward, making a wall hanging of himself. "Get on with it then. Tie me up."

He tipped his head to the side, considering. "I could throw you over my shoulder and carry you out."

"You wouldn't dare." I almost growled it.

He blinked. "I believe I will use the ribbon after all."

I took a step back to put space between us. I could hear the voices of the others gathering far off in the great hall, laughing and greeting each other, but all my other senses were focused in this room, in this moment. I gritted my teeth against the moment he might touch me, resisting in advance any contact. I closed my eyes against the sight of him, the warm cinnamon of his eyes, the new scar, the unfamiliar wiriness of his beard, the curve of his neck where it met his collarbone...but closing my eyes only heightened my awareness of his scent, warm leather and lavender soap and, yes, male sweat. My heart was racing like a greyhound, and I forced my eyes open again.

With swift movements, he brought the ends of the ribbon up around my hands and as he crossed the ends over, his fingers grazed the top of my hand. A jolt shot up my arm like a bee sting and I jumped, gasping. He jerked away too, the ribbon fluttering to the floor. He bent to retrieve it and I drew a deep breath, flexing and shaking out my fingers. As he straightened, I shot a quick, daring look at his face but I could not read his expression.

Good. Fine. This was nothing.

I laced my fingers together prayerfully and held out my joined hands toward him. I would not flinch again.

He took one end of the ribbon in each hand and lifted his hands up around my wrists. I noted how careful he was that this time, he would come nowhere near touching me as he crossed the ribbon, dropped the ends, then pulled them up again, wrapping it twice around. His brows drew together as he made a careful bow and pulled it snug but not tight.

"There," he said.

"I am your captive now," I agreed.

"Oh God. Beatrice," he started, taking a step toward the door and turning his back on me.

"What?" By keeping my bound hands clenched, I could ignore their trembling.

"Don't mock."

"Am I mocking? I didn't realize."

"This is ridiculous," he said, stomping to the door. "Come." He gestured through the doorway, his hand rigid and sharp, like a knife.

"Fine," I said, and sauntered by him.

He remained a stride or so behind me all the way back to the great hall where, it seemed, all the other young women had been captured. Mary was attempting to drink wine, holding the goblet precariously with her hands still bound, making a show of not quite spilling some on her bosom. Not only her captor, but several other men, gathered around to see if she did and, I suppose, to offer her aid in the form of clean kerchiefs. The princess, in contrast, sipped delicately from a goblet offered by the king, the simple act, and the way their eyes met over the rim of the cup, far more suggestive than Mary's loud display. With a suppressed sigh, I turned away from them, looking for Grace.

She spied me in that moment, pushing her way through the others with Lord Beymond on her heels. "Thank goodness you're here, Beatrice," she said, starting to hug me but unable to with her hands still tied up in Lord John's ribbon. Glancing over my shoulder, she saw Benedict. "Oh, look at us, all together again." Her words were innocent enough, but I saw

Lord John's face darken at her words, at the way he was excluded from the "us."

Benedict bowed, smiling. At least he could be easy with *her*. Suddenly, the Duke of Surrey was there as well, his smile wide as always, showing all his white teeth.

"My lady Beatrice," he said, inserting himself between me and Benedict, "I see that you have been captured despite all your brave words."

I glared sidelong at Benedict. "It is a poor hunter who follows another man to the quarry and takes what is left in the nest." Perhaps not the best insult, making myself into the leavings, but still...

"This fledgling has teeth," he growled in reply, "and is scarce worth bagging. I'll not get any reward for your capture."

The duke laughed, his head thrown back, while Benedict and I scowled at each other. "Lady Grace, come. Allow me to escort you to the table to take refreshment."

Lord John opened his mouth to object, but the duke was, after all, a duke. He watched, powerless, as the duke gently loosed the ribbon around Grace's wrists, tucked her hand into his elbow, and led her away.

I turned to Benedict and stuck out my hands at him. "Are we done, sir?"

He bit his lip against another sharp remark. In one swift motion, he drew his belt knife and slashed the ribbon between my wrists, so close I felt the whisper touch of the blade on my skin. The severed pieces of ribbon fluttered to the floor like tiny, distressed birds. Before they touched the stone, he had sheathed his knife and walked away.

CHAPTER 5

T hat evening, we ladies were invited to congregate in the cozy sitting room attached to the guest room the princess was using. I was surprised when the page in green and white opened the door for me to see that I was the first to arrive.

The princess sat in a chair by the fire, making it a throne by her mere presence in it. I curtsied low and she beckoned me in, gesturing to a seat beside her.

"Sit," she said. "I wanted to speak to you alone, Lady Beatrice, before the others join us and we must put on masks of formality."

I folded my hands in my lap and wondered at her words. Did she not understand that everyone wore a mask in her presence? Did not she herself wear a mask of royalty at all times?

She reached out and placed a hand over my hands. "Do not trouble yourself. You have done nothing amiss." Sensible of the honor of being touched by her, I said nothing and promised myself I'd keep my head down and my mouth shut. For as long as possible, at the least. "I merely wanted to advise you of my thinking on certain matters." She removed her hand from mine and sat back again. "The king plans to remove to Woking shortly, and I will return to Westminster, to reside with Lady—" She paused to correct herself with a wry twist of her lips. "With my-lady-the-king's-mother at her house Coldharbour, until such time as we are married. After Christmas, most likely, although I would like to preside over those festivities myself...but no matter."

I could imagine what my-lady-the-king's-mother had to say about her son the king's first Yuletide. This beautiful woman, born royal as he had not been, would not be permitted to outshine him in the palace in which she had been born. Lady Stanley would want the king to preside alone over the court, without the reminder that the House of York had been there first, and longer.

"No matter," she repeated. "I would like to be settled with my ladies by then, for certes before Henry—his majesty—returns to court." She paused again, and her silence was again heavy with meaning. She wanted the security of women around her, friends and allies against the king's mother and even, perhaps, as a subtle reminder to him that she was not friendless.

"And so we come to it, Lady Beatrice." She fixed me with her gaze, amber-gold and clear and intent, and so beautiful I had to catch my breath. "I came here with the design of choosing women for my court, and I would like to bring some of your cousins with me, although upon consideration, Mary may be yet a bit—unready—for court. And for certes I would not ask your aunt to part with Eleanor. But you would be my first choice, a wise and witty woman who entertains me and who would be a bright star in my court."

Blushing, I murmured thanks.

"*Would be*, I said."

She paused, letting me ponder the censure underlying her words. "And that is why I have brought you here before the others. I need to be perfectly clear with you, as you have always been painfully clear with me." I smiled at her choice of words. "I must surround myself with women of a certain temper. A certain disposition. A certain..." She paused again, searching for the word. "Humor. Your stated determination to remain unwed distresses me, as it goes so entirely contrary to the way of the world."

I opened my mouth to respond but she lifted a hand, just a fraction, and I silenced myself.

"Understand something, please. I take no exception to your thinking. I think it is refreshing. Daring, even. I almost envy you. In another world, I might emulate you. But I do not live in another world, I live in this one, and in this one I was born a princess of a royal house and I was destined to marry from the moment I drew breath. As were you, as the only child of a lord of the realm, though you may prefer to imagine you were not."

Under the weight of her words and her gaze, I wanted to squirm in my seat like a chastened child. I forced myself to remain still and listen, because she was far from finished. "You think you are the only woman who balks at being told what to do, whom to marry? Are you not aware that I have been promised to no fewer than four men in my lifetime?" She leaned forward, and her eyes flashed with anger. She ticked the names off on the fingers of her right hand. "The Dauphin of France. The Duke of Portugal. Henry Tudor. And..." She shook her head and snapped her tongue against her teeth, working to regain her composure. "Least said about the fourth is best," she said at last. "I say all this so you will understand something of these men whose names I just spake. I was given no say in whether I would or would not marry them. I never met either of the first two. I was betrothed to the Dauphin at the age of four. The Duke, well, I shall say no more about that. That was..." She shook her head again and pulled herself straighter. "My mother arranged my marriage to Henry while he was still an exile, along with my family's support for his claim to the throne. She was going to make me a queen, one way or another..."

She looked into the fire for a long moment, her fists clenching and unclenching on the arms of her chair. The more she spoke, the more uncomfortable I became, and I found my gaze drifting to the door, hoping it would open to admit some of the other women, ending this all-too-candid conversation.

"However," she said at last, "while my marriage may have been arranged for me, I choose to make the best of what was given me. With Henry, I am queen of the country of my birth. I rule as I was meant to rule. I am...content. And Henry himself is a good companion for me." I could not help but think of her keeping Grace with her the night before, and the time the princess and the king had spent alone in her room. She was binding him to her tightly indeed.

She continued, "My plan—our plan, Henry's and mine—is to make everyone forget the wars and pain of our fathers' and grandfathers' generations and bring peace to our kingdom. This is no dream. We mean to make it real, and that starts with us. One man, one woman, and one day, our children and their children succeeding us peacefully to keep this land safe. No more strife, no more war, no more fighting over this throne. We will not have it." When she said it, with such fierce passion and determination, I believed her. "We need people around us who want the same thing, Lady Beatrice. That peace. That continuity. That dynasty. And that cannot happen without alliances, without marriages, without children."

"I would never do anything to undermine that, your highness," I said.

"Your refusal to join us—to marry and be one of the steadfast allies of our house—undermines us."

My mouth dropped open and I had to force it closed. She was saying that she would leave me here and take Grace to court with her, easy, docile Grace who would marry where and when she was bid.

I struggled to devise an answer. Here among my family, I had long espoused the position that I did not want to marry—since I had lost my heart to Benedict, in fact, although none of them knew that was the reason—until it had become something of a jest. Indeed, my uncle loved to tease me, "Beatrice, we will never find you a husband if you are so shrewd of your tongue," but he said it with a laugh in his voice and a wink in his eye. He believed that one day he would give me in marriage to some worthy man. But Benedict was the only man I had ever wanted to marry, and if I could not have him, I wanted no one.

And now, here he was again. But what if he still would not have me? How could I bear it? And if he would not, could I marry another with the sole aim of achieving the prize the princess dangled before me?

"I do not wish to live out my days in my uncle's house," I said, my voice scraping out of my throat.

"Well then," she said, twitching her lips in half a smile, "you have some decisions before you, do you not?"

I could not allow her to leave me here, to look after my aunt and uncle in their dotage. "Your highness," I said, my words flying ahead of my thoughts, "I promise you this: when you are married and crowned, and when you have borne a prince for the kingdom, then I shall marry any man of your majesty's choosing." Though my heart fluttered in my chest at the thought of rendering up such a promise, it gave me at least a year.

To become a nun.

Or a pirate.

Or, perhaps, to find a way back into Benedict's heart.

The door opened before I could say aught else or the princess could respond to my words. One by one, the other women began to file in. Grace sat beside me on a cushion and gripped my knee with her hand. Placing my hand over hers, I shook off the dark mood that had fallen upon me with the princess' words and endeavored to join the jollity of the others, chatting about the day just ending and their plans for the next.

"Surely Lady Grace will be betrothed before we leave for Woking," the princess said as the fire burned low, "so diligent are the gentlemen in their pursuit."

Shy Grace ducked her head. "I do not seek their attentions," she protested.

"Nevertheless," the princess replied, "they flock to you like children to a sweet."

"I know I should enjoy it," Grace said, "but I never know what to say."

The princess leaned forward and squeezed her hand. "Then say nothing. Let them do all the talking."

"In my experience," Lady Viola said, "they prefer it that way."

Grace smiled. "I am content to speak with Benedict, as he is an old friend."

"And he does so adore the sound of his own voice," I added.

"But the other gentlemen who attend upon me... I don't know how to act or what to say. My mother always said that my silence would be a virtue when it came to courtship, but she was not jesting, Lady Viola, as you seem to be."

My heart squeezed in my chest at the sight of my dear cousin so discontented. Had we been alone, I would have tried to comfort her, but in truth I knew not what to say, for I was never one to cosset a man, nor to make his wooing easy by telling him what he wanted to hear. I would speak plain to everyone, and every person would know my mind, man or woman, king or princess.

"Lady Viola speaks not entirely in jest," the princess said. "Sometimes silence is the best reply. Better they not know what you are thinking."

"Silence?" I scoffed. "Never leave them in doubt of what you are thinking, Grace."

The princess smiled. "You do not believe in the power of mystery, Lady Beatrice?"

"I believe I shall leave mystery to Lord John and his melancholy."

The princess shook her head, chuckling. I took it as encouragement and went on, "In truth, I cannot even look at the man whilst eating, lest I be heartburned an hour after."

Amidst the laughter, Grace looked troubled, her brows drawn down, her mouth tight. She radiated unhappiness with the attention he had been paying to her. The princess made a tutting noise with her tongue. "Fie, Lady Beatrice, for mocking the poor fellow. He has good reason to be sad."

"I do not mock, your highness. I do own he is comely to look upon, or would be if he would but smile now and then."

"We have heard what Sir Edmund Benedict thinks would make a perfect woman. Tell us what qualities you think would make a perfect man." She leaned forward, her eyes bright with mirth.

I smiled at her and said, "It seems to me that the perfect man might be made of a combination of Lord John and Sir Edmund."

She looked around at her ladies for enlightenment. Grace, tilting her head, ventured, "The one dark and the other fair?"

I nodded. "Aye, that is but the beginning. On the one hand, you have Lord John—handsome, yes, but like a pretty picture, he stands there staring at one, saying nothing, making one uncomfortable—while Sir Edmund, well." I tossed my head. "Sir Edmund is like a spoiled child, forever prattling on even when no one wants to hear him. If only he would be quiet!"

The ladies chuckled. The princess said, "So you propose for your perfect man half of Sir Edmund's tongue in Sir John's head, and half of Sir John's melancholy temper in Sir Edmund's merry heart..."

"And add to these a shapely leg and a full purse dangling above..." Here I cupped my hand so that the ladies would not mistake my double meaning, and they all roared with laughter. "And nimble feet in the dance—well, such a man would win the heart of any woman in the world!" I concluded.

"You and Sir Edmund seem to agree more than you disagree, which I do find interesting," the princess said. "Both of you seek an impossible ideal, a paragon. Something that does not exist in this world, and mayhap not in the next, but do not tell my-lady-the-king's-mother I said such a thing." Everyone laughed, enjoying the feeling of being included in this small rebellion.

A gentle rapping on the door interrupted the laughter and good-natured teasing. "Enter," the princess sang out, and the door opened to reveal Benedict.

"Do come in, Sir Edmund," the princess said. "We were just discussing you, in a way."

To a chorus of repressed giggles, he entered the room, casting his suspicious gaze on each of us in turn. The court ladies concealed smiles behind their hands or looked at him from under their lashes, Mary was smirking, and Grace, poor thing, was flushed pink to her ears. No wonder every man was courting her. She was exquisite, even when she was unsettled, perhaps especially so.

And I? Inside, I was as struck dumb, as flushed and dazed as Grace.

"I am...delighted that I can provide a source of amusement to your highness, in any small way."

The princess preened with pleasure at having flustered him.

"Have you a message for me, sir?"

He blinked. "A message. Yes." He straightened and recollected himself. "His majesty the king has sent me to say that the hour grows late and that he will be retiring soon. He wonders if you would be offended if he paid a call to you before then, to wish you a pleasant night."

By my count, the hour was not that late at all, the sun having set only a short while before while we were enduring church services at the behest of my-lady-the-king's-mother. But one did not gainsay a king. And after Grace's experience the previous night, it was clear that "retiring" for the night did not mean going to sleep.

"I would be most pleased if his majesty did so," the princess said, rising from her chair. All of us, reclining on scattered pillows or perched on stools, scrambled to our feet. "My dear ladies, thank you for your attendance upon me today. I will have no further need of you this evening."

We all moved to the door, passing Benedict with varying levels of sobriety. I brought up the rear of the line, and before I could depart, the princess called out to me, "Lady Beatrice, wait, please, if you will."

I halted, startled. I was at the doorway, face to face with Benedict, but he was pointedly looking elsewhere—anywhere but at me. I turned back and curtsied with a feeling of dread rising in my gullet. "Your highness?"

"You will attend me this evening."

"Yes, your highness," I said, mindful of Grace's arrival back in our room from her attendance on the royal couple, flushed and tipsy.

The princess waved a hand at Benedict. "You may return to his majesty, Sir Edmund."

He bowed and departed. I glanced at the princess who was lacing and unlacing her fingers together. I did not feel it was my place to inquire after her thoughts, but standing in silence was not my habit. "What would have you have me do, your highness?" I asked at length.

She looked at me, almost as if surprised that I would ask. "You will keep us company," she said. "You and Sir Edmund will be our companions this evening. That is all."

She turned away and sat again in her chair by the fire. In a moment, there was a brisk knock and Benedict opened the door again to admit the king.

The royal couple embraced and I looked away, but that was no relief to my embarrassment, for my gaze collided with Benedict's. Stomach quivering, I glanced away again, turning my body away so that I saw nothing.

At last, after the faint click of a latch, he said quietly, "They've gone."

I let out my breath but was still reluctant to turn. "And now what?"

I heard the rustle of his garments as he moved, the clink of metal as he poured. "Wine?"

I thought of Grace, giddy and flushed. "No, I thank you."

There was a pause as he drained a goblet. I could hear the gulp as he swallowed the entire thing at once. Good, if I made him as uncomfortable as he made me.

"You know, Beatrice, I did not ask for this duty. I did not ask to be here with you. I would have preferred not to be here."

I turned then. "We are of the same mind, then. What are we to do, since we are not free to leave?"

He refilled the goblet and gestured to the seats by the fire. I scoffed at the implication. "Sit and converse like old friends?"

He shrugged. "We might play at tables, if you will hold this goblet and allow me a moment's peace to move the game between the chairs."

I bit back a sharp reply—I? Give him peace?—and instead took the delicate goblet from his hand, the stem still warm from his grip. Tables was a fine idea. A game would give us something to do, rather than staring at each other or worse, conversing.

He crossed to the far windows and tested the weight of a small round table that stood between them. The wood was dark and intricately carved, and some long-ago forefather who went on Crusade with King Richard the Lionheart had brought it home with him. I hid a smile as Benedict struggled to lift and carry the thing without showing the strain on his face. As if I wouldn't hear his loud exhale when he half-dropped it on the flags in front of the fire.

"Excellent," I said. "Shall I fetch the game, or..."

He straightened, sweeping a hand over his doublet to smooth it. "Pray, my lady, do not strain yourself," he said, his voice thick with sarcasm. He stalked across the room again, this time to a cabinet where items for guests were stored: extra goblets, a lap rug of finest sable, and a few games. I sipped at the wine while Benedict set the tables board between us, with its long dark triangles set into the board of pale maple, and watched him place the circles of ivory and slate in their clusters, three here, two there, five there.

"Are you ready?" he said, holding out a hand.

A shock jolted through me at the prospect of touching him again. I blinked, startled, clamping my lips down on a gasp. Hot color rose in my cheeks.

Then, of course, I realized he only meant for me to hand over his goblet. I hurried to hold it out, cheeks burning with embarrassment now, and in my haste our hands collided with the goblet between, my hand gripping the stem, his hand reaching for the bowl that was too suddenly in his reach, and the red liquid sloshed and slipped up the side, baptizing first his hand then mine. I gave a little cry. He leapt to his feet, reaching with his other hand to steady both our hands and catch the wine before it fell onto the board.

All our sudden motion became utter stillness.

Very slowly, very carefully, he removed the goblet from my grip. With equal care, he reached within his doublet to remove a kerchief, wrapping it around my hand and drying the wine before taking a step back to sit and set the goblet down so he could clean his own hands.

Only then did we resume breathing normally once again.

He did not look at me when he murmured, "Ladies first."

I know the rules of tables, and the strategies—I do—but they abandoned me in that moment and I gave no thought at all to what I was doing as I reached for the dice and threw, moving some number of my pieces some number of spaces toward his side of the board.

We played on in silence for a time, careful to allow each other to complete our moves before reaching for the dice. Careful not to touch, not to look, not to speak. It was maddening.

I stared down at the board. Black and white pieces on a patterned board, and in that instant, the very idea was infuriatingly pointless. We sat here in silence, pretending nothing was wrong between us, that there was nothing unspoken...

"'Well-loved among the ladies of France,' is it?" I said at last, addressing the top of his head.

He jerked so violently I thought he'd drop the goblet, or at least spill the wine again. Good. I wanted him angry. I wanted him as upset as I had been when he left. Was still.

"Sweet Jesus, Beatrice," he sputtered. I had caught him mid-swallow. "What kind of a question is that?"

I sat back, crossed my arms. "I think you heard me. I am simply repeating what you said. And the king alluded to your conquests last night as well. Ladies all over France weeping because Sir Edmund wouldn't marry them. *Les pauvres.* I rather know the feeling."

His mouth twisted. "Beatrice."

"No, I am sorry. Am I making you uncomfortable? Should I not remind you of the past? Should I not take you to task for your behavior? Perhaps I should go." I pushed off of my chair, and it tottered on its legs behind me, landing with a thump. "Oh, but I cannot. I am bound by the princess' command into this tangle from which I cannot escape without harm to my reputation or, worse, to hers. Yet among the king's men you seem to have achieved near-legendary status. How is that fair or just? Please, Sir Edmund Benedict, friend to a king, explain this to me."

He stared at the floor, or perhaps at the game board. I spun away, heading to the table where he had found the wine. I wanted to feel the rush of it in my veins. To replace the anger with something else.

"Why did you not marry?" he said at last. "After I left. You were free to. Why did you not..."

"I have no wish to marry," I said, turning back to face him with an overfull cup of wine in my hand. "Have you not heard me say it?" I scarce recognized my own voice.

"That was not always your wish."

I gripped the goblet tighter, making a fist around it. Were it a softer metal, I might have crushed it. "It is now."

"I am sorry to hear that," he said. I could almost believe that was true regret in his voice.

"Sorry?" I scoffed. "Go to, you care nothing for me. You made that plain when you left."

"Beatrice," he snapped, getting to his feet. "That is not fair."

"Do not speak to me of fair. Not now."

"I was trying to be fair to you, two years ago. I believed then, and I do now, that going away and leaving you here, unmarried, was the only possible—"

I drew my hand back, as if to throw the goblet at him. "I will not hear it. Not again. You have had the better of the bargain in every way."

His jaw clenched and he drew a lengthy breath in through his nose. "Beatrice. We could not marry. You are an heiress. I was no one, and your uncle would not have allowed it."

"And now?"

"And now, what?"

"And now what, Sir Edmund the Great? Now that you've achieved all that you sought and you are no longer a no one? Now that you are attendant of a king?"

He threw up his hands. "You made it quite clear that we were not going to renew our relationship upon my return—if I returned. I do believe you were not entirely hopeful that I would return at all—"

Something shifted inside me, melting, burning. "No, never that," I said, but he was angry now and I knew not if he heard me.

"—saying you would eat all of my killing, as if I could not acquit myself well in battle when all I wanted was for you to believe in me, to wait for me, but no—God in heaven, nary a woman in France was so shrewd of her tongue as you. How could I have forgotten?" He shook his head once, sharply. "No. This?" He gestured between us, back and forth. "This is fine."

I stared, stunned. "Fine."

He nodded. "Good."

I nodded. "Good."

"Shall we finish the game?"

I was spared from answering by the squeal of hinges as the door to the bedchamber opened. I had to curtsy with a full goblet of wine in my hand, the liquid sloshing right up to the rim. As the door scraped shut again, I peeked up under my lashes. The king stood there, his hose clumsily laced and his doublet askew, so I dropped my head again. "Ready, Benedict?" he said, and I was surprised to hear him use the same familiar name we used here where he was raised.

"Of course, your majesty."

I remained, head bowed, until I heard them pass by me, open the outer door, and leave. Then I rose, and with shaking hands I cleared away the goblets we had used and called for a servant to help me replace the game board and heavy little table. On the floor, I found the kerchief Benedict had used to clean up the spilled wine and almost—almost—handed it over to the servant to clean and return to him. Instead, I crammed it inside my sleeve, warm against my wrist.

CHAPTER 6

In the morning, the princess decided we all must rise before the sun so we could see off the men on their hunt. This put the whole household in an uproar, between the bustle of getting a dozen women roused and dressed in the half-light, and the scramble to get downstairs before the men were ready to leave, and the effort to look effortless as we walked outside.

"Goodness, 'tis cold this morning," Grace said, tucking her arm through mine and pulling me close as we proceeded out the main doors and down the stairs. At the bottom of the stairs, the princess stopped and, as had been arranged beforehand, we all fanned out behind her, right and left, bright jewel-toned sparks amidst the frost-tipped fallen leaves that littered the ground. Servants followed with trays of goblets and flasks of ale, ready to fill the stirrup cups we would offer, but they held back—as they had been directed—so as not to disturb the picture we were meant to present as the men rode past.

The king must have known to expect us, for his head was turned back towards the manor as the group of them trotted around the side of the house on the path up from the stables. The rest of the gentlemen were chatting and laughing, while their steeds snorted and tossed their heads, eager to be off. The serving men followed behind in a more somber group, mounted on more placid beasts, many of them bearing on gloved fists the hooded hawks that would do much of the hunting. Nearby, one of the

Ladies Katherine said, "I do so love the sight of a hunting hawk. So majestic."

On her other side, my cousin Mary giggled. "I do so love the sight of a man on horseback," she said.

The princess glanced over her shoulder. "Ladies," she said in a most placid voice, but her scolding was clear. Even Mary quieted.

The king pulled his horse up with a word, and behind him the other men stilled their mounts at once. Turning his horse's head, he walked it toward the princess. A servant came forward, almost invisible, to place a goblet of ale in her hand, and disappeared again. I shook my head, marveling. Was there some magic that came of being born to royalty? For sooth, I never had it.

The king leaned forward in the saddle and the princess reached up with the cup. I could not hear what she said but it made him smile, to quite pleasing effect. I reflected that he should do so more often. He grasped the cup, and for a moment they both held it, motionless. Then he took it from her, sat upright, and drained it all at once.

In that moment, as if released from a spell, everyone moved. A horse stamped its foot, a hawk bated, someone sneezed. The servants hustled forward, handing each of us women a goblet, and each of us in turn sought out one of the gentlemen to offer best wishes for a good hunt. Grace was meant to go first to the Duke of Surrey, though it was in fact my place, as the eldest of the family. But he had shown favor to Grace, and she was the daughter of the house... I laughed a little to myself, feeling a twinge of jealousy over a man I did not even want. I hung back a moment, watching how she managed it.

And was surprised when she passed him by for Lord Thomas Keighton.

Before I could reach him, my Aunt Ursula noticed and swept in to hand the duke a cup, and he pretended to appreciate the honor of being served by the lady of the house rather than her beautiful daughter.

The sole woman left standing on the steps, I looked around to see which of the men had not been offered a farewell cup. I noted that Benedict had stopped his horse almost directly in front of me. I could scarce believe it. He must have chosen to stop here, if only to torment me further.

I considered the other alternative. Lord John Beymond looked uncomfortable on a thick-limbed black stallion, squinting at Grace as she stood beside Lord Thomas' horse, her face alight with interest as he spoke to her. His hands twitched on the reins, making his horse jumpy.

Very well then.

Gripping my cup in a tight fist, I approached Benedict's horse, a sleek and muscular chestnut that—and I had to smile—perfectly matched his eyes. Ignoring the man, I greeted the steed first, stroking his velvet nose and murmuring sweet words as I rubbed behind his cheekbone.

"You always did have a way with them," Benedict said.

Keeping my eyes on the horse—he had very long eyelashes—I said nothing. Nothing to Benedict, that is. The horse and I were having a lovely conversation.

"His name is Cinnamon."

Of course, it was. The very color of his eyes, for certes.

With a final scratch between the fine fellow's ears, I turned at last to his rider. I took my time lifting my gaze, taking in his polished boots, his leather riding hose, his green jerkin—always a good color with his complexion—and finally his face, marred by a tightness around his mouth and eyes. "Do you have something for me?" he demanded.

"Do you want it of me? I'll gladly be off and leave you to one of my cousins."

He did laugh at that. "Oh, heaven spare me your cousins." He gestured with a gloved hand. "Here. I won't leave you with your task undone."

I moved closer, standing by his stirrup to hand up the cup. Of a sudden, I recalled the goblet we passed between us the night before, the wine spilling, the wildness of my feelings... I almost couldn't hand it to him and lost the will to speak. He hesitated in leaning down, seeing, perhaps, something in my face. "Beatrice?"

I nodded and lifted the cup higher. I managed to get out some strangled words. "A safe and prosperous hunt, my lord."

He took the cup from me and drained it. "I thank thee," he said formally, passing it back.

I turned and walked away before he had a chance to say anything else.

I knew I should look about to see if any other men had not been offered a cup but found I could scarce breathe. I hurried back toward the stairs, trying to look like I was not fleeing. I gestured to a servant to refill the cup as I cast my eyes over the men and horses, but I saw nothing but a blur. Were these tears? Impossible.

The sound of impatient hooves told me that the men were readying to depart. I spun around, foamy ale threatening to spill over the edge of the cup, to find Lord John's horse standing nearly atop my skirts.

I blinked. "Lord John?"

"Everyone seems to have forgot me," he said, his voice tight.

"I am very sorry, my lord," I said, handing him the cup. Standing on the step as I was, I was of a height with him, and I could see the anger and frustration flashing in his eyes. "God speed you on your hunt, Lord John."

He thrust the empty cup back into my hands. "I thank thee. I am not of many words, but I do thank you." He hesitated, his eyes half-averted as though he were uncertain whether to say more. "At least one of the daughters of this house has not forgotten her proper duty."

He jerked his horse's head around sharply, and I winced at the pain it must have felt, but also at his criticism of my family, righteous though it might have been. "I am sorry, my lord," I repeated, but he was already gone, following the other men out of the courtyard and out into the fields beyond the manor where they could hunt their hawks.

* * *

The morning we spent at needlecrafts again with my-lady-the-king's-mother, waiting for the men to return. At least she had not been up with the dawn to spoil our seeing-off of the men, and she had not insisted on our attending church services thereafter, though she and her women went to chapel several times a day as though they were nuns.

Aunt Ursula looked up from the shirt in her lap to glance at Grace, who was frowning at some intricate embroidery on a sleeve. "Did Lord Thomas say aught to you this morning at the leave-taking, my dear?"

Grace jumped, stabbing herself with the needle. She winced and stuck her finger in her mouth. Eleanor laughed at her. "No doubt he wanted to take you, not leave you," she said.

"Nothing, Mother," Grace said, glaring at Eleanor.

"Your father hopes that you will consider the Duke of Surrey's suit. Though Lord Thomas may be younger and handsomer, a duke is a far worthier match."

Lady Stanley sniffed. "If reaching above one's station."

To my mind, any claims of reaching above one's station were quite hollow coming from a Beaufort, daughter of a duke though my-lady-the-very-superior-king's-mother may have been. I was sorely tempted to mention that her own family line, on her father's side, had been born illegitimate, the children of John of Gaunt's liaison with his mistress Katherine Swynford.

For once, I held my tongue.

"The duke is so effusive," Grace said, continuing her complaint from the previous day. "He speaks, and jests, and I scarce know what to say in return."

Mary sat up straighter. "If you've no desire to see the duke court you, Grace, I'll gladly—"

"No," the princess, Aunt Ursula, and I said, all together.

Aunt Ursula looked at me, surprised. "I had no idea of your taking an interest in these matters, Beatrice. You have been absolute in your opposition to the very thought of marriage till now."

"I take no interest in the duke himself," I said. "Yet I would spare him Mary's tender attentions."

Mary threw a ball of yarn at me. I caught it and tossed it back. It bounced off her head and rolled under Eleanor's chair, and she dropped to the floor to chase it like an oversized kitten. My-lady-the-king's-mother, if possible, looked even more dour and disapproving than before.

"You are the eldest of us," Grace said to me, returning to her fancy stitching. "There is no reason you could not seek the duke's attentions, were it not for your well-known aversion to marriage."

"True," Aunt Ursula said. "The duke is a fine man, and well worth your consideration. If not for his interest in Grace." In her voice, we heard the end of the discussion.

My-lady-the-king's-mother sniffed again. Would anything ever please that lady? "In truth, it is better that Lady Beatrice maintain her policy against marriage. She is too cursed of tongue to make any man a happy wife."

I gritted my teeth. "That God has seen fit as yet to send me no husband, I am on my knees every morning and evening to give Him thanks."

She glared at me, and I could see that she was doubly offended that I would make mock of prayer, and that I would pray to give thanks for being so contrary and unnatural. As she saw it.

"Surely we can find someone to suit our lady Beatrice," Lady Katherine Howard said. She sounded disinterested, as though the princess had asked her to say it.

Thinking of Benedict, and his harsh reaction to me last night, I said, to cut off any suggestions in that direction, "I could not abide a man with a beard." To demonstrate, I rubbed the sleeve of my gown against my face and grimaced. "I'd as soon lie in a cupboard among the woolen blankets."

Over the laughter, the princess said, "The fashion is now to wear no beard."

I scoffed and rolled my eyes to the ceiling, making sure everyone saw. "What would I do with such a man? Dress him in one of my gowns and make him my maid? No, I thank you. I have enough maids in my service." The princess laughed loudest of all, though of course my-lady-the-king's-mother disapproved. I continued, "Hark to me. He that has a beard is more than a youth, and he that has no beard is less than a man. And he that is more than a youth is not for me and he that is less than a man…" I paused, shrugging, "Well, I am not for him."

Mary leaned over to her sister Eleanor and said, in an exaggerated whisper that everyone could hear, "Aha! The duke and his beard are not for Beatrice!"

My-lady-the-king's-mother clucked her tongue against her teeth and said, "Enough folly, girls. Attend to your duties." Waving her hands at her lap, she made it clear that the time for jesting was over and the time for work had arrived. With a collective sigh, we picked up neglected shirts and sleeves and altar cloths, threaded needles, and bent to our work.

* * *

At dinner that afternoon, Aunt Ursula made a point of saying to the table at large, "You have come to visit us at a happy time, for we always celebrate the harvest with a masque and revel with all of our neighbors and friends."

"Indeed," the Duke of Surrey said, "many a time have I joined in the revelry at Lady Ursula's excellent harvest celebrations. One must consider himself fortunate to be included among the guests."

Aunt Ursula inclined her head, pleased with his compliment.

Lady Stanley, her mouth pinched, looked less pleased. "Is tomorrow not the feast of the Nativity of the Virgin?"

Several people suppressed groans. Was my-lady-the-king's-mother going to spoil even this, my family's traditional revel, with her dour religiosity?

Princess Elizabeth reached over and tapped Lady Stanley's clenched fist with her own fingers. With that small gesture, the older woman's face eased, and in that instant, I realized that she was not yet an old woman—

certainly younger than either Uncle Lionel or Aunt Ursula, and younger than her constant piety, unceasing disapproval, and dour clothing would suggest.

Aunt Ursula's smile wavered but did not falter. She brazened her way forward, determined not to give way. "I assure you, my lady, we will do nothing to disrespect the holy day," she replied, "and we never would."

"The holy virgin's day," the princess said, "would be a most appropriate day for gentle revelry. And perhaps a betrothal or two?"

Around the table, there were cries of approval, a smattering of applause. I thought Mary would collapse from lack of air at the thought, and Grace shot a shy look toward Lord Thomas under her lashes. "Should we not see to the preparations, then, Aunt Ursula?" I said. "We have been much distracted of late."

"Oh yes," Mary said, jumping to her feet and dragging Eleanor after. "Tell us what we must do."

Aunt Ursula wiped at her mouth and glanced at them. "I had not meant this very minute..."

The princess looked at her. "I am no longer hungry, Lady Ashley," she said. "Have you had your fill?"

It mattered not whether my aunt had eaten enough or had just begun to eat. If the princess wanted to leave the table, we would all leave the table. Aunt Ursula rose and led the way, leaving my-lady-the-king's-gloomy-mother staring after us.

* * *

We followed my aunt to the great hall where several trestle tables and benches were being set up for our work. She issued a series of orders, reserving to herself the task of sending out new invitations to neighbors near and far, making sure everyone understood that the king was staying with us and would be attending her party. Servants were dispatched into the woods surrounding the manor to collect branches, vines, leaves, pinecones, and acorns, and indeed to dig up small trees to put in pots for our indoor forest. We ladies were not permitted to decorate the hall, my aunt decreed, but we could make the masks, and so we gathered around the tables to see what there was to be used. In addition to bits and bobs of fabric and fur, buttons and lace, there were deadheads of flowers, dried leaves of herbs, stalks of grain, wisps of straw, nuts in their shells, clusters of berries clinging to twigs, assorted bird feathers, and all sorts of other remnants of the gardens, woods, and fields around the house.

I stood with Grace, away from the court ladies, and pondered what disguise I would wear. It would need to be something special, something beautiful and bright, something that Benedict would never guess at...

"What are you thinking of, Beatrice?" Grace asked.

"I believe I will disguise myself as a star."

"A good choice. What disguise should I choose?"

I considered. "Something beautiful and precious as you are."

She smiled and pushed at my arm. "Stop it."

"Nay, I am in earnest. You must represent yourself as you truly are." I leaned closer to her. "Do you think the princess' remark earlier was in jest? For certes, she and the king and indeed your father fully expect that someone, if not more than one, will make an offer for your hand at the masque. They must recognize who is behind your mask, and further, your mask must reflect who you are. A gemstone, mayhap, or..." My racing thoughts tripped ahead of my tongue and my words took a moment to follow. "Or, given Aunt Ursula's theme, a snowflake. Unique and perfect, but also delicate and fragile, like to melt away if one touch it too roughly or speak too harshly nearby. Yes. That is the answer."

She was shaking her head, mayhap thinking that I spake in jest. She ran her fingertips over the items on the table without seeming to note what was under them. "Think you that I will receive an offer of marriage so soon?"

"I would be shocked if you did not."

She shook her head again, more decisively, and picked up a blank mask-face. "So," she said, "a snowflake. And a star. Yes?"

We began to work on our masks, standing side by side without speaking, lost in thought. "Beatrice," she said at last, "what did the princess say to you yesternight, ere we all arrived?"

I glanced up from the pile of ribbons I was sorting through, pulling out all the white, cream, and silver. "Nothing of import. Why do you ask?"

She too looked up from the table, her gaze meeting mine with a sharpness I was unaccustomed to from her. I sighed. "She spoke of court, of going to Westminster."

Grace drew in her breath and moved closer, glancing aside to assure we were not overheard. "Yes? She will bring you with her?"

I tilted my head from side to side. "Mayhap yes, mayhap no. She made it quite clear that she and the king only want married couples at court with them." I touched the tip of her nose. "And so, there is no doubt that you will go."

She ignored me. "You think you will not go? But why ever not? There are a dozen or more men come here to no other end but to find a bride. Why must you be so perverse as to resist the very idea?"

"Perverse, am I?" I swung a feather at her like a sword, but she was having none of my jests. "I am not perverse, nor am I determined not to marry, no matter what I have said."

"And yet?" she prompted when I said no more.

"And yet, I like not this unseemly haste, this desperation. I know marriage is an agreement, an arrangement, and yet..." Memories rose up, unbidden, and I thrust them aside. "You would prefer to have some say, would you not? To choose Lord Thomas over the duke, no matter what your father says?"

Grace slid her glance from side to side, again checking that we were not overheard. "Of course," she said, almost a whisper. "Is that what is behind all your defiant words? A choice my father will not allow you to make?"

A blow struck too close to the mark. I opened my mouth to deny it, but we were at that moment joined by the perpetually grieving Lady Viola. A blank mask dangled from one hand and she cast her gaze over the items on the table with a disinterested air.

I was not ungrateful for her interruption and turned to her with smile. "How now, Lady Viola," I said, "what will your disguise be, do you suppose?"

She looked at me with her great dark eyes. "I have no idea. Given my mourning state, I ought not to be attending a party at all."

I shared a glance with Grace. "Can you not break your mourning for one night? I'm sure one of my cousins has a gown that would suit..."

Viola fixed me again with that fierce gaze. "It seems I could count the days on these two hands since I lost my brother, though I know it has been longer. My father, too, is not long lost to me." She assayed a tight smile. "So, no, Lady Beatrice, I cannot set aside my mourning. I do not know if I will ever remove it."

Chastened, I did not reply. She shook her head, banishing the tears that had gathered. "I will make a raven's mask to match my mourning robes. That should discourage any young lord from making an overture of love, do you not think?"

I agreed. "Perhaps I should do the same, and dance by myself, undisturbed by suitors all night long."

Grace groaned. "Oh, heaven give me strength."

* * *

I know not what the gentlemen did all that day—perhaps they practiced their dancing—for we ladies were preoccupied with making masks and altering our garments to match the masks we planned to wear. We also made masks for the men: eagles and foxes, lions and wolves. By nightfall, we went exhausted and happy to the dining table. Everyone was full of excited chatter about the coming masque, sharing hints about disguises and promising dances.

Somehow, I found myself seated next to Benedict.

To judge by the smirks of those around us, it did not appear to be a happenstance. They seemed to be waiting for another outburst.

Lord John Beymond sat upon my other hand.

Greek sailors worried about being forced to choose between the man-consuming monster Scylla and the ship-crushing rocks of Charybdis. In the moment, I felt much the same.

Lord John leaned toward me, his lips so close to my ear as to make me squirm in discomfort. "My lady Beatrice, perhaps you can answer a question for me."

"Perhaps," I replied.

"It is something that has always puzzled me," he said, his fingers rubbing absently at his beard.

"Indeed," I said, wishing myself seated on the other side of the table with Grace. Yet she was deep in conversation with Lord Thomas and would likely pay me no mind.

"Sir Edmund's name. Benedict. It is such an odd family name. Was his family connected to the church in some way?"

I shot him a look, trying to determine if he had some hurtful purpose in asking the question. Seeing none, I shifted in my seat, turning my body to face him so as to block Benedict from our conversation. "Have you not asked him yourself, my lord?"

Having captured my attention, he likewise turned to face me. A small smile tugged at his lips. "If the answer is what I believe to be true, then he would not thank me to do so."

My spine stiffened on Benedict's behalf. "And what do you believe to be true?"

Again, his fingers played over his bearded chin. Then he reached for his goblet and took a drink. I gripped the edge of the bench upon which we sat, waiting. At last, he answered me. "That he is bastard born, the name belonging not to his father but made and bestowed to cover for his birth. *Benedictus*, meaning blessed. Is the name not something of a jest?"

I allowed myself to smile even as my fingernails dug into the wooden bench. "Say that to his face. His gauntlet will meet your words."

He tossed his head. "Precisely why I would never say such a thing to him."

"Instead you hide behind a woman."

"My lady, I assure you," he said, leaning toward me again, his eyes dark and hard, "I have not survived these recent years by being a coward." Though his hold on his goblet was loose and relaxed, his other hand gripped the bench beside mine, and I could feel the raw strength there.

"His father was a priest," I said at last, "now the Bishop of Lincoln. Benedict has not seen him in many years. He was a boy when the man left him here as my uncle's page."

"And so you have known him all your life," he said.

"Very nearly. I came here to live when I was five, when my father died."

He nodded, seeming aware of my family history. "But if you are such old friends, what can be the source of such discord between you?"

"What do you mean, my lord?"

Still holding the wine in his hand, he pointed a finger at me. "Do not try to play the innocent. You and he have been publicly feuding since the moment we arrived."

I loosened my grip on the bench and waved a hand. "It is but an old jest. My uncle calls it a merry war, and so it is."

He nodded, but with a quirk of his eyebrows conveying an air of disbelief. "If you say so, my lady." He angled his face to look out across the table, seeming to scan the entire party but I could see that his gaze alit upon Grace, lingered there, and then jumped to the duke, who sat at my uncle's right hand. I could imagine his thoughts even before he spoke. "Your cousin seems quite to favor young Lord Keighton."

I turned back to face the table, but I did not allow myself to relax. Not with this man. "They do seem to enjoy one another's company."

"The king was under the impression that the Duke of Surrey was going to make an offer for her."

I reached for a piece of bread, simply to have something to do. "I have not heard that he has done so."

"Nor I," he said, as if we would both have been the first to know such a thing. "I would imagine that your uncle would condone the match."

"I suppose he would," I said, "but I do not suppose my cousin would, given the favor she shows to Lord Keighton."

He turned to look at me again. "My lady Beatrice, you astonish me. Are you suggesting that a young girl should say whom she is to marry?"

I spread some cheese on the bread. "Why ever not?"

"A woman needs to know her place. A woman must be obedient to her father's commands, and then to her husband's."

"Why should a father know better a woman's mind when it comes to choosing a husband?"

He scoffed. "Oh, please, my dear lady. Now I am sure you jest." When I did not laugh, he continued. "Marriage is far too important a matter to be left to the weak and fickle hearts of women. Marriages unite kingdoms, pass titles, secure fortunes... Why, just look at the head of this very table to see the importance of marriage. Should our king and princess be free to marry where their hearts lead them? A stable boy for her, a kitchen wench for him? Where would England be then?"

I forbore to mention that this king's grandfather, Owen Tudor, had been wardrobe-master to his grandmother, Katherine Valois, once princess of France and then queen of England, who had no doubt followed her heart in marrying him. Instead, I said, "They appear to be quite content with what fortune has handed them, both in uniting their kingdom and in uniting their hearts."

"Rubbish. Do you not see that it matters not? If they hated each other, yet they would be required to breed heirs for the throne."

Now I reached for my wine. "Oh, do go on, Lord John. I am quite seduced by your words."

"Why would I expend the effort to seduce you, Lady Beatrice? If you were to be my wife, you would perform your duties as required."

"As in the dance, sir, a willing partner is preferable." I pinned him with a glare. "Or so I have heard."

He chuckled. "Now I understand why Sir Edmund enjoys crossing verbal swords with you. It is most entertaining."

"I am glad to provide entertainment for you, my lord. Willing partner or no."

He saluted me with his wine glass and turned his attention to his meal. I allowed myself a deep breath and a deeper draught of wine.

"Well, well, Beatrice," came Benedict's teasing voice from my other side. *Was I not to have a moment's peace?* "I had no idea you found Lord John Beymond so appealing."

"Hardly that," I growled through my teeth.

"Ah, has he offended you as well? Is there any man here who has not?"

I grinned at him. "The king has behaved most kindly toward me."

He smiled as well, and my eyes were caught by the tiny white scar under his eye. This close, I could see that it was not as small as it had seemed but slid down his face. What appeared to be a flaw in his beard, a line of pale blonde among the copper, was in fact an extension of the scar. I caught my breath. That must be why he grew the beard, to cover the scar. How much he must have seen, how much he must have experienced, and how much I longed to ask him about it. And yet, we could not seem to speak in civil tongues. I frowned a little and gulped more wine.

"I do not like your beard," I said.

He laughed, making a sound rather like one of Lord John's mocking snorts. "I had heard that you have decided opinions on beards."

"Have you indeed?" I had made that quip to a room full of women. Who had told tales out of school?

"Aye." He shifted a little closer on the bench. My heart skipped in my chest and I tried to move away but was trapped by the presence of Lord John on my other side. "You said that kissing a man with a beard is like lying in the woolens."

I lifted one shoulder to indicate how little I cared for the comment, yet my pulse had begun fluttering in my throat. "I may have said so."

He inched closer again.

"Have you much experience kissing men with beards?" he asked.

To my chagrin, my cheeks flushed. A twitch in the corner of his mouth revealed that he saw it. Growing angry, both at him and myself, I blurted out, "Beards are out of fashion. Only old men wear beards these days."

He flinched a little.

Oh, this was intolerable.

I raised a hand and felt his intake of breath. So. He was not made of stone. With a tentative finger, I touched the line of the scar—an impossible, impermissible intimacy at table—from his eye to his jaw. His skin was rougher than I remembered, and there were fine lines around his eyes. The hairs of his beard were cropped short, just before they could curl, and of a texture rougher than his hair. Richer in color than his hair also, they were a multitude of tones, mainly copper, but also brass and gold and a few strands of mahogany.

A shudder ran through him and he blinked. "Beatrice..."

A cup struck the table somewhere far away, and the buzz of conversation swelled. I snatched my hand back. My-lady-the-king's-mother stood. "I am going to the chapel," she said, scraping every one of us ladies with her eagle-sharp gaze. "Which of you will join me?"

All along the table, men and women sent nervous glances darting, one to the other, rabbits dashing to escape her. I looked to the princess and noted that tiny crease between her brows that indicated displeasure. She did not want to attend services any more than the rest of us. Would she prevent it from happening?

As she opened her mouth, the king set his hand over hers where it lay on the table. "My lady mother," he said, in a voice that would brook no argument. "Princess Elizabeth has promised to accompany me to a private service later this evening. Release her and her ladies for the nonce."

Her eyes narrowed but she could not gainsay her son the king. Lady Stanley curtseyed and left the room. After a moment's hesitation, Aunt Ursula followed, perhaps thinking to protect the rest of us from my-lady-the-king's-angry-mother's wrath by appearing obedient. A whisper of released breath whooshed around the table, followed by nervous laughter. The princess, concealing a smile behind her goblet, leaned back against the high back of her chair. "Let us have a story, something of King Arthur and his valiant knights," she said, before taking a sip of her wine.

Several of the young women clapped, and Eleanor, who was still a child at heart in many ways cried, "Oh yes!" Benedict began to rise from his seat, smoothing his doublet, a self-satisfied look on his face that spoke of being called upon in this fashion many times in the past. The man beside him patted him on the back, and some of those further away pounded fists or knife-handles on the table in approval.

Mayhap I only imagined, or mayhap I did indeed see, the slightest flicker of displeasure on the king's face. He cast his gaze over the rest of the company, looking away from Benedict. "Where is Lord Howarth? Will, favor us with a tale."

Startled, Lord Howarth nearly choked on his wine. Recovering quickly, he placed his goblet on the table and wiped at his mouth, rising from his seat. Beside me, Benedict froze, taking in what was happening. Their gazes collided and held for a moment, and I could nearly feel it, like sparks flying off two swords in combat. Then Lord Howarth pivoted slightly toward the king and bowed. "I am honored that your majesty should ask." Benedict had no choice but to bow, his back stiff, and then sink back into his seat. His face was shadowed with something close to anger, akin to resentment. I sensed that he was not used to being shunted aside.

What had brought about the shift in storyteller? Clearly the other men had expected him to be chosen; clearly this was his accustomed role.

Was Benedict, like me, being punished for his stated resistance to marriage?

The blood roared in my ears so that I could hear nothing else, not a word that Lord Howarth spake. Benedict sat silently fuming beside me, staring down at the table. After a few moments, he pushed himself up off the bench and walked out of the hall without a word. An unpardonable rudeness in ordinary company, it verged upon treason when done in the presence of a king. Yet no one stopped him or even seemed to mark him.

Before his shadow had faded beneath the high archway, I rushed after him.

I almost caught up with him on the stairs leading up to the gentlemen's quarters. "Benedict, wait."

Three steps above me, he turned, his hurt so palpable I shrank back. "What do you want, Beatrice?" he asked, biting off his words. "Come to gloat at my downfall?"

"No," I said. "I want to—" But what I wanted I could not say.

He waved a hand at me. "Begone, will you? Please. Just leave me be."

He turned and charged up the stairs, where I could not follow.

CHAPTER 7

As the sun faded from the sky, strains of music drifted up from the great hall, reaching the nursery where we had all gathered to dress for the dance. Aunt Ursula stood in the doorway, hands on her hips, a sentinel keeping us in as much as she was keeping intruders out. "After all my hard work," she kept insisting whenever Eleanor or Mary would plead to be released, "I will not have you spoil it by running down the stairs like impatient children. You are ladies, and you will behave like ladies."

At last she was satisfied that we were ready to be seen and that the party below had gone on long enough that our arrival would be noted and appreciated. She arranged us in a line according to our rank, a familiar enough occurrence, with Grace as always in the lead. My cousins could scarce contain their excitement as we walked down the stairs, the music growing louder with each step and with it, the sounds of voices, mostly male.

"What of the princess?" Grace whispered to her mother. "Shouldn't she take precedence over all?"

"The princess is already down," Aunt Ursula said in a soothing tone. "She, as well as Lady Stanley and the other married ladies, wanted to join the festivities before you maidens."

"To enjoy some peace before they let slip the hunting hounds," I said, only half intending to be heard.

"Fie, Beatrice!" my aunt scolded. "If any of the gentlemen pay their attentions to your unmarried cousins—or indeed to you yourself—that is right and just. It is the way of the world. It is time you ceased fighting it or you may find yourself most unhappy indeed."

I had a sharp reply ready but had to stay my tongue for we had reached the ground floor and the broad archway opening into the great hall. Grace paused to put on her mask, a glittering white snowflake, and as Aunt Ursula tied the ribbons at the back of her head, I peered through the archway beyond them.

The great hall had been decorated to look like a forest glen, with trailing vines and slender branches draped along every beam and wrapped around every pillar. Richly scented pine needles had been mixed with the rushes that were strewn on the floor, and small seating areas, perfect for intimate conversations, were concealed by clusters of branches arranged to resembled bushes. Trestle tables lined the walls around the outside of the room, draped with cloths in rich, autumnal colors and laden with treats, and candles sparkled everywhere in tall, branching candelabras. The center of the room had been left clear for dancing. Music drifted out over the room from a group of minstrels that was concealed on the dais behind a stand of small potted pine trees. It was positively magical.

Eleanor and Mary pushed past us, masked and giggling. Lady Viola, her mask a dark, sharp-beaked raven to match her mourning garb, paused beside me to admire the room. "I don't know if I can do this," she murmured.

I touched her arm. "You don't have to dance," I said. "You can make an appearance for an hour or so, just to show the king you have obeyed his command, then go back to your room."

She nodded and stepped across the threshold, joining the party with the air of one going to her doom. I raised my own mask toward my face. I was quite proud of it, in fact. Its many points and streaming rays concealed my face quite well and would doubtless prevent any man from seeking to court me. As I tried to put it on, however, I found that its silken ties had become entangled among the rays, which were after all only more gold ribbons, stiffened with starch. I couldn't pull them free without risking damage to the delicate construction.

"Grace," I said, stepping back beside her and hoping for the help of an extra pair of hands. "Could you spare a thought for your poor cousin? If I can't put this mask on, Aunt Ursula will not permit me into the party." My aunt nodded in mock seriousness.

Grace held the mask in her hands as I pulled and tugged at the long silken ties, unwinding them from the starlight rays. When I looked up, I could see that her eyes, in the deep shade of her mask, were large and round. Rather than excitement, however, they were filled with trepidation. "It's only a party, dearest," I said, "and no binding promises need be made tonight."

Aunt Ursula sniffed and threw a parting shot at me before striding into the party, masked as an owl. "Speak for yourself, Beatrice."

"Everything is beautiful," Grace whispered, securing my mask. "Everyone is so beautiful."

"As are you," I said. How many young women was I going to have to prop up this evening? "I will tell you what I just told Lady Viola: all you have to do is dance a few dances, spend an hour or two, and then you can leave."

My mask on, she turned me by the shoulders to face her. Her mask, unlike mine, did not cover her entire face, and it was easy to tell who she was. "You misunderstand me, dear cousin. I have no desire to leave. At least not if..." She paused, pressing her lips together. "I only wish I had your wit to protect me. Or that courtship could occur in silence."

She knew not all she hinted at. Or mayhap she did. "Say not that aloud," I urged. "Not where your mother can hear, nor any man."

"Why?"

"A courtship in silence?" I repeated, adjusting her mask. "To a man, that would mean a courtship of hands, and lips, and tongues that do not speak..."

"Beatrice!" she squealed, cutting me off.

I laughed and slipped my arm through hers so we could go in together. Walking into that room was like stepping into the current of a fast running stream. We were pulled in, swept along with the flow of people strolling, chatting, swaying, laughing, dancing... Aunt Ursula must have invited every family within riding distance, for the room was full to the walls with masked people.

In the light of dozens of candles, in her white kirtle embroidered with silver, Grace positively glittered. Beside her, I must have appeared a dim shadow, for all that I'd chosen a golden star as my disguise.

Despite the number of people in the room, our entrance did not go unnoticed. Heads turned our way, all of them masked, and it was quite disconcerting to realize I could not tell who anyone was, excepting of course my uncle with his greying hair and his limp, and the king, garbed as a red dragon, a nod to his Welsh heritage. All others—wolf and fox, pheasant and peacock, bear and swan—were unknown to me. For once, I felt as Grace did in a crowd. There was nothing for it but to set about learning who was who.

Men began to approach us, and Grace shrank back. But the first to reach us was Uncle Lionel, his mask a snarling lion, who took Grace's hand and pulled her away from me. "Daughter," he said, his voice deep and rumbling, "you remember what I told you?"

"Yes," she said, squirming under his firm grip. "I remember."

"Good." He cast a look at me and pivoted her farther away to keep me from overhearing. "Lord John Beymond has made some overtures to me, and the king's right hand would be a good match, but I believe you can reach higher. Far higher. If the Duke of Surrey entreats you to dance, you shall agree with good will." He leaned in closer. "I do not want to hear any foolishness about this young Lord Keighton. You shall not refuse a duke."

"No, Father," she whispered.

He released her and nodded, satisfied. "Beatrice. Remember, you will never get a husband if you are so shrewd of your tongue."

"What man will know who I am in this mask, Uncle?"

"Two minutes of speech with you will teach him who you are. For once, be mild and see what comes of it."

I laughed at the thought. "Wherefore? To catch a man I do not want and who would not want me once I removed my mask?"

My uncle shook his head. "I will see you married ere I die, niece."

I did not gainsay him again, for after the princess' demand, I was beginning to think I might have to make some compromises.

As he left us, a man dressed all in black with a mask of a cat covering his entire face emerged from the shadows near the wall and came towards us. Something about his carriage uncovered him to me: Lord John Beymond. At the same time, from the other direction came a group of men led by a tall and mysterious gentleman clad in a doublet and hose of deep red-brown, with a half-mask crowned with the glorious antlers of a mature stag. Spying us, the stag broke into a broad smile. He must be the Duke of Surrey, which meant that among the gentlemen with him were Lord Thomas and Benedict. Glancing from the men to my cousin, I had no time for further calculation, for she had flushed pink with pleasure at the very idea of Thomas, her lips curving into a tremulous smile, her gaze sliding right past the duke.

Trouble, trouble, I thought as I stepped forward to intercept Lord John.

"Good even, Sir Cat," I said, giving him my full attention and prettiest curtsy.

He scarce bothered to conceal his annoyance as he gave me a perfunctory bow. "My Lady Star," he replied. "You shine most brightly tonight."

"I thank you," I said, striving to behave like one of my flirtatious cousins, looking up from under my lashes and tilting my head, all the while feeling foolish. "I believe cats can see in the dark, is it not so?"

He glanced past me, toward Grace. "Yes, and your shimmering presence is making that rather difficult at the moment."

"I beg your pardon. You are not a stargazer? Is there some other thing that you would wish to gaze upon?"

He did not restrain an impatient grunt, seeing that his chance with Grace had been cut off by the duke. "No. Never you mind. In fact, I would be honored if you would dance with me this evening." He bowed again and departed without allowing me the chance to reply. I stood there staring after him with my mouth gaping open, more fish-on-land than fallen star.

I turned back to Grace and found her still surrounded by the duke and his men. Her color was yet high, her smile yet bright, and she said little as their words spilled over and around her. Elbows out, I forced my way between two large fellows and took her arm again. Ignoring the other men, I focused my attention on the stag—the Duke of Surrey—who was the greatest threat.

"Gentlemen," I said, "snowflakes are delicate things, and like to melt when so much hot wind strikes them."

"What fierce spirit descends from the heavens to your aid, fragile one?" the duke asked Grace in a teasing tone, white teeth flashing in the dual shadow of mask and beard.

"No spirit, noble stag," I replied, "but a star fallen from the firmament and carried hence on a gentle zephyr." I waved my hands to demonstrate.

"Perhaps the star will dance with you this night, your grace," one of the men said.

I laughed and said, "Only if I do not return to the heavens before your grace has a chance to prove your grace in the measure."

Shaking his head, the duke looked at my cousin and held out a hand to her. "Now that your protector is here, will you walk a while with a friend?"

Grace turned to me, her eyes wide and almost frightened. I knew she feared the question her father had prepared her for, but there was little I could do to spare her. She could scarce refuse him.

I deflected. "Why, sir, how are we to know you are a friend?"

To the chuckles and guffaws of his men, the duke-as-stag spread his hands out wide, a pose of harmless innocence. "What harm could such as I be to a maiden?"

I scoffed. "You have the look of Acteon about you, my lord. Perhaps you were caught spying at places you should not and were punished for it."

As he was wearing a mask, I could not read his face, and so I could not tell if my joke had perhaps been ill-advised. Not that he did not understand it. Surely he was educated well enough to remember the tale of the youth who had spied upon the goddess Diana bathing in her moonlit pool and had been turned by Diana into a stag to be hunted and killed by her hounds for the sin of witnessing her nudity. But perhaps my suggestion that he might have offended in such a way had crossed the bounds of permissible jests. But then he turned his head to the left and to the right, looking behind him in an exaggerated manner, though heedful of his great antlers. Then he turned back to me and said, "I must keep a careful watch for the goddess' hounds tonight, in that case."

I allowed myself to breathe and smile. "Never fear it, noble stag. No pagan goddess can hold sway on this night when we celebrate the Blessed Virgin."

Grace spoke at last, and her voice did not waver. "I will walk with you, sir, but only if you walk pleasantly and speak quietly, and expect me to say nothing dazzling."

"Your mask is all too dazzling, lady, for me to expect anything more," he replied.

"That is not quiet speaking," I scolded, shaking a finger at him, and Grace giggled.

"Already I fail," the stag exclaimed in mock anguish, but Grace held her hand out to him. He took it and they glided away, a handsome pair. I sighed to see them go, my small and innocent cousin with the tall, worldly duke and hoped, for her sake, that he would not ask for more than a dance.

The duke's men, now that he was gone, began to drift away as well. Yet I became aware of someone behind me, just over my right shoulder. Forgetting I was masked, I shot him a fierce look, attempting to send him on his way, but he remained. "Do you know how the Lady Beatrice is masked tonight, Lady Star?" he asked, his voice low and muffled.

I turned my head to see him better and noted that his entire face was concealed by a fox mask, ruddy red and furry, complete with pointed ears and a jaunty white stripe between the eye holes. Some instinct urged me to be cautious with so many men in disguise this night, and so I also kept my voice low when I replied. "I do not know her well, Sir Fox, and cannot say."

"Ah," he said. "Pity. I had hoped to meet with her tonight."

I was immediately suspicious. "Has Sir Edmund Benedict set you on?"

"Sir Edmund... Who is he? Benedict is an odd name, is it not?"

I cocked my head at him, wishing my gaze could penetrate the mask. "No odder than any other name given by any other father. But you must know him. He is one of the king's men and served under the Duke of Surrey in France."

He shook his head slowly. "I do not know the man."

I scoffed. "Well then, I am surprised. I thought everyone knew him. He is never quiet and loves the sound of his own voice." Why was I abusing Benedict to a stranger? I knew I should not but could not stop my tongue. "He might as well be the king's jester, for he never utters a word of substance and thinks only of mirth. In faith, I think even the king tires of him."

The fox's posture stiffened, and I thought he must know Benedict after all. "He sounds a shallow and useless fellow."

"It is worse than that, sir. Be careful, if you have a wife, not to allow Sir Edmund anywhere near her, for he is faithless, and a notorious seducer. You will end a mockery, with the cuckold's horns on your head." I clamped my lips together. I had not expected my words to come out in so acid a tone. But his words from our first meeting still stung. *I am well-loved among the ladies of France.*

The fox dipped his head in acknowledgement. "I am well warned." Then he looked straight at me, his eyes glinting sharply, fiercely, behind the mask. "If I ever meet him, I'll tell him what you said."

"Oh, please do." There was something about those eyes, dark and shadowed as they were... "Pray, tell me, why do you seek out the Lady Beatrice?"

The fox stepped back, drawing a slow breath. "I seek her from my own curiosity. I have heard tell of her, and I had hoped this night to see if the stories were true."

"What stories have you heard, sir?" I asked, as if it mattered not.

He leaned closer, the better to share his wicked gossip. His mask grazed mine, the fur catching on the sharp edges of my star's rays. His breath stirred my hair, brushed my ear. Yet the harshness of his words dragged me back from the thrilling sensations that moved across my skin.

"I have heard that she is disdainful and haughty. I have also heard that she wields her words like a cudgel, and that though she is famed for her wit, she takes unholy joy in the cruelty of her words."

His words sent ire boiling up from my belly, searing my throat. "Now I will not believe that you do not know Sir Edmund. Only he would speak so of—Beatrice." I took hold of his arm. He started, pulling away. "I would that he had come here and tried his wit upon me. I'd give him more than he bargained for."

The fox stared at me for a long moment. Between the mask and the dim light, I could not read his thoughts in his eyes. At last, he bowed low. "When I know the gentleman, I will tell him you have said so, Lady Star."

"Please do, Sir Fox." I dropped a hasty curtsy, then leaned in and flicked the leather tip of his fox-nose. "And you would do better than to carry tales about a noble lady."

His mouth twitched as if he might respond but instead, he turned away. The light of torches and candles caught fire in his hair and for one horrified moment, I thought that perhaps the man in the fox mask did not merely know Benedict but was Benedict himself. But I assured myself that could not be, for Benedict never had any compunction about speaking honestly to my face, so why would he not reveal his identity at once? No, I would not regret anything I had said, whether Sir Fox was Benedict himself or a friend who would report my words back to him. If the rift between us could not be healed, let it become an abyss.

Looking around for my cousins, I noted Eleanor and Mary dancing with a pair of men masked as birds of some sort—pheasants, perhaps, or partridges? It warmed my heart to see them so happy. Then I saw that Grace stood with Aunt Ursula and Uncle Lionel in one of the brushy hollows that had been created for private conversation. The intensity of their parley made me look around for the stag, and found him standing nearby, looking well satisfied.

My heart leapt and dropped, landing somewhere around my stomach. Did this mean...?

I made my way toward Grace, slipping between laughing and chattering couples and clusters of merry-makers.

As I passed a small knot of men near one of the hearths, I heard them speak my cousin's name, which made me stop in my progress. Ducking behind a nearby tree, I paused to listen to their conversation. The tall, slender one wore the mask of a peregrine falcon covering his entire face, while the broad, stocky one was masked as a handsome hunting hound, which made me think of my teasing of the duke earlier. Beside him was a wiry fellow who had chosen, for some unfathomable reason, the guise of a rat, complete with trembling pink nose and wiry whiskers. Perhaps there had been no other masks left when he came to make his choice.

"The lady dressed as a snowflake is the fair lady Grace, I am sure of it," one of them had been saying as I passed.

"And the gentleman who is talking with her is Lord Thomas," Rat-face said. He gestured with his hands, making claws, and gave an impressive roar for good measure. "I know him by his bearing."

I opened my mouth to correct him—how this person could confuse my old, limping uncle, garbed tonight as a lion, with the lithe, youthful Lord Thomas was beyond reason—but then I recalled that I was, in fact, eavesdropping and did not intend to be noticed.

Hound-mask tilted his head at the man masked as a peregrine. "You sir, are the noble Sir Edmund Benedict, are you not?"

He was not. Even masked, anyone could see that. What was this foolish fellow playing at?

The peregrine flinched, almost bating like a falcon would when startled. He shifted his weight, pivoting toward Hound-mask. "Yes. Yes, I am," he replied. "You know me well." His voice and bearing revealed—to me, at least, I could not speak for these fools—that the peregrine was, in fact, Lord Thomas. What on earth was happening here?

Hound-mask grinned, shining teeth just visible beneath the flocked mask. "Good sir, you are very near in love to the great and gracious Duke of Surrey. Tell my friend here, who does not believe me, that the duke is enamored of the Lady Grace."

The peregrine—Lord Thomas—froze. "I—" he stammered. "I cannot —" Hound-mask seemed, or pretended, not to notice. He put a friendly hand on Thomas' stiff shoulder.

"In truth," Hound-face added, "I have been watching him since his arrival, when he bowed so prettily over the Lady Grace's hand and asked her to walk with him. I'd wager it was then that he asked for the lady's hand in marriage." Hound-face chuckled and punched Rat-face playfully on the arm. "I told him, Sir Peregrine, but he does not believe me, that the duke would use this evening's entertainment to ask for the lady's hand in marriage. And look you there, the great stag is with the lion now. Lion for Lionel, you fool." Hound-mask laughed and punched his friend again. The Rat punched him back, teeth bared. He did not seem to be enjoying this conversation as much as the Hound was. "You'll owe me a crown before the night is over, my good fellow!"

Thomas looked green under his mask. "How do you know that the duke is masked as the stag?" His voice came out thickly, as if he were strangling.

"Can there be any doubt?" the hound said. "So noble, so proud in his bearing... And he sought her out as soon as she entered the room."

Thomas clenched his fists and made as if to leave, but Rat-face stayed him with a hand on his shoulder. "You, sir, as you love the duke, do your best to dissuade him from his choice. Any man can see that she is not worthy of him."

Through gritted teeth, Thomas demanded, "Why do you say this?"

Rat-face sniffed, making his nose tremble. "She is far beneath him in birth. Why, even her cousin the lady Beatrice is of a superior rank."

Thomas looked down at the man and shook the man's hand off his shoulder. "Far be it for you to speak so of your betters."

"True, so true, sir," Hound-mask exclaimed. "But a man may do things for love that he may come to regret."

"How do you know he loves her?"

Hound-mask shrugged. "Would he stoop to marry her else?"

Thomas, it seemed, had no answer to that. "Your pardon, good gentlemen," he said through gritted teeth. "I must away."

They bowed as he strode away. Hound-mask and Rat-face slipped away themselves, snickering, but I had no time to ponder their game because I watched as, halfway across the room, Sir Fox accosted Peregrine-Thomas. The fox took him by the shoulders as a man greeting a friend, but Thomas reared back like a skittish colt. The fox held his hands up, as if to say, "How have I offended?" I drifted closer as they spoke for a while, and Thomas appeared to explain his anger at Hound-mask and Rat-face. Sir Fox gestured with one hand in the universal sign for "come with me," but Thomas shook his head vigorously and stalked off. The fox raised his hands in frustration and went in the opposite direction.

All this male intrigue had distracted me from my intent, which was to get to my cousin. I looked back to the spot where I had seen her before, only to find her approaching me, once more on the arm of the Duke of Surrey. Even at a distance, I could see her broad smile beneath the edge of her sparkling mask. As I hurried towards her, she released the duke's arm and skipped to meet me, taking my hands in hers.

"Cousin," I said, "you do look happy."

She did a little caper and squeezed my hands, spinning me in a circle. "I am happy, Beatrice. I am!"

I could scarce imagine that a proposal from the duke would put her in such a mood. "What brings this on?"

She tugged me close to whisper in my ear. "The duke did tell me, as we were walking, that Lord Thomas is enamored of me, and that he will ask Father this night for my hand!" She danced me around again, tipping her head back in delight.

Her happiness enveloped me, but I could not deny the blacker feelings in my heart. Concern for her...and mayhap a twinge of jealousy?

I pulled her to a stop. "I am delighted for you, and Lord Thomas is a noble man, and handsome for certes, but Grace, are you certain?

"Certain enough," she said, a stubborn lift to her chin. "Enough to know that I prefer to choose for myself—as you have urged me often enough—than to wait for my father to decide for me."

I sighed. How could I argue against myself?

My aunt and uncle arrived, Uncle Lionel arm in arm with the duke and Aunt Ursula sliding between us, beaming at both of us. "Well, girls, it is a happy night. Are you well satisfied, dear Grace?"

"I am, Mother, I am," she replied, putting her arm around her mother and giving her a light squeeze. "I hope you are as well." Her voice trailed up in question, in hope.

"I am, although I must say I could have wished you a duchess."

Grace's eyes flashed beneath her mask and she said, "Mayhap Beatrice is more suited to a coronet than I."

"Grace!" I said, and "Grace!" her mother exclaimed, an outraged echo. But Grace, with her own wishes so near fruition, could not be silenced. She laughed and fairly skipped away, slipping her arm through her father's.

"Now all that remains is to find Lord Thomas and tell him the news," the duke said. "I sent Sir Edmund for him but he has not returned..."

I am well-loved among the ladies of France. I could not get the image out of my head: Benedict in some dark corner, leaning close over some young woman, touching her face, kissing her...

"Lady Beatrice, would you undertake this office for me?" The duke's voice broke into my thoughts.

"Of course, your grace," I replied, slamming the door on that picture. "How will I find him?"

"He is masked as a peregrine falcon, a swift and true hunter." The duke hid a laugh in his voice, but I did not comprehend the jest. I was thinking of the peregrine whom I had seen earlier. What had Rat-face and Hound-mask been thinking when they spoke of the duke and Grace? Had they known that the peregrine mask hid Lord Thomas when they deceived him? Were they trying to make him think that the duke was proposing to my cousin? But wherefore? Were they attempting to breed jealousy there? To what end?

I curtseyed, unable to decipher the mystery. "I will fetch him hither, your grace."

It was not difficult to find him, for he had doffed his mask and sat brooding in a corner, firelight from the hearth casting shadows upon his face that only served to highlight his sharp cheekbones and brows. I almost left him there, for he seemed so content in his misery. But I had my orders. One disobeyed a duke at one's peril, and of course, there was Grace's future happiness to consider.

"How now, my lord? Why are you sad?"

He glanced up at me and down again, frowning at the peregrine mask in his hands. "Not sad."

"Are you unwell?"

He shook his head.

I huffed out my breath, blowing air up under my mask. It was hot standing so near the fire, and he was not making this easy on me. I put my hands on my hips, deciding to treat him like the child he was acting. "Neither sick nor sad, but neither merry nor well either, sir. You shame your hosts with your behavior."

He looked up at me, genuine pain in his eyes. I took pity on him and sat beside him on the bench, yanking at the ties on my mask so he would see it was I. "My cousin is waiting for you. You have promised to dance with her, and she is disappointed that you have not kept your promise."

"What good is a promise if it can be handed from one man to another?"

I bit back harsh words, feeling proud of myself as I did so, and said, "Why, then, you are merely jealous, and wrongly so." He glared up at me and I glared back. "You misapprehend, sir. The duke has wooed on your behalf and gained my uncle's consent to the match as well. Grace awaits you with her father and the duke to share with you the good tidings."

His entire face lit at the news, and in the purity of his expression, I could see why Grace adored him so. He leapt to his feet and could scarce contain his eagerness enough to offer me his arm and escort me across the hall to my family.

By the time we arrived, the duke and my aunt and uncle had also removed their masks and were smiling and raising goblets together. The duke spotted us first and opened his arms to Thomas, his white teeth showing bright in the low light.

"Ah, Thomas! Lo, I have wooed in your name, and the beautiful Grace is won!" They embraced, and someone pressed a goblet into Thomas' hand. The duke continued to speak. "Moreover, I have spoken with her father and won his good will. Name the day and you shall be married!"

Uncle Lionel stepped between them, looking far more serious now that the young man was before him. "Lord Thomas, in taking from me my daughter, you take the best of me and of her mother. She is the most precious gift I can bestow, not only because she is my sole heir but because she is a dear and gentle woman in her own right. I charge you to be fair and faithful to her, and never give her cause to grieve this night."

Thomas looked from him to Grace and I was touched to see his eyes shining with unshed tears. Mayhap he really did care for her. Mayhap it was more than a passing fancy after all.

Uncle Lionel seemed to be waiting for Thomas to say something, but all the besotted fellow could seem to do was gaze upon Grace. I cleared my throat, but he took no note. "Speak, my lord Thomas," I prompted him. "That was your cue."

He blinked and shook himself a little, looking at me with a bemused laugh. "Silence is the most perfect herald of joy," he said. "I would be only a little happy if I could express it in words." Yet he bowed to my uncle and said, "Full well I acknowledge the debt I owe you, and I vow never to bring harm nor trouble to your daughter. I will love her better than I love my own self."

At last, he turned to Grace and took her hands in his. Her eyes shone as she looked upon him. Indeed, it was as if her entire being had been set alight. "Lady," he said, "as you are mine, I am yours. I give away myself for you, and gladly so."

Grace shot a desperate glance at me and I knew what she sought: words. I shook my head gently. Of all times, this was not the time for me to speak for her. "Speak, cousin," I prompted. When she looked lost, I remembered what she said earlier about speaking without words. "If you will not speak, then stop his mouth with a kiss, and don't let him speak either."

Aunt Ursula gasped through her laughter. The duke clapped his hands together, drawing the attention of the party-goers around us. Amidst the cheers and applause of her family and many others, Grace went up on her toes to press her lips softly to Thomas'...with a familiarity that I hoped, for her sake, only I noted. After the kiss, Grace whispered something in Thomas' ear.

"She tells him," I said to the duke who was at my side, "that he is in her heart."

Now Thomas was blushing, and I wondered whether sweet Grace hadn't said something less innocent than I thought. "Indeed, she does," he said, and added, winking, "cousin."

My heart squeezed. *Cousin*. He was to marry my beloved Grace. The world seemed to shift under my feet, though I had not consumed much wine.

I would lose her. I had lost her.

Leaning close, the duke said, "Truly, lady, you have a merry spirit."

"Good Lord, for alliance," I murmured, then roused myself. I smiled up at the duke, taking note of his words at last. "Thus goes everyone into the world save I, two by two, partnered and paired. I shall go sit in a corner and cry like a fish-monger, 'hey-ho, bring me a husband!'"

The duke chuckled and said, "I had not thought you interested in being partnered and paired. If you want a husband, Lady Beatrice, I will get you one tonight."

I gave him a dubious look. "Here? A masked fellow I know not?"

"Think of the fun you'll have discovering all the ways in which you exceed him."

"Partnered, I said, your grace. A partner is a mate, a match, an equal." I faced him, hands on hips, and gave him a good look up and down. "Have you no brothers, your grace? Your father got excellent husbands, if a lady could come by one."

He laughed and swept an elaborate bow. "Will you have me, lady?"

For a moment, I wondered if he could be serious...but no. Though my family kept proposing the match, in truth he was a duke, and I was no one, an orphan, the daughter of a baron who had disgraced himself long ago. True, the princess had shown me some favor, and I would inherit a great fortune but yet, he could not be serious. He had seemed to favor Grace until this evening.

And I did not want to marry him...did I?

On the other hand, he was well respected by the king, and had been brave in battle by all accounts, and was wealthy and not ill-favored, and witty and wise. And all around me, voices clamored that I must marry if I did not want to end an unmarried encumbrance in my uncle's household. If I wanted to join this king and queen's witty, glittering court. To be more than nothing, growing old, alone, here in this house, always wondering what might have been. My uncle would require me to accept this proposal and the princess would call me a fool if she knew I had hesitated for even a heartbeat. Would it be so bad?

The duke looked up at me from the depth of his bow and in his eyes, I saw sparkling humor. This must be a jest. An exercise in wit at a party. A flirtation with no substance.

My breath caught in my throat as I struggled to understand my emotions. Was it relief or disappointment I felt? I sank into a deep curtsy to hide my face from him and took solace, as always, in a jest of my own. "No, my lord, unless I might have another husband for working-days. Your grace is too costly to wear every day."

He straightened and took my hand to lift me from my curtsy, kissing it as I rose. He was shaking his head, a wry smile twisting his lips. Though I was usually so astute, so confident at reading people, I could not tell. Was he perhaps a tiny bit disappointed? I found my heart was heavy, despite my teasing words. "Forgive me, your grace, for it seems I was born to speak always in jest, to say nothing of substance."

He waved a hand, still holding mine with the other. "There is nothing to forgive, dear Beatrice. To be merry most becomes you, and your silence most offends. By my troth, you were born in a merry hour."

Before I could stop my tongue, I said, "No, sure, your grace, my mother cried." Well I knew it. Her crushing disappointment at being presented at last with a living child, only to learn it was merely a daughter? I had been reminded of the weight of that disappointment every day until she died, not long after my father's death, and so, in misery and disgrace, I had come to live with my uncle Lionel, her brother.

Shaking off the tears that were suddenly welling in my eyes, I gestured with the star mask in my hand. "But then a star danced," I said, swaying a little, "and under that was I born."

A figure all in black moved at the edge of my vision, and I reached out to grasp at her sleeve. "Lady Raven," I said, "you must dance with this most noble stag, else he shall fall into a deep melancholy from which he will never return."

"Oh, I hardly think…" Lady Viola began.

The duke was busy strapping his mask back on. "Yes," he said, "my lady, you must rescue me from despair. Lady Star has failed utterly to make me happy. You must avail me."

Viola stared, her eyes dark and mysterious behind the feathered mask she wore. "Most noble lord," she said at last, "I am yours to command."

He bowed and took her hand, leading her off to dance, and I found myself able to breathe again.

What had I nearly done?

Turning away from my family, I found a seat in one of the little groves and fanned myself with my mask, drawing in great gulps of air. Blurred swirls of color swept by, dancers whirling and striding in time with the music, but I couldn't see details of figures or faces. Their masks were grotesques, gargoyles in the shape of demons, taunting and haunting me. How close I had come to throwing myself into life with a stranger, handsome and rich though he might be.

I watched the dancers for a time, letting my thoughts drift, and their shapes slowly solidified into men and women, dressed in their finery for a happy night among neighbors. Not all problems need be resolved in one evening, I chided myself, and I drew in a breath, determined to enjoy the rest of the party.

The duke and Viola—Stag and Raven—finished their dance and I mused that they looked well together for all that she scarce reached his shoulder. He bowed, and I saw him say something as he escorted her from the dance floor. She shook her head and left him with a hurried curtsy. With a disappointed air, he looked about, seeming lost. Seeing that I had not moved, he made his way back to the little grove where I sat.

"An odd girl," he said, looking back over his shoulder at her. I was glad there was no awkwardness between us. His proposal had been a jest, then, or at the least, he was content to pretend it was.

"She has suffered great losses," I told him, "and she is afraid of what the future may hold for her."

"The king will see to her future," he replied. "She has no cause to fear."

"Did you tell her so? I am sure she would have been quite relieved to hear it."

He gave me a quizzical look as though he was not sure if I was teasing him. "I confess I am not having a satisfactory evening at all, my lady Beatrice." When I made a sympathetic noise, he held up his hands. "No, no, do not pretend that you care. You are part of the problem. You have scorned my very pleasant, very proper proposal of marriage, and you have set me onto dancing with that dreadful raven. My friend Thomas is lost to me, and I cannot find my other companions, and here I stand with you! My torture is endless!"

I peered up into his face. "Just how much wine have you imbibed this even, your grace?"

He wagged a slightly unsteady finger at me. "I am not so deep in my cups that I cannot tell a hawk from a handsaw." I giggled. I could not help it. What did he even mean by that?

"You are not the only one who is disappointed in this evening's entertainment, your grace."

He leaned in closer, his breath flowery with wine. "If you had accepted my proposal, we might both be engaged in some activity that would render the evening much less disappointing."

I pressed a hand to his chest and pressed, rocking him back. "No doubt tonight would be most enjoyable, but the disappointment would strike us soon enough. If not on the morrow, then the next, or the next. Marriage, I believe, is much like a dance: it begins with wooing—a jig, hot and hasty." I danced a few quick steps to demonstrate. "Then the wedding, a stately measure." I swayed around him in a slow, decorous dance. "Then," I finished, standing before him again, "comes the repenting, a cinquepace." I grabbed his hands and spun him in a circle. "Faster and faster it goes, until finally, any love there was at the beginning falls down dead."

I let go of his hands and he staggered to an unstable stop.

Zounds, Beatrice, what are you thinking?

"Forgive me, your grace," I said, but he was laughing.

"My dear lady," he said, "the wooing with you would be worth any amount of repenting."

"Not everyone thinks so," I muttered, looking around for a servant in hopes of getting some wine. I was much too dry for all this flirtatious banter with a powerful man.

"What ho! Is that why you're so disappointed in this evening? Do tell me."

I shook my head. "Nay, it is no matter. A trifling." *Where were all the servants?*

He sat on the bench and grabbed my hand, pulling me down beside him. "You must tell me. As your liege lord, I command you, for if you are unhappy, I am unhappy, and I must put it to rights." His voice softened then, quieted, and he said, "In sooth, dear lady, what is amiss?"

I looked at him, searching for the eyes behind the mask. It was difficult to confess to a man wearing the mask of stag, false antlers branching above his head, but on the other hand, the entire evening had a feeling of unreality about it. "Someone I spoke with earlier told me that he heard tell I am cruel and disdainful, and that my wit is false, and that..." My throat squeezed and my voice cracked. The duke reached out to rest a hand on mine. "And I think it was my old—friend—Benedict, Sir Edmund, who said these things about me." I shifted on the bench so I could face him. "Am I cruel, your grace? Is he right to say it? Should I examine myself, change my ways, silence my tongue? Should I do as the princess demands, as my uncle desires, and make myself into a good and proper wife?"

Why had I wished for wine? Words were spewing from me as if I was sodden drunk.

"Beatrice..." he began, but abruptly he stood, stepping in front of me. Confused, I tried to peer around him.

"Your grace!" A crowd of masked men approached. His retainers. He was attempting to conceal me, to protect me. I drew in a shaky breath, trying to collect myself, and wondering whether I could slip behind one of these bushes unseen.

"What ho, lads?" he said, all blustery good cheer. They all spoke at once, and the clamor gave me time to recover my composure.

But then...

"The Lady Beatrice has a quarrel with you, Sir Edmund," the duke said. "A gentleman this evening told her tales that suggest she is much wronged by you."

Amidst chuckles and jeers from the other men, Benedict burst out with a howl of objection. "Oh, no, your grace! She has misused me past all endurance! She said—not thinking me to be myself—that I was the king's jester who capers like a fool."

"Well, a fool is not always a fool, to be sure," the duke observed.

Ignoring him, Benedict charged on. "She said I do nothing but devise slanders—"

"Indeed, a strong word," the duke said.

"She called me a notorious seducer—"

"You must admit that appellation to be true," the duke said.

I peeked around the duke's leg and saw Benedict, his mask in his hand. He was furious. Though the duke and the other men thought this was a delightful performance, he was genuinely angry, and the less credence they gave his anger, the more his fury grew. I could see it in his eyes, which flashed and flamed, in the heat of his cheeks, in the tightness of his jaw. I could see it because in his hand he grasped his mask. A fox.

So. I had indeed abused him to his very face. But then, he had been just as cruel to me, whether he knew it or not.

"She is unstoppable, your grace, yet she must be stopped. All I did was speak to her, and of a sudden, I stood like a man at a mark with an entire army shooting at me! If her breath were as bad as her words, there would be no living near her. Indeed, even as she is, it is near impossible to be in a room with her."

The duke laughed, and I think only his rank and position as Benedict's overlord saved him from Benedict's fist in that moment. After a pause, Benedict said, in a fervent tone, "Will your grace command me any service to the world's end? I will undertake any errand to the Antipodes that you can devise to send me on. I will fetch you a toothpicker from the farthest inch of Asia, be your ambassador to the Moors, fetch you a hair from the Great Khan's beard. Anything." There was real pleading in his voice now.

"No, Sir Edmund. Your place is here. With me, in service to the king." I could hear the smile in the duke's voice and knew that would not appease Benedict's mood.

He clenched his fists and released them, rolled his shoulders, and pulled in a breath. I could hear it in the silence that fell between dances.

"Oh God, give me strength." They were all still laughing, but I did not find it funny. *All I did was speak to her...* He knew it was me, and I did abuse him. I abused him first. Suddenly the duke in front of me, the branches surrounding the bench I sat upon, all seemed too close. I could not breathe. I waved my mask for air.

The motion must have drawn his attention, for when I looked up again, his gaze was locked on me. "Your grace, here is a dish I like not. I cannot endure my Lady Tongue."

I rose from my seat to face him. I would not sit, sheltered by the duke, whilst he spoke thus. I opened my mouth to reply. I scarce know what words were framing in my mind to speak, but they would have been harsh. Benedict held up a hand, addressing his words to the duke while still looking at me. "I would risk my life at the gates of hell rather than hold three words further conference with this—" His eyes blazed, and he stabbed a finger at me. "This harpy."

He did not wait for a reply but spun on his heel and charged away. "I suppose he's off to the Great Khan," one of the gentlemen said in an attempt to be witty, but the jest fell flat and no one laughed.

Harpy.

The word hung in the air like the shrieking half-woman, half-bird itself.

The duke watched Benedict walk away and shooed his retainers after, sending them for wine and sweets. When he turned back to me, he looked thoughtful. "My dear lady, it appears you have lost the heart of Sir Edmund."

It was in me to object that I had never had it—at any other moment, I would have—but I was wrung out, tired of banter and wit. I was shaking—with anger, humiliation, regret, with a thousand feelings I could not name. I chose instead to tell the truth, or as near to it as I could manage. "Indeed, my lord. He gave it to me once, and like a moneylender, I gave him a good return on it, a double heart for his single one. But I soon learned that there was no value in the contract and I had paid interest while earning no benefit. Thus, you may say that I have lost it, but I say that I never had it." I sighed. "I had thought I had not had enough wine this night, but now I think I shall retire without any. Would that be unpardonably rude?"

"Of course not," he said, bowing. "Good night, my dear lady."

I rushed for the doors, the dancers once again a blur of color and forms around me. Aunt Ursula called out to me and I waved, showing her a smile, and at her side was Grace, still shining with happiness. "God give you joy," I called to her, and fled.

CHAPTER 8

I slipped out of the room at first light, sliding out from under the covers and leaving Grace to sleep undisturbed. She had returned to the room well after the bell rang for Matins, stomping in like a baby elephant escaped from the royal menagerie. She was all clumsiness, jangling the door latch, tangling herself in her clothes, fumbling everything she touched, stumbling over her shoes, and laughing at every mishap.

Her joy set my teeth on edge.

I pretended to be asleep, though I had been staring at the rough ceiling of our room for hours since returning from the ball. Even when she stuck her frigid toes against me, I did not flinch and forbore to scold her. I just let her snuggle against my back, humming a half-remembered tune as she tumbled into sleep.

The morning air held a chill, and the edges of leaves were rimed with frost as I strolled along the gravel path into the garden. I had thought to settle on the bench in the bower hidden at the far edge of the garden, but in the sudden autumn morning, the stone bench would be too cold for comfort and I had neglected to bring more than a light shawl. Walking would keep me warmer, I decided. Besides, I doubted that I would encounter anyone else so early, after the masque the night before.

I tried to enjoy the brightness of the sunshine, the glitter it cast on the edges of the frosted plants, the little puffy clouds my breath formed in front of my lips, the busy chirps and trills of birds surrounding me. I tried not to think that the next time this garden bloomed, Grace would be gone, married, mistress of her own home.

In two years of determined preaching against the estate of marriage, I had not allowed myself to think about what would happen when my cousins married and I was the last one left.

And after all, I could have been the first to marry if Benedict hadn't...

"There you are!"

I turned at the sound of Grace's voice and saw her hurrying toward me.

"What are you doing up so early?" I asked as she pulled me into a tight embrace. "I thought after last night, and all the wine you drank..."

She waved a hand. "I was drunk on happiness, not wine. I scarce slept at all! And when I did wake and you were gone, I had to come look for you."

I gestured to the path and she walked with me. "I needed some air. It's a lovely morning, but a reminder that winter is nearly upon us. So, Grace, you enjoyed the night of your triumph?"

She wrapped her arms around herself. "Oh, Beatrice, it was everything I've ever imagined, but at the same time, it was like nothing I have ever dreamed of. He held me close while we danced—at least, when Father wasn't looking—and we kissed and talked..." The happy glow from the night before had not faded. "We have the same thoughts, the same feelings, the same words... When I begin a sentence, he finishes it. When he moves, I go with him. It's like nothing I've ever felt before."

I halted, struggling against the twisting coil of emotions rising in my belly. I used to be the one who finished her sentences. Once Benedict and I had moved and breathed as one. Now I had lost them both. I forced myself to smile. "I wish you all happiness and every blessing. Has he spoken to your father about a wedding date?"

She grinned. "He asked if we could marry today, but Father denied him, saying it was unseemly haste."

"I should say so!"

"But then at King Henry's suggestion, Father agreed that we may marry this week, even before he and Princess Elizabeth depart!"

"How wonderful!" I exclaimed, though my heart sank to hear it. So soon would we be parted!

She tucked her arm through mine and we resumed walking. "We will all be very busy at our needlework for the next few days as a result."

I rolled my eyes. "Only for you, my dear cousin, would I spend the last warm days of the year indoors of my own free will and endure hours in the company of my-very-superior-lady-the-king's-mother."

Grace sighed. "I am sure she will instruct me on how to dress, and what to say, and how to comport myself as a bride."

"And as a wife as well," I said. "But never you fear, she'll not be there for the wedding night."

Grace, halting, flushed bright red and covered her face with her hands. I burst out laughing. "Lucky for you, there will be no need for words that night."

She squealed and swatted me. I laughed again and fled from her, and we raced like children along the path until we reached the circular center of the garden where there sat a little stone bench and a statue of a nymph from classical legend. Wouldn't my-lady-the-king's-oh-so-rigid-mother be scandalized to see her, in her stone half-nudity, smiling that secret, knowing smile. What god or satyr was she escaping? In the summer, she was surrounded by roses, but now all the plants had been harvested, the hips for making tisanes and medicines, and the petals for making rose water and for scenting soap.

Grace collapsed onto the bench, still laughing and gasping for breath, making bright clouds in the cold air. "Why did you quarrel with Benedict last night?" she asked.

Her question startled me. "What do you—how do you know? Who spoke of it? Did he complain to you?" My heart began to hammer in my chest. I could not tell if I was angry, or with who.

"Of course not! He would not. But you do not quarrel quietly, Beatrice, and many people heard of it. Lord Thomas heard it from the duke, and of course he asked me about it..."

"Oh, of course. Is there no discretion in these men?"

Placid Grace, sweet Grace, scoffed at me. "Fie, Beatrice, this has naught to do with them. What is to do with you and Benedict? You were ever friends before he went away. What is toward?"

I stared. What had this Lord Thomas done to my Grace?

"Nothing. 'Tis nothing." She fixed me with a look, waiting. I threw up my hands. "We quarreled. He said harsh words, I said them back. What does it matter?"

"Because there is something at the root of it that I do not understand. A thing that makes no sense. Something to do with your protests against marriage and men and—" She cut herself off, eyes widening. "Zounds,

Beatrice," she exclaimed—she, Grace, who never cursed—"are you in love with him?"

"No!" The word burst out of me, which, of course, served to negate my protest. I turned my back on her to collect myself, drawing a long, deep breath of cold air. "I am—" I bit off my words. There was nothing I could say, no way to finish that saying, that was not untrue. I was nothing to him any longer. *Harpy.* The word still rang in my ears.

I walked a few steps away. Sharp, dying iris leaves poked skyward, swords waiting for me to fall upon them. But I had carried this for so long, would it not be a relief to set the secret down? "Yes," I said, turning around at last. "That is, I did love him, before he left."

Grace rose from the bench. "But no longer?"

I sighed. "How can I tell you? I know not. I tried to put aside those feelings when he left but I fear I have failed. And it is worse now that he returns with all his dreams realized, while mine are crushed..." My voice broke, so I silenced it.

Grace's eyes were wide with surprise. I could see her turning over in her mind all I had said, retracing the paths of her memories to consider what she had missed. "But did he leave you with no assurances at all?" she asked at last. "I cannot believe he would dally with you in such a manner."

My heart ached in my breast as it broke anew. This was why I never spoke of it; this was why it was better to feign disinterest in marriage and love. Would that he had stayed away...

"I believed in my heart that we would marry." My voice still wavered. I scarce sounded like myself. "My feelings bent in that direction, and I believed—I still believe—that he inclined that way too. But when the time came for him to depart and I wanted him to speak to my uncle before he left...that was when he refused."

"On the eve of his going away? Why?"

I rubbed a hand across my forehead, which was damp with sweat despite the cool morning. "He was worried. He feared that Uncle Lionel would refuse us."

Grace scoffed. "Benedict is like the son he never had. He would never refuse Benedict anything."

"That was what I thought, but Benedict was certain I was wrong. He thought that Uncle would be angry that he had dared to reach so high."

"Because you are an heiress."

"A great heiress. And he had nothing."

Grace kicked at a pebble on the path. "So he went away to gain his fortune in war. Threw in his lot with a rebel king and hoped to rise."

I could not speak, only nod.

"Could you not have married in secret, without his permission?"

I gave her my most disbelieving look. "Would Benedict have ever done such a thing? And, despite what the world thinks of my willful nature, would I?"

She touched my hand with hers. "Of course not. And so he left."

"And so he left."

She was silent again, thinking. "You know, if you had married, and then the rebellion had failed, you would have very different things to be unhappy about. At least he's alive and not attainted of treason."

"I know, I know. He was not entirely wrong. I know this. But, Grace, he has returned and..."

"And? You have done nothing but fight with him. Have you thought to ask him how he feels now?"

I sighed again. "I can't seem to keep from arguing with him. I can have every good intention, but something about being in his presence reminds me of the way we parted. It was not a happy time, Grace."

"And yet you shared none of it with me," she said. "The one you say you love best in the world."

"I am sorry. I could not. I—I am sorry," I repeated.

"Well, I know now, and I promise you, I will despise him on your behalf."

I tried to laugh but managed only a hollow sigh. "You need not. I do not despise him." Hardly that.

"All right. But you must tell me how we feel about him. I am yours to command."

My voice fled once again and I wrapped my arms around her. We stood there for a long moment, holding each other close, and I could not bear to release her, knowing that she would soon marry and leave me. When at last she pulled away, I almost believed I could marry anyone just to go to court with her, for how could I live without her?

"I shall leave you for now," she said, "for Mother has no doubt been searching the entire house for me. There are many arrangements to be made. For my wedding." Her eyes sparkled when she said the word. "Do not hurry inside. Take your time. And we will deal with Sir Edmund Benedict, I promise you. All right?"

I nodded and sat on the bench while she made her way back to the house. The rising sun painted a pale rose-gold cloak over the nymph statue. The bare branches of the rose bushes rattled and scraped against each other in the slight breeze. A sudden rustling behind me, a light foot-fall on the gravel path, revealed to me that I was not alone. I twisted on the bench, suddenly afraid that someone had been spying upon us the entire time, that they had heard all I had said...

Instead of a spy, I found a young goat rummaging in what was left of a patch of daisies, nibbling at their dead heads and broad leaves. It looked to be one of this year's stock, leggy with youth, all white with a few blotches of warm brown on its back and over one eye. Its horns were short, rounded nubs atop its fuzzy head.

Sweet as it was, it did not belong in Aunt Ursula's beloved garden.

I looked around for a stable hand or other worker from whom it might have escaped, but no one was in the area. "How far have you wandered, my girl?" I asked, and she looked up at me, her long ears flop-ping alongside her glassy-bright eyes. She must have determined I was of no concern to her, for she dropped her head and went back to feeding on flowers.

Aunt Ursula would have her roasted for dinner, and Aunt Ursula detested goat.

"Come, now, young mistress. Time you were moving on."

This time, she did not deign to glance at me, just kept grazing.

I clapped my hands. She flinched but didn't stop eating.

"Here, now. Move along." I clapped and stamped my foot. She jumped, danced away, and promptly set to eating something else. Rosemary?

"No!" I shouted. I waved my arms at her, shuffling my feet on the gravel. The stones ground with a loud clatter. She gave an annoyed bleat and trotted a few strides along the path.

Better. I followed after, still dragging my feet.

She jerked her head sideways and danced away again. I was herding her deeper into the garden, opposite to the direction we needed to be going, but I couldn't see any way of turning her back. I looked ahead, hoping we would come upon some herder searching for her.

At the turning of the path, a chunky boxwood had been trimmed into a neat sphere. The path formed a circle around it, offering me the oppor-tunity to herd the goat in the direction of the barns at the rear of the castle grounds. She skittered away from me toward the boxwood then stopped, startled by its sudden bulk in her way. With tiny, mincing steps, she turned back toward me, tilting her head with a confused air.

"Now, now," I said, "you can go 'round." I waved my arms to show her the way.

She stamped one sharp little hoof at me.

I stamped my foot right back, feeling rather foolish but at the same time glad to have a safe outlet for my emotions. "Off you go," I said, louder. "Go!" I shuffled toward her, shaking my skirts at her.

She stamped her hoof again, and I began to doubt the wisdom of bothering. Mayhap I should turn back now, find someone who could handle this…

She lowered her head and suddenly she was charging, her little feet flying, those nubby short horns aiming straight for my knees.

I gathered my skirts in both hands and fled.

We made a thunderous noise charging down the gravel path. Gasping with ludicrous laughter and looking for a place to step off the path, I also kept glancing back to be sure she was not too close…and in such a moment, I stumbled, and began to fall, and slammed into a man's velvet-clad chest.

He grunted, and his arms went around me as we tumbled into a low hedge. My hip slammed into the ground, starting tears in my eyes. The goat flew past, and I swear it was laughing.

I pushed off the man's velvet chest, heedless of who it might be, and found my skirts snagged in the myriad snatching branches of the hedge. He, too, was endeavoring to rise whilst thrusting me off of him, which meant neither of us could gather ourselves properly. "Oh, go to, sir," I cried. "Be still a moment, I beg you."

From farther down the path, another man cried out and I looked up to see what was toward. The goat, which had not stopped its charge, had collided with a yeoman soldier, who now held the squirming creature in his arms. It writhed, aiming kicks at his ribs and legs. "My lord," the fellow called out, "what shall I do with this…thing?"

"To the kitchens," I called back, not caring that he had not addressed me. "I hope it makes a tasty stew!"

The man in black velvet had managed to extricate himself from the hedge and was now standing over me, hands on his hips. "Lady Beatrice," he said, disapproval dripping from his words.

I twisted to look up at him, wincing at the branches poking into my flesh. Dark hair, dark beard, dark eyes. My heart sank. "Lord Beymond."

With that acknowledgement, he reached out one gloved hand. I put my hand in his and allowed him to haul me, like so much baggage, to my feet. I brushed leaves and twigs from my clothes, knowing my cheeks to be red with embarrassment and discomfort to have been placed in this situation.

"I do not believe," he said at last, "that your uncle would do us the dishonor of serving goat stew at his board."

Saints above, was the dour Lord John Beymond making a jest? I peered into his face, trying to discern the truth of it. It would not do to laugh if he did not mean me to.

"Indeed not, my lord," I ventured, "but that was a most troublesome goat."

He made a sound deep in his throat that could have been a chuckle or mayhap a strangled cough. It was impossible to tell with this man. "May it trouble you no longer, then." He waved a hand at his guard, not deigning to look at the poor fellow who was like to have bruised ribs if not a blackened eye from the goat's struggles. "To the barn with it," he said, loud enough for the man to hear. The man's bootsteps departed in that general direction, crunching the gravel and covering the sound of his muffled curses.

"May I escort you...somewhere?" The question, from his lips, sounded almost sordid.

I suppressed a shudder. "I was merely enjoying a walk in the morning air," I said. "I neither desire nor need an escort."

"I believe my lady would be safer with an escort," he said. "To prevent further trouble with goats."

I forced myself to smile. "Indeed, my lord, I do appreciate your concern. But I feel perfectly safe now that you and your man have come to my rescue." I hoped I was doing a fair imitation of my cousin Mary's brand of flattery, the kind that distracted a man from the knowledge that you did not, in fact, enjoy his company.

He glanced out across the garden, toward the bright sun that now shone over its high wall. The air was growing warmer, the touch of frost disappearing from every green thing. "I believe I will join you nonetheless." He took my hand again and placed it on his arm, then set off down the path, taking me with him.

I gritted my teeth and allowed it. He was high in the king's favor, I told myself, and I had already displeased the princess enough. Let him carry back a tale of my biddable nature.

"You promised me a dance last night," he said, his tone light enough but it carried a note of displeasure.

"I do apologize, sir. I was feeling unwell, and so I retired without dancing."

"Hmmm. The news of your cousin's betrothal, perhaps, unsettled you?" *Tread carefully, Beatrice.* "How so?"

He waved a hand. "That she should so easily come by that which you, being older and well-dowered, are entitled to but seem unable to obtain."

There was a wealth of insult in his words, but I would not rise to it. "Nay, sir. I am exceeding happy for my cousin. I am but sad that we will so soon be parted."

"So soon?" he echoed, tilting his head toward me.

"Aye. My uncle has agreed to hold the wedding this week, while the king is still visiting. It is a great honor."

He made a sound—was he grinding his teeth?—and replied, "A great honor indeed for your family. Tell me, Lady Beatrice—" He halted and turned to face me. "What would your cousin like for a nuptial gift? Have you any thoughts? If we are all to be present for the event, I must give the matter some thought, and as I don't know the couple very well, your counsel would be much appreciated."

I was stunned by the sudden shift in the course of his inquiry. I had no idea how to counsel him, for I had no knowledge of his wealth or what he would consider impertinence on my part. "I...I believe..." I stammered. "Many folk give a bride cloth or items for the new home."

He looked thoughtful, "For their home? Perhaps I will give them a goat."

I burst out laughing, and for the first time, I saw Lord John smile. A true, genuine smile. It rendered him something handsome.

"Your pardon. I fear I am interrupting."

The words were sharp, clipped. Still smiling, we both turned in the direction of the voice.

Benedict stood on the path, arms crossed, jaw clenched. The sight of him made my very bones ache.

I dipped an impertinent curtsy. "Sir Edmund," I said. "Forgive me. I thought you had departed for Asia on an errand for the duke."

Beatrice. Why must you always...

Lord John cast me an uncomfortable sideways glance but said nothing.

Benedict pivoted on his heel and almost, *almost* began to walk away. I could feel how close a thing it was. But then he stopped his other foot from falling and instead turned the step into a bow, giving my feisty obeisance back to me. "My lady," he said, "how could I ever leave you?"

Lord John frowned, unable to read the subtle currents of this deep-flowing stream between us. "Sir Edmund..." he began.

Benedict glanced at him, seeming to notice him for the first time. "My lord John. If you would be so good, there is something I must say to the Lady Beatrice." Lord John hesitated, looking at me. Benedict narrowed his eyes. "In private, my lord. If it pleases you." The air around him fairly hummed with tension. I kept my eyes downcast and would not look at either of them.

"As you wish, Sir Edmund." Lord John took my hand in his and raised it gallantly to his lips. "I will not be far away, Lady Beatrice, should you have further need of my assistance."

I forbore to mention how he had left me lying in the bush when he stood and instead said nothing, only watched as he brushed past Benedict, dangerously close to bumping his shoulder.

At last, when I could no longer hear his tread on the gravel path, I focused my attention on Benedict. "You wish to have words with me, sir?"

He ground a heel into the grit. "It has come to my attention..." He trailed off, looking over my shoulder. "Last night, what I said..."

I would not help him. I would not make it easy for him. "Yes?"

He heaved a sigh. "Last night, I was an ass. I admit it. All right? I was a dolt, a clodpate, an idiot. But I was not unprovoked—" He bit off the words. "Sorry. You called me a fool, and I acted a fool in response. I apologize."

He held out a hand. "Shake hands? Friends again?"

I tilted my head, gazing at his hand as though he offered a viper in it. "You called me a harpy."

He winced. "Can I blame the wine?"

"No, you may not."

He huffed again. "I have said I was an ass."

"I am not yet done hearing you say it."

He rolled his eyes at me. "By this hand, Beatrice, I said I was sorry." As he swore by it, he withdrew it. "And it is not as though you have nothing to apologize for."

"Apologize?" I sputtered. "For but speaking the truth of you, to you?" I cringed to hear myself utter the words, but I could not stop myself, or withdraw them once spoken. He hurt me, over and over, and I could not stop hurting him.

He threw his hands up. "You are right. I am a fool," he said. "A fool for thinking we could ever be friends again."

He spun, tiny stones flying up around his boots, and stalked away back toward the castle.

Wait, I called after him in my heart, *come back!* But the words never passed my lips.

CHAPTER 9

A ll that morning, the household was atwitter with plans for Grace's wedding and I hid in my bedchamber. By the noon meal, I dreaded the prospect of sitting at the big table with everyone and their cheerful chatter. I took a place at my uncle's groaning board, sitting between my younger cousins. Yet we could not begin, for most of the male members of the family were missing. I looked along the table, trying to catch Aunt Ursula's eye and ask about the delay, but she seemed determined to ignore me.

At long last, Uncle Lionel, the Duke of Surrey, and Lord Thomas burst into the hall, all laughing and pounding each other on the back as though they had just heard the most wondrous jest. As Benedict was not with them, I could not imagine what had entertained them so well.

Uncle Lionel passed behind us on his way to his seat, patting each of my cousins and me on the shoulders and kissing the tops of our heads. I could hear him as he lowered his head close to mine. He was giggling, an occurrence as rare as snow in summer. "What on earth has made you all so pleased with your yourselves?"

He shook his head. "Never you mind, niece."

Lord Thomas, taking a seat nearby, heard my question and laughed louder. "We have been listening to some very fine musicians."

The Duke of Surrey, seated beside him, grinned. "Oh aye. Music is the food of love, as much as this fine meal is food for our bodies. Would you not say, my lords?"

The three of them burst out laughing again. I caught Aunt Ursula's eye then, expecting her to be as annoyed at their childishness as I was, but she looked upon them all with an indulgent air.

Uncle Lionel slapped his hands against his stomach, ready to tuck in. "Wait," he chided himself. "Are we all here, dear wife?"

"As you know, my lord, the king and princess are taking their meal together in the king's chamber." She looked up and down the long table. "For the rest of us, only Sir Edmund is missing."

My uncle frowned and leaned forward to look along the table. "Fie, where is he hiding? We cannot begin without him."

My stomach twisted and groaned. *Must we be still delayed?* I found my hand creeping toward the roasted pigeons on a platter in front of me.

"Beatrice!" my uncle bellowed, and I snatched my hand back.

"Yes, Uncle?"

"Go and find Sir Edmund Benedict. Tell him dinner waits upon him, and the good duke will begin to eat the table itself if he tarries longer."

Over the general good humor, I complained, "Good uncle, must I go? Can you not send one of his friends?" I cast a sharp look at Lord Thomas, lounging at Grace's side and looking smug.

Uncle Lionel smiled at me, also looking rather smug. "You are one of his oldest and best friends. And I have asked you, my good child." He laid a rather heavy emphasis on the word "child."

I did not need to be scolded twice.

I rose and bobbed my head to show my obedience. Amidst the buzz of quiet conversation, I left the hall.

If they had been listening, as my uncle said, to musicians, I guessed they had been in my uncle's private study. A realm of men, as my aunt's solar was a realm of women, it was just inside the gates, near his steward's office. I was not often permitted to set foot in there, and it had been strictly off limits during our seek-and-find game the other day. Yet it was the logical place for the gentlemen to have retreated to for a private performance before the musicians, hired for last night's fete, departed.

When I arrived, I found the door to the study half-open, so I peeked inside to see Benedict sitting on a large tufted stool in front of the fire. He propped his elbows on his bent knees and supported his head in his hands as though it weighed as much as a frigate's anchor. His aspect was so bereft, I nearly left without going in, but he must have heard a sound—my hand pushing the door, my footfall on the floor—and looked up. His face appeared feverish, beaded with sweat from the heat of the flames, but pale behind it. I glanced back over my shoulder, certain that I should return alone to the dining table.

"I beg your pardon, Sir Edmund," I said, giving him more deference than I had since he'd returned. "I should not disturb you."

"Nay," he said, clearing his throat when his voice seemed to fail him. "Come in."

As I approached, he stared at my face with gleaming eyes. I wondered if he was indeed ill.

I stopped at the edge of the rug, as close as necessary, as far as possible. The intensity of his perusal was making me uneasy. "My uncle..."

He raised his eyebrows, waiting.

Familiar snappishness returned. "Against my will, I am sent to bid you come in to dinner." I enunciated each word precisely. So that he would not mistake my meaning, I gestured with one hand in the general direction of the hall.

He said nothing, but a slow smile lit up his face. He no longer looked ill, though still flushed.

"Fair Beatrice," he said, then paused, his voice soft and nearly swallowed by the fire's sizzle. "I thank you for your pains."

His sudden politeness in the face of my rudeness surprised me. I almost forgot to be sharp with him. "I take no more pains for your thanks than you take pains to thank me. If it had been painful, I would not have come." Well, that was not entirely true. It was painful, always, now.

He rose and took a step toward me. I took a step back. "You take pleasure then? In the message?"

What was this? Where were the barbs, where was the wit wielded like a rapier? Whither *we can never be friends again*? What was wrong with him? I eyed him warily, like a bull that might charge if provoked.

"Aye, as much pleasure as you may take upon a knife's point." He said nothing, just continued to look at me with that placid glow. "Zounds, Benedict, will you not come away from the fire? I think it has given you a fever." I bit off my words. "If you are not hungry, fine. Don't come."

I turned about and hurried back toward the dining hall, determined to forget the look in his eyes.

And forget I soon did, for instead of going back to the jollity of the hall, I determined to get my own dinner from the kitchen and dine alone in my room. But as I passed behind the hall in the serving corridor, I heard my Aunt Ursula say, over the rumble of voices, "But are you certain that Benedict loves Beatrice so entirely?"

I stopped short, almost falling out of my shoes. *What?*

"Oh, yes," my cousin Grace replied. "I have it from both the Duke of Surrey and from my betrothed, Thomas."

Aunt Ursula chuckled. "I think you just like saying 'my betrothed.'"

"I confess, I do. But they are his closest friends, so they must know the truth."

I pressed my spine up against the wall for support as my mind raced with this news. The cool, solid stone could not stop my racing heart or quell the sudden fever that seemed to possess me.

One of the serving maids shot me an annoyed look as she passed with a basket of bread. I shot her one back. This was my life, my *heart*, they were talking about.

"Indeed, we do," Lord Thomas said, and I remembered he had been sitting beside Grace at table.

"But what do you suggest we do with this revelation?" Aunt Ursula asked. "Are you going to tell her?"

Tell me? Yes, tell me!

"Dear Thomas and his grace the duke did ask me to let Beatrice know of Benedict's feelings so that something might come of it." Grace replied.

"We would all very much like for the two of them to join us at court," Thomas said, "and that cannot be if they do not marry."

Aunt Ursula scoffed. "My Beatrice need not marry *him*. She could marry anyone. She could marry the duke himself, if she put her mind to it."

I cringed, hoping the duke himself had not heard, and hoping my aunt never heard of his jesting proposal.

"It matters not if he loves her," Grace said, "for she will not hear of it. She closes her ears to him and can scarce speak a kind word to him."

Me? Unkind? Ha! Harpy still echoed in my ears.

"We have counselled him to wrestle with his feelings and never to let Beatrice know of them," Thomas said.

"'Tis mayhap for the best," Aunt Ursula mused. "For though Benedict is a fine young man, and now high in the king's favor, he may not yet be deserving of our Beatrice."

"Yet is not Benedict as deserving of love as anyone?" Grace objected. "And Beatrice would be an excellent match for him in wit and wisdom, if not in lineage and fortune. Surely his place in the world is not now so far beneath hers..."

"True," my aunt said. "You know how I love my niece, but no woman was ever born whose heart was framed of prouder stuff!"

"Indeed, even so," Thomas replied with an air of finality. "Let Sir Edmund's love consume itself like a covered fire, die away in sighs and crumble in on its own embers. Better that than to die of her mocking."

I thought I might die for want of breath, right there in the corridor outside the hall. They thought me cruel. They thought I would hurt him rather than hear him speak of love.

What did they think of me? Was I a heartless harpy indeed?

"Still," my aunt mused at length, "what if you were to tell her of it? Hear what she will say. What harm in that?"

"Nay, I will not. Rather, I will go with Thomas to Benedict and beg him to fight against his passions. And—" Grace paused, apparently thinking, then said, "I will invent some tale of her that will turn his heart against her."

"You would not," Aunt Ursula said. "You will not."

"Oh, Mother, fear not. It would be nothing terrible. Nothing to stain her forever. But you know that an ill word can poison liking."

Aunt Ursula made a disapproving noise. "Do not do your cousin such a wrong."

"Well, then, perhaps I shall tell him that she loves another. That would put an end to it."

"You are an innocent, my dear, if you think so," Aunt Ursula said.

I pushed away from the wall and stumbled away from the dining hall, away from the clatter of knives and goblets, the rush of conversation. Away from anywhere I might meet with people and be forced to speak politely and cover my shattered emotions. Like a blind woman, I made my way up to my bedchamber, and I have no memory of how I got there, staggering up stairs, along corridors, past servants and closed doors.

They say that when people speak of you when you are not there, your ears burn. I had never known it to be true until that very moment, for my ears, aye, my face flamed at having been so spoken of. And it was my own family who said such things of me and made such judgments. Those I loved and trusted above all others!

How much better not to know what people truly think of you.

Oh, but then too, they had said that which made my heart skip a beat and dance again to a lighter tune.

Benedict loved me.

Could it be so? It must be, if the gentlemen had told Grace. What reason had Thomas to lie to her about such a thing? And would he not be the one to know, being his closest friend for so many months? He and the duke had been Benedict's constant companions for the past two years. Blood, danger, pain, battle, they said such things bonded men into kin for life.

He loved me still.

Here we were, arguing like fishmonger and fishwife since he'd arrived. Was it possible that harsh words could hide a tender heart?

I stood at my bedchamber window, looking out over the same fields and woods I'd grown up with but not seeing any of it. My blood raced in my veins. My skin flushed hot then went shivering cold. I hugged my arms tightly around myself.

The answer was so clear. Before Grace said anything to Benedict to prevent him from speaking, I would show him I could change. I would change. The faults laid against me by Grace and my aunt Ursula were not irreparable. I could be sweet and gentle; I had Grace to model myself after. I could be mild and loving and kind. At least, I could try. If I changed myself, Benedict would be emboldened to speak, and once he spoke, we could be united. The truth was—not that I would ever have said —I had only refused marriage these past few years because he had refused to marry me. But if he would have me... What would I not surrender for a chance to be his once more?

Grace came looking for me after dinner, bringing some food wrapped in a cloth for me. "You never came back to the hall to dine with us," she said. "I was worried. Are you unwell?"

I lay back on my bed, staring at a spot on the ceiling. I scarce glanced at her or the food she offered. "Yes, I am well. Thank you."

She frowned. "You don't look well. You look pale. Here, eat." She thrust her bundle at me.

I ignored the food, but I did sit up. "I have no stomach, thank you. Grace, what would you think if I said I wanted to get married?"

She sat next to me on the bed. "I would think you truly are ill," she said, laughing a little.

"Grace. What if I were to marry?"

"But you have said—"

"Forget what I said. If someone asked me."

"Have you changed your mind about the duke, then?"

I flung myself back down on the bed. "Never mind. I can see you think this is a jest."

"Nay!" she protested, lying beside me. "I promise. You...you have been so adamant that you will never marry, 'tis hard to imagine..."

"If you do not believe such a thing is possible, I suppose I must expect utter incredulity from the rest of the world. Not to mention everyone sharpening their wits upon me. But," I said, sitting up again, "does not the appetite alter? Does not a man love a sweetmeat in his youth that in his age he cannot abide? Even Saint Paul tells us we must put away childish things when we become of age, does he not?"

"Oh dear," Grace said, pulling a grave face. "When Beatrice quotes Scripture, we are indeed in dire straits."

I hit her with my pillow. She laughed, swatting me with hers.

Our conversation ceased after that.

* * *

Grace went forth from the room with a tale that I felt unwell and left me to my brooding. At some point, I ate the scraps Grace had brought me from dinner and considered that it had been no accident that I had been sent from the hall, and no accident that I had overheard the conversation about Benedict. Deceptive and dishonest, if you asked me.

Still.

If they thought me as proud and willful as they said, they must have thought that confronting me head on was the worst possible approach.

And if I were truthful with myself, they were probably right. Would I have listened if they had spoken the truth? When his words from the masque were still hot in my ears?

Nay. Like as not.

A knock on my door roused me from a drowse. It was late, later than I expected, and I had to rub my eyes and touch my hair in the hope of looking refreshed rather than ridiculous.

A small boy in the king's green and white livery stood there. With a perfunctory bow, he said, "Her highness Princess Elizabeth hopes you are feeling better, Lady Beatrice, and requests your presence for the evening."

"Oh, of course. Give me a moment and I shall come presently."

I wished—mayhap for the first time in my life—that I was as lovely as Grace. That I could rise from bed looking refreshed and didn't need a maid to help me look presentable. There was no time, while the boy waited outside my room, to send for a maid and water for washing, to change my kirtle or even my sleeves, to dress my hair or apply a bit of color to my lips or kohl to my eyes...so I must do the best I could and go.

As the page opened the door into the princess' room, I recalled Benedict's comment from the masque the night before when he said he felt like a man at mark, my words like arrows. Here, I was the target, the intense scrutiny of the people in the room the arrows. Had Grace told everyone of what she had learned from Lord Thomas and what I had said to her earlier about marriage? Did they all now know that Benedict loved, and that Beatrice would requite him? Everyone watched in silence as I entered the room and curtsied to the princess—to my relief, neither the king nor any of his gentlemen were present—and took a seat beside Grace.

"I am glad to see you looking so well, Lady Beatrice," the princess said. "I would be sad to be without your excellent wit for too long."

I inclined my head to acknowledge the favor of her attention, but as I began to thank her, a sharp voice cut me off. "A lady has no use for wit, only wisdom," my-lady-the-king's-ever-sour-mother said, fixing me with a grim stare.

The princess pressed her lips together and all but imperceptibly rolled her eyes in the direction of her future mother-in-law. "Surely there is no harm in a jest, my lady," she said.

"When a maid treats words lightly, she treats all things with lightness, including those precious things that ought not be surrendered without consequence. Those things that ought to be protected at all costs and not yielded without proper sanction."

"None of my ladies is light of reputation," the princess insisted, a tinge of irritation creeping into her voice.

Lady Stanley sniffed. "That may be, for the nonce. But one hears stories, and one sees hints. In such a fevered season as this, when the household is rushing pell-mell toward a wedding? Pah!" She twisted her lips in a grimace, settling back in her chair like some ancient hag pronouncing a curse. "What rein can hold licentious wickedness in check when it begins its breakneck charge downhill?"

I felt Grace bristle beside me, but I knew she would not answer back. Aunt Ursula looked as if she had swallowed something foul, and I feared she, as hostess, would say something unforgiveable. Which meant I had to defend my family.

As I drew breath to say I knew not what, the door opened, admitting the king and his gentlemen. In a sweet agony of anticipation, I searched for Benedict in the group filing through in twos and threes. Where last night we had sniped at one another like a pair of fighting hawks, I feared speaking to him tonight. How could I frame my thoughts? What could I say?

But he was not with them. My heart sank. At the opening of the door, it had leapt into my throat, fluttering like a wild bird, but now it dropped like a stone below where it normally sat, down and down, until it seemed to strike the very boards of the floor. Nay, I told myself, it is for the best, for what could you say to him before all of these people, knowing what you know.

He loves me.

My heart lifted itself up again, singing.

The king stood, speaking at length with the princess and his mother, graciously including Aunt Ursula in the conversation, while the other gentlemen spread out through the room, bowing, greeting, settling onto chairs and pillows. The soft buzz of conversation surrounded me like the drone of bees on a summer afternoon, soothing my agitation as I waited for him, wondering at his delay.

Suddenly, the door flew open. It crashed into the wall with a loud bang, causing all conversation to cease. Everyone looked up as Benedict burst into the room. He skidded to a halt as his feet came up against the edge of the rug, arms out for balance. Everyone stared.

He flushed red.

His beard was gone, his cheeks shaved clean.

"Benedict," the king said at length. "What have you done..." He circled his hand around his face.

Grace jabbed me in the ribs with her elbow. I realized my mouth was hanging open, and I snapped it shut so fast my teeth clicked together. The slight pain jarred, and I put a hand over my lips.

Benedict glanced around the room, saw me, blushed redder—if that were possible—and directed his gaze at the king. After a rapid bow, he said, sounding pained, "Your majesty, I am not as I have been."

No one seemed to know what to say or how to react. "Indeed not, Sir Edmund," the king replied. "Will you not join us, changed as you are, or will you stand in the doorway all evening?"

Keeping his eyes on the floor, he picked his way across the room to sit in the only spot available, a small stool near the king.

I couldn't take my eyes off him. The Duke of Surrey seemed to have the same affliction. "Good heavens, Benedict!" he said. "Were they in need of stuffing for new tennis balls, that you visited the barbers today?"

The comment broke the tension, and everyone burst out laughing. "Indeed, he is younger by years tonight than this morning, for the loss of a beard," Lord Thomas teased, rubbing his own bare chin. "Younger than me, mayhap."

Benedict, sitting behind Lord Thomas, who lounged on the floor, kicked him in the shoulder. "Never younger nor more foolish than you, my lord Lackbeard. I can still grow a beard should I choose to."

Grace leaned close to my shoulder, turning her head so that her mouth was right next to my ear and no one but me could hear what she said. "Did you ask him to shave his beard?"

I shook my head, unable to speak. I had not asked it of him and would never have done so. But he had teased me just the other night about my distaste for beards. And he had not had a beard when he had left for war, when he had left me...

I am not as I have been...

Was that a message meant for me?

I wanted everyone to leave, for the room to empty of everyone but Benedict and me so that I could ask him, not outright, of course, but somehow find some words to learn the truth of what I heard, and what he had just said, and what this all meant.

When I next caught hold of a snippet of conversation, like catching a grasshopper in midflight on a sunny day in a grassy meadow, I realized that the king was in the middle of proposing the evening's entertainment.

"A game of lords and ladies," he was saying. "The duke of Surrey dreamed it up this afternoon."

The princess shot a glance at him, and he bowed. "Of course," she murmured. "What is the nature of this game, your grace?"

"Each person present will speak in praise of another, the gentlemen in praise of a lady, the ladies in praise of a gentleman. No names, of course."

"Of course. That would be indelicate," the princess replied, fluttering her lashes at him.

He inclined his head, managing to conceal a grin. Only the duke of Surrey would dare flirt with the king's betrothed right in front of him. "Your highness and his majesty will judge who offers the best praise. His majesty has offered a jewel for a prize." The king held aloft a pearl set in gold that I had seen pinned to his hat earlier in his visit. A dear prize indeed. "Who will begin?"

"Mischief and nonsense," Lady Stanley muttered, rising from her seat. As expected.

Aunt Ursula sniffed. "I shall begin, your grace." Her bright gaze swept the assembled company. "My highest praise of a lord, any lord, is this: that when the day's work is done, he doesn't ask me to take up the distaff and work some more." She stood. "And with that, my good lords and ladies, your majesties, I shall leave you to your game." She made a stiff curtsy, shallow out of age, not disrespect, and offered Lady Stanley an escort out of the room. The two older dames exited, all stiff-backed dignity.

We were all silent, wide-eyed, watching them go. Mary, stammering, ventured, "Did she just...?" but did not dare to finish her own question. "*Mon dieu!*" the princess exclaimed, lapsing into the French she had often spoken in her youth. She was right. Only French seemed appropriate for what my aunt had seemed to suggest.

"Well," the duke said, for once flustered. He stared for a long moment at the closed door then recovered his usual good humor. "Perhaps a gentleman would like to go next?"

Someone snorted. "After that? What can a man say to follow that?"

Over the mutterings and chuckling that created a low hum in the room, one voice rang out, "My lady is so fair, she would teach the torches to burn."

Every voice was silenced once again, and every face turned toward the speaker.

Benedict reddened but did not flinch. After all, he did like to be the center of attention.

My stomach fluttered. He was looking at the princess, at my cousins, at anyone but me.

The duke turned toward him. "Well said, sir."

Benedict looked at me at last, and the touch of his gaze was like the spark to ignite those torches. I would have run to him that instant, had we been alone. He must have seen it. The corner of his mouth twitched but he didn't smile. The caprices of his whims were so easy to see now that he had shaved that beard. So too was it easy to see the near-miss of that scar.

"She is like to a snowy dove among the crows, like a jewel amidst the dust."

The duke's brow twitched. "Very well, sir. We have heard you speak your piece."

"An angel among harpies," he finished.

An apology, of sorts. I had to look away, for my eyes were burning. Grace cast me an inquisitive look. I shook my head at her.

"Next," the duke called out. "Next!"

Eleanor sat up straighter and a smile stretched across her whole face. "A lord is gracious and tedious, senseless and disheartless, strong and brave."

There was a pause as everyone tried to decipher her meaning and moreover whether she was jesting. Mary, as always, came to her rescue. "Oh, well said, Eleanor, dear!" she cried, clapping her hands. I noted several people leaning their heads together, whispering. Those of us who knew Eleanor and her difficulties explained to those who did not.

"Next?" the duke said, eager to move on. "Lord John?"

Seated near the back of the crowd of men, he looked as if he smelled something bad, like cow manure or rotting fish. "Pray, allow someone else to speak," he said, his words far more gracious than his expression. "I am not a man of many words."

"Lady Viola?"

Lady Viola flinched. "Forgive me," she said, bowing her head. "Though I attend upon their majesties, I am yet in mourning. My heart will not allow me to indulge in games." Her glance touched up the duke and slid away. I watched her watching him as he bowed to her and called upon another. "Much as I might desire it," she added in a whisper that no one heard save Grace and I, sitting near her.

Others spoke, some witty, some clumsy, some obvious in their praise of this lady or this gentleman. Meanwhile, I watched Benedict. His face was painted with golden light on one side where it caught the glow of the fire, but his eyes were lost in shadow. I could not tell if he was looking at me. I could not read his expression. My family said he loved me still, and his words tonight seemed to suggest it, but since his return, he had not revealed any signs of love, and indeed last night, he had been most cruel.

If the duke called upon me to speak, as he surely would, I would have to decline. Any other time, I would have relished the chance to cut a man's pride to ribbons with my words. But farewell, contempt. Adieu, Lady Disdain. For once, Beatrice, so famed for her wicked tongue, would be silent.

The voices around me dulled to mere sound, a rushing hiss rather like the tide at the shore. The duke glanced at me often, but I steadfastly avoided his gaze and always there was another to speak up in my place. I did not even notice when the prize was awarded, clapping along with the others in a pleasant fog of my own thoughts.

The princess made a delicate yawn, waiting long enough to cover her mouth to ensure that it would be noted, and in a rush of motion everyone was on their feet, hurrying to take their leave. She beckoned to me. "Stay," was all she said.

I sat on a pillow beside her chair as the room emptied, watching the servants clear the wine and goblets, waiting as the gentlemen all took their leave, including the king and his closest companions. I could scarce make myself look at Benedict. What would my eyes reveal if I did?

When the room was empty at last, and the servants had moved into her bedchamber to attend upon her there, she rose and stretched with a sigh. "My dear lady Beatrice," she said, "am I right in thinking that your views on marriage may have changed during this last turning of the sun?"

"I—" I could scarce frame my thoughts into words. "Mayhap it is true, your highness. Mayhap, they are changing."

She smiled, that slow, warm smile that would make a person swear to follow her into hell itself. "Glad I am to hear it," she said. "Will you wait here, to attend me until I fall asleep?"

I bowed my head. "Of course, your highness."

Her request meant the king was returning. Which meant...mayhap...

I sat on the rug by the fire while her attendants helped her change for bed, then watched as they left, extinguishing all the candles behind them so that I sat bathed in a small, glowing circle of golden light. My skin tingled with anticipation, every sense heightened, my ears yearning to hear the door open again behind me to admit the king once again.

Despite my intense anticipation, I found myself half-dozing in the warmth and dark before the latch rattled and the door swung open. I scrambled to my feet, dropping into an awkward curtsy on feet numb from sitting so long. King Henry, having doffed his gown and doublet, swept past in his shirt and hose, ignoring me entirely.

"We must pretend that these nights are not happening," Benedict murmured, shutting the door and leaning against it.

I nodded. My heart was racing, and I could scarce draw breath. At last, we were alone, and words unspoken hung in the air between us.

"You shaved your beard," I said at last.

Really, Beatrice? Is that all you can think to say?

He smiled, but it was a soft, indulgent smile, not sharp with disdain or wit. He slid his fingers along his jaw, exploring the sensation. I had to press my own fingers together, entwining them to resist the desire to do the same.

"'Tis an odd sensation. I have not been without a beard since—well, in some time." He glanced at me, and when our gazes met, they skittered apart, like rocks colliding on ice. He still had not moved away from the door, nor I from the hearth.

"Will you not come in?" I asked, with a weak gesture toward the large chairs where, earlier, the princess and the king had sat together. He looked long at the seat as though it was as great a challenge to cross the flagstone floor as it had been to survive the battle that put Henry on the throne. At long last, he walked to the chair but did not sit. Instead, he stood behind it, gripping the back with his hands.

"Grace and Thomas will soon be wed," he said, his gaze fixed on the fire dancing in the hearth. "You will feel her loss keenly, I think."

"I will," I said, "When the royal court continues on to Woking, I will lose all."

"Surely not all."

"Near enough."

His lips parted as though he would speak—I was watching his face so closely I noted every flick of an eyelash—but he said nothing, just shifted his weight from one foot to the other and back again. Then, abruptly, he turned to face me. "Lord Keighton and the Duke of Surrey were talking to your uncle today, and they said the most—"

He cut himself off and tilted his head toward the door, listening. I did too, my heart pounding from what he had—mayhap—been about to say and from wondering why he had not said it. At first, I heard nothing, but then I could just make out the sounds of voices raised in anger and concern. A door slammed.

Benedict moved like silent lightning, crossing to the door and pressing his ear to it, one hand on the latch. With great care, he lifted the latch and slid the door open just enough to peek into the hallway, and whatever he saw there was enough to make him rush to close it again. He beckoned urgently to me, whispering, "Come here!"

Much as I wanted to ask what was toward, I held my tongue and hurried to his side. From here, standing beside the door, I could hear what he heard: the distinct rap-tap of shoes coming closer. My eyes widened, and I could feel the blood draining from my face. At this hour, there could only be one person coming to the princess' rooms.

Lady Stanley. The king's mother.

Benedict looked down at me, and in his deep, cinnamon eyes, I saw the same emotions I felt: hesitation, apprehension, something akin to fear. If it were Lady Stanley, and if she forced her way past us, and if she discovered her son with the princess...

It did not bear thinking of.

I glanced at the door to the princess' bedchamber. Loathe as I was to disturb them, knowing what I would find when I went into the princess' room, I knew I must. I opened my mouth to speak.

Benedict grabbed my hand and raced back to the chairs by the fire.

"What are you doing?"

"Shh!" He hushed me, a finger to his lips as he settled down in one of the chairs.

"Are you mad?" I said, dragging back against him, trying to pull him back to his feet. "She will be upon us at any moment—"

He grabbed my arm with both hands and yanked me onto his lap. I was startled speechless, and he took advantage of the moment to rearrange me around him, pulling my legs across him so they dangled over the arm of the chair, draping one of my arms around his shoulders, placing one of his hands on my waist, raising the other to glide like falling snow along my cheek.

"Oh," I whispered, so close that my breath brushed his skin and he blinked at the touch. "I see. Yes, this is a fine ruse."

He nodded, barely. "A fine ruse," he repeated, the words rough, half-strangled.

He stroked my cheek again, lingering, sliding lower. His fingers splayed out along my neck, bending to its shape. In the play of the firelight, his eyes were very dark, the pupils very large. My lips parted, and I leaned in toward him, yearning for a taste.

"Lady Beatrice!"

Like a newborn stork, I flailed off Benedict's lap and curtseyed low and deep. He stood too, far more gracefully, and bowed his head, looking quite shamefaced.

My-lady-the-king's-interfering-mother fixed me with a glare that could have shattered steel. If the king had brought her to Bosworth, he wouldn't have needed any knights to fight for him. "Lady Beatrice," she repeated, scorn dripping from her words. "I am sore disappointed to find you here."

Several replies flitted through my mind, but I decided that she would not appreciate any odd quirks or remnants of wit at the present moment. I remained silent.

Her lips twisted. I could see she had expected me to give her a tart response, and she was further disappointed that she could not add that to her reasons for disappointment. She flicked her hand at me, allowing me to rise.

"It seems that the notion of marriage is setting this household off kilter," she said. "First your cousin Grace coerces her father into accepting her betrothal to Lord Keighton, with no time for her father to know the young man or his family, and then the plan for an over-hasty wedding, again, at the young woman's urging—" She looked at me, daring me to deny what she said. "And now this!" She waved a hand at us. "Today I heard talk of another wedding before long, isn't that right, Sir Edmund?"

She could not have shocked me more had she punched me in the stomach. I glanced up at Benedict, but he stared straight ahead. Only the clenched muscles of his jaw revealed his tension, but I knew that was not for me or himself; it was for the king in the next room, who might, at any moment, walk out.

"I scarce believed it, given the determination I had heard expressed by both of you against marriage in the short time we have been in this place, but well do I know how foolish girls are when a handsome man looks at them twice. Propriety!" She barked the word, and I jumped. "You will not besmirch the princess' reputation! I went to your room this night to assure myself that your conduct remained beyond reproach, as is required of a lady companion to the future queen, and what do I find? Hmmm? No, you are not in your room, and your little cousin does not know where you are. Except her cheeks are very pink, and she cannot look me in the eye, sure signs of a liar. So, I seek you out, and I find you here, indulging in sinful pleasures."

She looked like a demon, her face red, her eyes black flashes beneath her stark white wimple, the fire casting her in grim shadow. I could not frame a response.

Benedict took a large step away from me, separating himself from the temptation of "sinful pleasures" I supposed. "Nay, my lady," he said, speaking rather loudly. Indeed, rather more loudly than needful to reach her ears. "Say not that Lady Beatrice is at fault." He raised his voice even further. "Her highness Princess Elizabeth would never condone such behavior." There was a small thud and a gasp from beyond the bedchamber door.

Lady Stanley made a sour face at him. "There is no reason to shout at me, young sir. If it is not Lady Beatrice's fault, I suppose the fault is yours?"

"Indeed," he replied, "for I am known to be a wicked fellow."

I had to bite my lip to keep from laughing. Much as I wanted to strangle him over that wickedness...

"There is only one cure for wickedness, Sir Edmund," she said.

"Oh, aye."

"I suggest you avail yourself of it now."

"Now?" he squeaked.

"I will escort you to the chapel myself. We will wake the chaplain, and I will wait while he hears your confession. Then I will join you in prayer for an hour."

He bowed his head. "You are too kind, Lady Stanley. Your efforts on behalf of my immortal soul will surely not go unnoticed."

She frowned at him. "Better you kept silent, young man." She pointed a long finger at me. "And you, young lady! Get you to bed this instant and pray for your poor dead mother's forgiveness. I will speak to your uncle and your aunt about your shameful behavior in the morning."

I bowed my head and curtsied low, a picture of regret. "Yes, my lady. Thank you, my lady." An hour of discomfort for Benedict tonight, any punishment I might suffer at my uncle's hands, these things mattered not. But if she were occupied long enough for the king to safely depart from these chambers and return to his own with his mother none the wiser, well, that was worth anything.

As Benedict followed her out, he cast a quick glance over his shoulder, flashing me a brilliant smile. One that promised much, and more.

CHAPTER 10

"This is my wedding bower," Grace said.

We stood just inside in the doorway of a room that had been opened and aired over the last few days in readiness for Grace's wedding.

Her wedding that was to happen on the morrow.

Three days had elapsed since my-lady-the-king's-meddlesome-mother had interrupted Benedict and me in the antechamber to the princess' bedchamber. Three days in which I had not ceased to feel his touch, imagine myself once again in his arms, conjure the touch of his lips that I had been denied by her interference. I was like to drive myself mad with the thought of it, yet I could not stop. And to make matters worse, the close call had instilled a new caution in the king and the princess, who had put a stop to all our evening entertainments and even much of the daytime contact between the gentlemen and the ladies. The men rode out every morning to the hunt, while we women dedicated ourselves to preparing for Grace's nuptials—necessary, of course, but far less diverting to me now that I longed to see Benedict again. But we saw each other across the table at mealtimes or exchanged longing glances in corridors. Now that I longed to go sneaking about at night, drinking too much unwatered wine and staggering back to my room dizzy from kisses, the opportunity was denied me.

This wedding bower, in one of the little-used towers in the older part of Uncle Lionel's manor, had been prepared for Grace's nuptial night, and for the nonce, I must drag my thoughts from when I might speak with Benedict and keep them here, with her.

The many linens we had stitched with both speed and dedication had been strewn upon the bed in an abundance of luxury: sheets, pillowcases, even a hastily patched-up quilt. Heavy drapes were pulled back to let sunlight in through the narrow unglazed windows (this part of the manor was quite old) and thick rugs covered the flags on the floor. When the night came, the now-empty hearth would glow merrily with a welcoming fire.

"It would be nice if we could find a tapestry or two," Grace said at last. "To warm up the walls a bit."

I chuckled. "I don't think you'll be looking at the walls, cousin." Then I laughed harder as she flushed pink, not just her cheeks but her entire face, even down her neck.

"Beatrice," she said, trying, and mostly failing, to chide. Then she sobered. "Tomorrow I marry Thomas, and the day after that, we will depart with the king."

The knowledge was a stone in my gullet. "I know," I said, putting an arm around her.

"I can never remember a time when we were apart. And soon we will be separated forever."

I gave her shoulders a quick squeeze combined with a little shake. "We knew this day would come, for you if not for me. Do not think of it as forever. You will visit your father and your family from time to time. And just think, there will be children for me to teach all my bad manners to."

"Children!" she squealed, nudging me with an elbow. "I'm not even married yet!"

Our ladies' maid, Margaret, bustled through the open door, humming a tune under her breath. "Oh!" she exclaimed. "Pardon, miladies, I did not know you were in here." She set down the large basket, overflowing with clothes, that she had lugged up the stairs.

"I only wanted to see it," Grace said. "I don't mean to be in your way."

Margaret's smile was wide, enveloping in its warmth. "Milady, you could never be in anyone's way." She hefted the basket again and moved past my cousin toward one of the chests, trailing behind her the scent of lavender that Grace favored in her clothes. I realized that she was moving some of Grace's belongings from our room to this one.

I had not expected this to be so difficult.

As she passed, I plucked a garment from the top of the pile, a night-time gown of frothy lace and pale linen, accented with ribbons in yellow and pale pink. "For your new husband?" I teased, waving it about. Grace squealed and tried to snatch it from my hands. When I swung it away from her, Margaret cried, "Give it here, milady!" Startled by her vehemence, I froze and allowed her to take it from me. She folded it into a rumpled mass and put it back atop the basket.

"Margaret," Grace said, "I think the sleeve of that gown was torn. May I see?"

"No," Margaret snapped, pulling the basket away. Grace and I stared, shocked. She pressed her lips together, sliding her eyes away. "I—your pardon, milady. I will see to the gown if anything is amiss."

Grace tilted her head, searching Margaret's face for understanding, but the maid kept her eyes down, her face closed off. "All right, Margaret. See to it that it is ready for tomorrow."

Margaret bobbed a curtsy and turned away, lifting the lid of the chest to begin placing Grace's clothes within.

Grace and I exchanged a look of puzzlement but neither of us knew what might be troubling our maid. Perhaps it was the thought of leaving here with Grace after the wedding that made her snipe at us.

"One other thing," Grace said slowly, as we turned to leave Margaret to her work.

Something in her tone made me apprehensive. "Yes?"

"I have decided to sleep here tonight, alone, rather than in our room. If that's all right with you." She shot me a quick glance, seeming afraid of my reaction. "I need to become accustomed to being without you."

I put an arm around her waist and pulled her to me. "Of course," I said, though my heart sank. We would not have one last night together as girls, as the sisters we were in truth. "If that is what you need, you shall have it."

We walked together, arms encircling each other's waists, toward the twisting stairway that descended to the main part of the house. My heart seemed to squeeze in my chest at the thought of my cousin's leaving, of the end of moments like this.

A sudden commotion echoing up the stairs caught our attention and diverted me from becoming entirely maudlin. I glanced at Grace and she raised her brows, showing she shared my curiosity. We moved together, descending the worn stone risers, to see what was toward.

Several of the gentlemen rushed past us, roaring with laughter and scarce begging our pardon for nearly knocking us over in their hurry. I tossed a few angry words at their backs as Grace pulled me in the direction they had come from. "Beatrice, look!"

A small crowd of men and a few women had gathered around an open doorway about midway down the corridor. With a start, I realized we were in the area reserved for the king's gentlemen. "We aren't permitted here." Having stated that aloud, however, not only did I continue to follow her, I hurried my steps until I was half-racing her.

"What have you done?" Benedict's voice boomed over the general hubbub, quieting the voices to barely stifled laughter and whispers.

Grace skidded to a stop, her arm linked through mine pulling me with her.

The crowd parted to allow him closer to the door. He approached from the other end of the corridor than us. At the front of the gaggle, nearest the door and facing out, stood Lord Thomas and the Duke of Surrey. Naturally. Both of them were giggling like children.

Under my breath, I echoed Benedict: "What have you done?"

Benedict came to a halt before them. He crossed his arms and tilted his head, and in that moment, I saw the man he might have been on the battlefield, implacable, steady, resolute. Something melted in my knees, and I was glad I had Grace to help keep me upright. The duke, at least, tried to sober himself, pulling his lips down and drawing his brows together. But then he sidled sideways and pulled the door shut behind him. It was Benedict's door, which now all could see had a large cloth sign tacked on it. Large, sprawling letters had been painted there, some of them still glistening damp and dripping.

"EDMUNDUS BENEDICTUS," it read, "GOOD HORSE TO HIRE."

I watched his face as he read the sign. The message made no sense to me, but it was clearly a jest between the men and meant to pierce sharp as a lance through Benedict's armor.

Thomas, studying his face, pouted, seeming disappointed that Benedict did not instantly respond, whether with an outburst of anger or a wicked jest. He prodded his friend's chest with a finger.

"Remember?" he asked, and when Benedict still did not reply, he put his hands up near his head, making horns with his pointing fingers. "Make a sign with letters as big as they write 'Here is good horse to hire'?"

The duke leaned closer, his voice quieter but no less teasing. "Here you may see Benedict, the married man?"

Benedict reared back, putting distance between them. Grace gripped my arm tighter. The crowd, stifling their humor, quieted, waiting. What would he do?

His jaw worked. Even from where we stood, I could see the muscles clench. I knew him so well, I could see the words spin through his mind as he sifted through appropriate replies. Then, in an instant, he relaxed and reached out to his friends, one hand on the duke's shoulder, and one on Thomas'. And he laughed.

He laughed.

I gasped, but the sound was lost in the confounded murmurings of the watching crowd.

Benedict dropped his head, squeezed his friends' shoulders, and turned so he could address all of them. Scanning the group, he said, "It seems I must learn to curb my tongue—to train it to the yoke, as it were. You may think to taunt me with my own words, but I say I am made of stronger stuff and cannot be mocked out of my good humor. And let me be clear— when I said that I would die a bachelor, I did not think to live till I were married."

Laughter and applause greeted his words, and he bowed gracefully. Grace murmured in my ear, "Did he just say..." but I did not hear the rest of what she said because as he rose from his bow, his gaze collided with mine like swords clashing, like lightning striking.

I could not look away, nor could he.

As the fellows realized that their fun was over, they began to drift away in twos and threes, murmuring and casting suggestive glances my way.

I cared not a whit.

Grace released my arm and slipped away to join her betrothed. Together, they and the duke made their way to the other stair.

I scarce noted her departure, for it meant that Benedict and I were by ourselves in the corridor.

Benedict heaved a sigh. "I think there has ne'er been a man so turned over and over by a woman as my poor self."

A smile tugged at my lips but I fought it. "Seek you my pity?"

"The gods alone have enough pity for a poor soul like me."

"Poor fellow," I said. "Too bad for you I am not a god, only a woman."

"There is no 'only' about you."

I felt my cheeks warm with his words and ducked my head to hide my reaction from him. He took a step toward me. "Beatrice." In his hands was a worn, much-folded piece of parchment, marked with water stains and wine, ash, and something dark that might have been blood.

"What is that?" I asked.

"Your letter," he replied, turning it over in his hands, rubbing it with his thumbs. Judging by the condition of the parchment, he must have done this very thing a thousand times. A thousand, thousand times.

"My letter?" Though I had written it when he left some two years before, I knew what it said. I could have recited it chapter and verse from memory. It was no love note to be kept and savored. "Why have you not burned it, buried it, torn it in a thousand pieces?"

"I should have," he said. "I meant to, many times. But it was all—" He glanced at me, a quick, furtive look, with the ghost of a smile in it. "It was all I had of you."

We both looked down at the ratty parchment for a long moment. At last, he said, "Why did you write it?"

"I should have thought its purpose was obvious from the words," I said wryly.

"Yes," he said with a smile. "But when we parted..."

I shook my head. "I do not want to go back."

"Beatrice," he said, taking my hand. "I think we must."

I stared down at our hands, concentrating on the warmth of his skin, the sword-roughness of his palm. "I was hurt, Benedict, and wanted to return it in kind. I wanted never to hear from you, never to see you again."

He moved away the distance of a breath, and my hand was cold when he withdrew his. "I thought you understood. I tried to explain, over and over. You refused to listen."

"I listened, but you made no sense. I thought that you loved me and we would marry. Instead, you decided to leave, and you claimed it was because my uncle would never permit us to marry because of your status."

"It was true then. It is not true now. That is why I had to go."

The old fury flared in my breast, so sudden it threatened to strangle my breath. "There it is, that Benedictine confidence. You are so sure of yourself, so confident that only you are right. How do you know? How dare you think you know my uncle better than I? Yes, I was an heiress, but he loves me as he loves his own daughter, and look, he is allowing Grace to marry Lord Keighton rather than the duke whom—as you know—he has intended for her husband for her entire life. And even if he had denied us, I would have defied him for you, you know I would. I would have left everything for you." I could hear my voice rising, ringing in the corridor, but I could not rein it in, now that I had loosed it upon him at last. My entire body was tight as a crossbow, ready to fire.

God bless him, for once he was silent.

For once, he placed himself before the target and spread his arms wide, waiting for the arrows to strike. Accepting them. He aimed no weapon back at me. He did not try to evade or dodge or shield himself.

I shook my head and drew a sharp breath through my teeth. He glared at the floor, jaw set. The sign, glimmering with damp letters, mocked him for showing any tender emotions before his friends. I pulled in another breath and forced my body to release its tension, to unwind the crossbow. Extending a hand, I did not quite touch him; I was not sure he would permit it. "I understand," I said, and at last I meant it. "I do understand. Look at you. *Sir* Edmund, well-loved and trusted by a duke, in favor with the king. Could you have risen so high had you not gone away? You had to take chances with your life, and you were better served—we were both better served—by your not being bound to a wife at home."

I swallowed hard. Had I truly forgiven him for leaving me?

I took the letter from his hand and crushed it. It felt like mud, like a rotting, smelly French cheese. I longed to destroy it, burn it. Unmake it, so that it had never been. "I am only sorry that we lost our friendship in that time," I finished, blinking against the tears pricking at my treacherous eyes.

"I was never not your friend," he said, once again twining his fingers through mine.

"Oh," I groaned. "You would ever have the last word!" But I was laughing as I pulled him toward me. His eyes lit with surprise then darkened with desire. I ran my hand up his chest. He released my hand so he could pull me close to him, our legs tangling. I rose on my toes to kiss him, weaving my fingers in his hair, relishing the fire shooting through my veins, a sensation at once familiar and entirely new. He had indeed learned some things while abroad. We were impossibly close and yet not close enough, the layers of my kirtle and chemise suddenly stifling.

"Beatrice," he murmured, pulling back with effort. "We should—be careful. That's my open door right there."

I glanced at it, and for a moment I considered flinging everything away. Go in, shut the door...the princess did it, why not me? It must be marvelous, for so many people to risk so much.

The moment stretched.

"Good horse for hire?" I said at last, ending it.

He hesitated, and I could tell from the quirk of his lips that he sensed my true thoughts before the question. He ran a gentle finger over the full- ness of my lower lip, and I almost forgot what I had asked. "I may have boasted that I would never marry." He rolled his eyes. "I may have said that a married man was like an ox with his head in the yoke, or a good horse for hire—placid, dull, boring. No will of his own."

"Oh," I said, afraid to ask but needing to know. "Is that what you think?"

"I may have thought so, once. But now, I—" He brushed a lock of hair away from my brow, continued the caress down my cheek. "I have seen that it need not always be the case."

"That is—" I leaned into his touch. The pulse in my neck fluttered under his fingers as he drew them down, down toward my collarbone, lower... His touch was making it hard for me to breathe, to think, to frame words. "That is good."

"I think so, too," he said. "And what of you? You've been saying that you will never marry. Anyone."

I tilted my head to look deep into his eyes. I was so used to seeing guardedness there since his return—that, and anger—but now he held nothing back. I saw his desire, and his fear, and the pain of the past two years, and I almost looked away. My heart ached from the sight of it. But if he was going to let me see what he felt, I had to do the same.

I let out a shaky breath. "Mayhap," I said, losing myself in him, "I might be convinced to marry."

He smiled. And kissed me again.

CHAPTER 11

The sun rose the next day, dull and inauspicious, glowering over the fields like a discontented old man, displeased with all he saw, attempting to pull the covers back over him and return to his slumber. The air was thick and the clouds hung low, making it hard to breathe freely. Still, all the household was up and scurrying, for there was a wedding to prepare for.

Upon my arrival at Grace's new chamber, I could scarce fit through the doorway, for the room overflowed with family and servants seeking to be useful. Our maid Margaret was there, of course, but also Aunt Ursula and Eleanor and Mary, and even several of the princess' court ladies. Aunt Ursula and my cousins stood beside the bed, deep in discussion over a trio of dresses. The princess had also sent over one of her maids whose name I did not know, and as I squeezed into the room, she was engaged in a silent battle of wills with Margaret, trying to arrange Grace's hair into a more elaborate style than was her wont. Grace paid them no mind, sitting on a padded stool with her eyes shut.

"I still think this one's lovely," Eleanor said, stroking a pale apricot kirtle with gentle fingers.

Mary shook her head. "Nay," she said. "This one, for certes." She lifted her choice, a deep violet velvet, from the bed. "Grace? What say you?"

Grace opened her eyes to see Mary's choice and smiled when she saw me. I smiled back, trying to embrace her with the warmth of my gaze since I could squeeze no closer.

Mary shook the kirtle to draw Grace's attention. "This one?" she repeated.

Grace wrinkled her nose. "The color of royalty, Mary? In the presence of royalty? Even you would not be so presumptuous."

Mary glared and tossed the dress back on the bed and sat beside it. "Very well, then. What have you in mind?"

Grace rose, pulling the maids along behind her, their fingers twined and tangled in her locks, distress on their faces. Eleanor clutched the pale apricot in her fists, and Aunt Ursula sought to untangle the delicate silk from her hands lest it be crushed beyond saving. I took advantage of their movements to slip into the room.

Grace moved without hesitation to the kirtle she wanted, pointing at a pale blue silk trimmed about the neck with pearls. "The color calls to mind the Holy Virgin, and I go to my husband a pure maid. Also, it is simple and well-made, not fashionable or vain, just as our love is, as our marriage will be." She raised her eyebrows at Mary. "With the plain white chemise, I think."

With a scowl, Mary rose from the bed and stomped away. I reached out to soothe her and forestall her from leaving the room, and over the hum of voices raised to agree with Grace's choice, I heard our maid Margaret say, quite clearly, "Are you sure, milady?"

Everyone turned to look at her, the buzz of conversation dying. Margaret kept her gaze locked on the floor, her hands still wound through Grace's hair, her jaw tight with the stress of speaking out.

Grace alone seemed unconcerned at the question. She ran her fingers down the fabric once more. "Yes, Margaret," she replied. "I am quite sure."

"Of course, milady," Margaret murmured. "As you wish." But she looked miserable, and there was no reason why she should.

"Sit, my dear," Aunt Ursula said, stepping into the center of the room, placing her hands upon Grace's shoulders to turn her back to the dressing table. "Let the maids finish your hair and then you can get dressed."

A servant began passing wine around and a minstrel strummed a lute in the corridor outside—there were too many of us in the room for him to find even a corner—and the mood relaxed once more. Grace sat, as bidden, and the maids resumed brushing and looping her hair, tucking pearls and tiny clusters of white alyssum flowers into it. One of the princess' ladies queried whether a strand of pearls around Grace's neck would be too much, given the dress' ornamentation, and Aunt Ursula fished around in the jewel box on the dressing table to find one. Margaret finished one last braid and tied off the end with a pure white ribbon, leaning close over Grace's shoulder as she did so.

"Please," I heard her whisper under the general discussion. "Will you reconsider?" Grace jerked her head to look at the maid. The poor girl looked almost panicked. Words of explanation flew out of her mouth, tumbling over each other in a rushing hiss like water in a mill race. "What I mean to say, that is, it is only that Lord Thomas has spent so much time with the king and the court, and he has become accustomed... Her highness the princess sets a high standard... Mayhap something less symbolic and more elaborate would please him."

Grace stretched out a hand to take the strand of pearls from Aunt Ursula and lay them across her throat for the group's opinion, but she held her focus on Margaret alone. "I am quite certain about my choice, Margaret, and *you* would do well to remember your place."

She made an unhappy curtsy. "I beg your pardon, milady. I only wish you happy."

Grace reached out and touched Margaret's arm. "We will be happy, dear Margaret. Today, and every day."

I could see, though, that her mistress' kindness did nothing to make Margaret feel better, and in fact seemed to make her even more unhappy. The cause of her misery was unknowable, however, though I resolved to ask her about it later.

Unfortunately, it was not until much later—too late—that I found out.

* * *

An hour—perhaps two?—later, we were gathered just outside the doors of the little chapel at the rear of the manor. Common folk held their services at the church in town, but our family always worshiped here in private. We would not forget them, however. Later, after the ceremony and wedding breakfast, the bride and groom would go down into the town and show themselves to the people who would be enjoying food and wine at Uncle Lionel's expense. Lord Thomas would distribute coins, and his new lady would allow them to wish her health, happiness, and many children, to touch her and tear scraps off her expensive kirtle to stitch into patchwork, tiny bits of memory of this day.

In the end, that would never happen.

One by one, we three cousins—first Eleanor, then Mary, and finally I— wished Grace well with a kiss on her cheek and a squeeze of her hand, then left her to walk into the chapel. I said nothing, for what could be said that would not bring us both to tears? This was the last time for, oh, so many things.

I left her with her father and hurried down the aisle to stand with my cousins, next to my Aunt Ursula, who was already wiping slow tears from her eyes. Eleanor patted her hand, smiling with a sweet joy. I felt strangely dislocated, unreal, as if this could not be happening or it were happening to someone else. Even the familiar chapel seemed strange today, ablaze as it was with a hundred fragrant beeswax candles and draped with an expensive altar cloth provided by the royal couple. The king's own private confessor waited at the altar to perform the ceremony, his gold- and gem-encrusted chasuble fairly creaking with his tiniest gesture.

I glanced across the aisle to the groom's side, where Lord Thomas stood with the king, the princess, and the king's mother in the first rank beside him. Behind them stood the Duke of Surrey, Benedict, Lord John Beymond, and behind them, the other young men and women of the court. The image was clear: arrayed behind Thomas, all the strength and power and youthful vitality of the crown, and on Grace's side, mere women and old men. I was chilled by the contrast, though I had no reason —at the time—to be concerned. As my gaze flitted over the court, I sensed someone's gaze upon me and caught Benedict looking at me. He smiled, sending shivers over my skin and setting my heart racing. I smiled back and glanced away, my entire body engulfed in a wave of heat. Surely it was a sin to think of kissing in a church...

With the slightest wave of his hand, the priest bid Grace and Uncle Lionel forward, and they proceeded down the aisle at a sedate, ceremonious pace. Grace's joy could have lit the entire chapel, no need for candles.

Lord Thomas twisted to look back at her, and emotions flickered over his face in a conflicted dance that spoke of more than just a bridegroom's nerves. First there was longing and admiration—for of course, she was beautiful—but then something else... Anger? Disappointment? Contempt? *What was this?*

The duke leaned forward, his jaw set as though he tasted something bitter, and put a hand on Thomas' shoulder to steady him. Thomas nodded. Perhaps he had been concerned about Grace's dowry? Or had had second thoughts about marrying altogether? And perhaps the duke had convinced him of the propriety of the match and encouraged him hither? Here, with the king beside him, after all.

While my mind swirled with these troubles, Grace had taken her place at Thomas' side, and Uncle Lionel had taken his seat beside his wife. I glanced once more at Benedict and tilted my head, eyebrows raised, in the direction of his friend. He raised his shoulders and let them fall. He didn't seem to know anything either.

The priest had begun to speak. The wedding was beginning, and I was fretting the moments away. I turned my attention back to what was being said.

"Who gives this woman in marriage?" he asked.

"I do," Uncle Lionel said.

"And you, Thomas, Lord Keighton, do you come here today to marry this woman?"

There was a moment's pause in which Thomas seemed to be considering, then he said, "No."

A gasp rippled through the company. Grace went white as the pearls on her gown. I started forward to her defense, but Aunt Ursula grabbed my wrist. Uncle Lionel forced a laugh. "No, of course not, Father. He comes to be married *to* her. You come to marry her."

Everyone laughed in relief, but I watched Thomas' face. His lips were a tight line and his color was high. That was not what he had meant. For a wild instant, I pondered grabbing Grace by the hand and fleeing the chapel with her. But of course, I couldn't. Of course, that wasn't my choice to make.

I should have. I should have done it anyway.

Clearly not amused, the priest silenced the audience with a quick gesture, and went on. "If either of you, or anyone here present, know of any impediment to this marriage, or any reason why these two should not be joined in holy wedlock, I charge you on your immortal souls to speak it now."

The silence was total for the space of a heartbeat, and then Thomas asked, his voice tight, "Know you any, Grace? Any impediment to this marriage?"

"None, my lord," she whispered, her hurt and confusion palpable.

Scowling at everyone's lack of commitment to the proper forms, the priest demanded, "Know *you* any, Lord Thomas?"

Uncle Lionel, his worry clear in his quick words, declared, "I dare make answer for him. There is none."

"Easily said, my lord," Thomas shot back. "Easy to swear when you know not of what you speak."

Uncle Lionel moved with painful dignity to stand again beside his daughter, the limp from his old wound apparent in his stiff gait. "Speak plain, son."

Thomas drew a deep breath and glanced back at the duke, who nodded. Facing my uncle, he said, "My lord Lionel, will you, freely and with an unconstrained heart, give me this maid, your daughter, for my wife?"

Uncle Lionel took Grace's hand in his. It looked so small and frail, and I could see she was trembling. "As freely, sir, as God did give her to me." He held Grace's hand out to Thomas, who stared down at it before reaching out to take it and pull her toward him.

I held my breath. Something still was not right.

"And what can I give you in return as recompense for this rich and precious gift?"

"Nothing," Uncle Lionel protested. "You need give me nothing."

The duke, standing behind Thomas, was shaking his head. "The only true recompense is to render her back again," he said. Thomas cocked his head in the direction of the duke, heeding his words but not seeing him, not seeing anything but Grace's face as though he was imprinting it for all time.

I looked from Thomas to the duke and back again. Their faces were closed off, emotions sealed behind invisible helms. They spoke their words as if by rote, like actors in a play. A chill fell upon me that was colder than a castle rampart in winter, colder than a snowmelt stream in spring. This was a show, they had planned it entire. Thomas had no intention of marrying Grace, no matter that he had come to this sacred place decked head to toe in his finery.

I yanked my wrist free of Aunt Ursula's grasp and dove forward just as Thomas shoved Grace wildly back toward her father. He was not prepared to catch her, and she fell past him to the floor, cracking her head against the heavy carved railing in front of the altar. I scurried around the railing, dropped to my knees, and wrapped my arms around her. Her head lolled against my chest and her eyelids fluttered.

"Thus, take her back again," Thomas yelled, his composure breaking, the words torn from his throat. "I beg you, do not give such a vile gift to someone you counted a friend. All who look upon her might swear that she were a maid, but she is none! She has known the heat of a lustful bed."

The priest stepped back, scandalized. Gasps echoed from the rafters and my cousins squealed as they raced to join me, clustered around Grace. Uncle Lionel, looking from Thomas to Grace, seemed dazed, lost. "What can you mean, my lord?"

"I *mean* not to be married," Thomas said, on the verge of tears. "I *mean* not to bind myself in holy matrimony for all eternity to a woman who is proved a whore!"

I surged to my feet, tipping a swooning Grace into Eleanor's arms, and flew at Thomas, beating my uncle to him by a hair's breadth. "How dare you?" I hissed, grabbing the front of his fine doublet in my fists and shaking him. "How dare you?"

The Duke of Surrey stepped in and, with exquisite control, removed my fingers from Thomas. No longer the smiling courtier, he said in clipped tones, "Desist, gentle lady. You know not all the facts."

"I know all I need to know," I said. He kept hold of both my wrists, and a good thing too, for I was ready to do all sorts of violence to his friend. "Grace is the sweetest, kindest, most innocent lady any of you have ever met. This is a slander most foul!"

Though he had remained silent till now, the king rose and came forward. He looked at each of us in turn, and under his steely blue gaze I found myself compelled to subside and wait for his judgment. We all did. At last, he took Lord Thomas by the arm and steered him to one side of the altar, away from center of it all but still close enough for me to hear. He spoke softly, calmly, reasonably.

"Thomas," he said, "my dear fellow." He shifted his grip, slinging an arm around Thomas' shoulders, like two old friends having an ale at the public house. "Mayhap you mistake me…mayhap I have presented an… example that you have followed and now, in the face of this company and standing before God, you feel remorse. Mayhap even anger and shame. Mayhap you blame her for your own weakness." He glanced back over the assembled company, at Grace's limp form, at the horrified members of the court, at the princess, who stared, wide-eyed and disapproving. And last, he looked at his mother, standing beside her, almost rejoicing at the spectacle of sinful lust brought low. Pitching his voice even lower, he unleashed his words, letting them run. "If you yourself have defeated her virginity, there is no shame in that for you were lawfully betrothed. But you must complete the act now and take her to wife. Else you are an oath-breaker and defiler."

Thomas threw the king's hand off his shoulder. "Nay!" he cried, spinning away. "It was not I. I never sought to be more than a friend to her before our wedding night." He stumbled back towards Grace, spitting his words at her. I placed myself between them, forcing him to yell at her around my body. "I was like a brother in my care of her and took myself away when the temptation became too great for either one of us."

Grace moaned and lifted her head, tears streaking her pale cheeks. "I was the same. I don't understand, Thomas. Are you unwell? You must be, to make such accusations."

He jerked away at her use of his name. She buried her face in her hands, giving herself up to weeping. I had to speak for her. "How can you say such things?"

Thomas' eyes flared with righteous pain. "I know what I did see."

"And what did you see?" I demanded.

Uncle Lionel turned to the duke. "My lord, will you say nothing?"

"What can I say?" he replied. "I am dishonored here as well, as I have worked to bring about the wedding of my friend to a—" He stopped himself before saying the word. "To an unchaste woman."

Uncle Lionel recoiled. "Am I truly hearing this, or do I dream?"

"I promise you, sir, all that we say is true."

Thomas, though he had turned away, seemed unable to stay away from Grace. He returned to her from where he had been pacing near the altar, kneeling beside her. Though Eleanor, cradling her, cringed away from him, Grace made an effort to sit up, looking at him straight to show that she was not intimidated.

"Answer me this, Grace," he said, his face so close a hand would not fit between their noses. "And Lord Lionel, I pray you bid her answer honestly—"

"Upon my life, I need no instruction," Grace snapped. The two who had come to marry, who had been so happy together for the past days, now stared at each other with fury and betrayal blazing in their eyes.

"Then tell me," said Thomas, "who was he whose chamber you visited last night not long after Compline?"

Grace scoffed. "There was no man, at that hour or any other."

"You lie!" Thomas cried, and jerked away from her again. Grace struggled in Eleanor's grasp, but I knelt to hold her too. It did no good for her to go to him now. Unless she wanted to slap him or kick him. That, she should do, and gladly would I help her to it.

The duke shook his head. "Upon my honor, I say to you all that we saw it last night—myself, the king's loyal secretary Lord John Beymond, and this good, grieving lord. We saw her, in this very dress that she sullies by wearing in this holy place, smelled her pass by us wearing the self-same fragrance she is wont to wear at all times, and go into the halls where the guards stay." His voice was nigh to broken with all the scorn and bile he put into it. "She knocked upon a door, whispered when it opened, and was admitted into the arms of a man who—and it pains me to say it, my lord —" Here he turned, one hand out to stay anything Uncle Lionel might interject, before continuing, "A man who wore no shirt and pulled her into his embrace." My aunt whimpered, clasping both hands to her mouth in horror, and my uncle growled, low in his throat, like a cornered dog. But the duke went on, an avalanche of bad news. "A man whose company she had clearly enjoyed before, more than once."

Thomas, unable to bear any more, groaned and dropped to his knees, grabbing fistfuls of his hair, tearing at it. Benedict came forward to comfort him, placing his arms around his friend.

"How can this be?" Uncle Lionel moaned. In this weak response, I heard the unraveling of his certainty. As his shocked gaze slid from the duke's implacable face to Thomas' tormented form to Grace's huddled body, unknowingly echoing Thomas' posture with head in hands—not from shame but from the blow to her head—I realized how it appeared to him. Her lack of resistance he took for guilt.

I stood to defend her. "This is fantastical! Impossible!" I exclaimed, but no one seemed to mark me above the buzzing chatter of the onlookers.

"Moreover," the duke said, fixing me with a sharp look, "after the deed was done, Lord John confronted the villain and reports that he did not deny their wrongdoing, but even bragged of these encounters they have had a thousand times!"

"That is preposterous!" I cried, and Grace cried out wordlessly in objection, but nothing could be heard over Uncle Lionel's howl of fury.

Shaking his fists in the air, his face red and sweaty, he was more distraught than I had ever seen him. Spinning around, he reached down and grabbed her wrist, the grip so tight his knuckles turned white. Gasping, she looked up. "Why do you live?" he cried and slapped her face, hard, with his free hand. The sound echoed in the stunned silence that befell the chapel. She reeled away from him, falling back against Eleanor, but he maintained his grip and held her fast, dangling by her fragile wrist.

I feared to hear the bone crack.

"Lionel!" Aunt Ursula cried, her voice sharp as glass.

I dashed forward to yank on his other arm. "Uncle! Let her go!"

The duke took a step back, reaching a blind hand behind him toward Thomas. "Come. There is nothing more we can do here. Let us go."

Aunt Ursula charged up behind me, placing her hand upon Uncle Lionel's where it encircled Grace's wrist. "Lionel," she said, "stop this now."

My uncle, his wounded leg shaking, released Grace's wrist. She slumped to the floor like an empty sack. Seemingly against his will, Thomas reached out a hand toward her but snatched it back, and instead grasped the altar railing to pull himself to his feet. "Fare thee well, Grace," he said, his voice thick, though with suppressed rage or suppressed tears it was difficult to tell. "Fare thee well. I will never love again." Supported by the duke, he staggered down the aisle and through the chapel doors. After a moment's hesitation, the congregation rose and hastened to follow.

Aunt Ursula gathered Mary and Eleanor to her and drew them off to one side of the altar next to the priest, who clutched at his bible like it would save him from contamination. I went to Grace and helped her to rise. She clung to me with one hand and placed the other on the altar rail for support. The chapel was empty and hollow, the many candles funereal now instead of joyful.

Uncle Lionel ran a hand across his face and drew a shuddering breath as though waking from a dream. "Is this real?" he said, looking around the deserted chapel. "Can this truly have happened?"

He lurched toward Grace again, his bad leg betraying him in his emotional state. She flinched against me but did not shy away from him.

"How can you have seemed so fair and been so vile?" he spat.

"Uncle," I said, striving to keep my voice steady, "Grace is falsely accused. You must know this!"

"Know? What do I know? I know what the duke and Lord Keighton have said. Is that not enough?"

"What they have said? They said they saw a woman in a dress embrace a man." My blood was on fire with the injustice of it. There was no proof of anything, just their word against hers, and she had not even been permitted to speak. "Have you even asked your daughter to speak for herself?"

But instead of asking for Grace's word, my uncle shook his head. "They are men of honor. Why would his grace the duke lie? Why would Lord Thomas lie? Why embarrass and dishonor themselves in this way in front of all this company?" He flung out an arm to encompass the now-empty chapel. "In front of the king himself? No. No, it must be true! Foul, deceitful, wicked child!" He reached for Grace again, and she fell back against me with a cry. I stumbled backwards, and I feared I might fall, but suddenly someone was there, catching me with strong hands about my waist, bearing me up. I had no need to look back. All my senses, my very heart knew it was Benedict.

He pressed a steadying hand to my back, then stepped forward, between me and my uncle. "Be easy, good my lord," he said, positioning himself so he blocked my uncle's view of Grace. "I hardly know what to say in the light of what has passed here, but there must be a way to get to the truth." My uncle, his jaw tight, nodded. Benedict mimicked the gesture and turned to face me. "My lady Beatrice, were you not your cousin's bedfellow last night?"

My heart tumbled into my shoes. Of course, that was the one question —the very question—that should yield the answer to save Grace, but alas, he did not know that it would yield the wrong answer. My eyes locked on his, I had to deny it.

"No, sir. Though I have been for all these many years since we were children, last night I was not. Last night, Grace spent in the bridal bower alone." How were we to know that her desire to prepare for married life would shatter her hopes for a marriage?

Uncle Lionel leapt upon it. "You see," he cried, "it is proven! She sent you away so that she could indulge her lust!"

Grace whimpered and sniffled beside me, sinking down to sit upon the altar rail.

"Uncle," I said, "that makes no sense. If, as the lords claim, this fellow brags of having been with Grace a thousand times, but I have been her bedfellow for years, it gives the lie to his story. When could they ever have been alone?"

Benedict's brow furrowed. "And who is this fellow that claims to know Lady Grace so intimately?"

Grace pointed to the doors. "Them that accuse me know. I know not."

"My lord Lionel," Benedict said, "Lady Beatrice is right. Something is not right here."

I could have hugged him, heedless of the others watching. Instead, I wrapped my arms around myself.

Uncle Lionel shook his head vigorously. "But how could Lord Thomas have been so misled? And why would the duke uphold him without strong proof? What about the dress, this very dress she wears to be wed in?"

That detail niggled at me, though I knew not yet how to explain it away. Benedict looked as perplexed as I. "On both sides, everyone swears that he is the only one in possession of the truth. Yet we know that cannot be. It is a puzzle that must have an answer."

My uncle's lips twisted as he seemed to fight back more hateful words. He shook his fist at Grace, reaching around Benedict to threaten her. "If it is revealed that this story is true—that there is a *word* of truth in it—I will kill you myself! Do you hear me?"

My cousins now burst into tears. Aunt Ursula again protested, "Lionel, for the love of all that is holy, cease your threats. This is our daughter. Our child!" She shuffled the other girls toward the exit, but seemed torn between removing them from the scene and staying to protect Grace.

Benedict took hold of my uncle's arms and pushed him back, away from Grace. Uncle Lionel growled at him but with his weak leg, he had not the strength to resist. "My lord Lionel," Benedict said through gritted teeth, "such words do not help us uncover the truth. Look at your daughter's face. Does she seem anything but innocent?"

Uncle Lionel looked at Grace as though an abyss had opened between them. His eyes filled with tears. "It is a mere semblance of innocence, a showing of grace. Oh, why were you ever lovely in my eyes? Why were you ever born to grieve me so? All the ocean has not enough water to cleanse this sin from your soul."

"Uncle!" I cried. "She is belied! You must believe it!"

The priest, at last, stepped forward and placed a hand on my uncle's shoulder. "My lord, if I may, rest you a moment, and hear what I would say."

My uncle blinked up at him like an owl in daylight. Mayhap this was a voice he would heed. The priest took his silence for consent to continue. "I have observed your daughter all this while, and I have noted her silence, which I know your lordship has taken for admission of guilt." Here, he raised his voice, speaking right over my uncle's renewed complaints. "Rather, sir, I noted the thousand blushes on her cheeks as they spoke, and the angelic whiteness of her countenance beneath, and the fire blazing in her eyes that would burn away the errors that those gentlemen spake against her maiden truth." He looked from Uncle Lionel to Grace and back again, an iron certainty in his countenance. "Call me a fool, but the experience of my years teaches me to trust in my reading of these signs more than in the words of men. These indications said more than loud protestations would have of her innocence."

"Say you that the duke lies? That his friend the lord Thomas lies? Such honorable men, friends of the king himself? Wherefore would they do so?"

"Wherefore indeed, my lord? Yet as your niece and this young gentleman have said, the tale does not make for fair reading. Something is amiss."

"Aye, uncle, heed the good father," I cried. "Something is indeed amiss, and we must uncover it."

The priest cast a reproving glance my way. "The proper authorities shall uncover whatever is toward, my lady. You shall leave it to the king and his secretary to inquire into the matter." Nodding, I subsided. "In the interim," he continued, "allow me to advise that you send the young lady away until such time as the matter is concluded, for good or ill."

Grace looked up, eyes wide. "Away?"

"Yes, away. I suggest the priory at Horsley. They are an old and respected house, and they have a place for lay visitors. The young lady need not take any vows nor even consider such a course until it may become advisable."

Grace frowned. "But will not my flight, my willingness to take holy vows, be seen as an admission of guilt?"

"What would you prefer, my lady?" he replied scornfully. "That we give it out that you died, as if a woman might die of a false accusation any more than she might die of a broken heart?"

I was beginning to like this priest.

I took Grace's hand, offering her what support and comfort I could. She alone could decide what to do from here. She and my uncle, who still wavered betwixt anger and grief.

"Good my lord, let this holy man advise you." Benedict set a hand on my uncle's shoulder and spoke gently. "You know that my love and my loyalty are with the duke and Thomas, yet I will deal justly with your family always. Shelter and protect your daughter, that we may uncover the truth and perhaps renew these nuptials at another time."

Uncle Lionel swayed, as though the weight of Benedict's hand and of events had finally become too much. "To a man caught in an ocean's tide, any hope of a rescue is welcome, even if it seems unlikely." He looked up at the priest. "Let it be as you say, and heaven help those who are false!"

CHAPTER 12

G race's room had been overcrowded and overly busy in the
morning as we prepared her to be a bride, but now that she was
making ready to be a nun—even as a ruse—she was abandoned
and alone. Only Aunt Ursula was there, sitting in silent sorrow on the bed,
seeming unable to summon the strength to move. Not even Margaret
attended her.

Grace, however, was a whirlwind of motion. All the trunks and baskets
that had been so carefully packed, she had pulled apart, tossing kirtles,
chemises, stockings, and slippers willy-nilly around the floor, like so many
limp, unstuffed scarecrows.

"Grace, love, what are you doing?"

She looked up at me from where she crouched beside a trunk, spewing
fabrics forth like a fountain. "A nun needs no such finery, would you not
agree?"

"You are not going to be a nun. You're only going away for a time, not
forever."

She moved on to another box, dumping out the contents and hurling
the box across the room. Aunt Ursula and I both flinched as the box hit
the wall with a crash.

"Oh no? How can you be so certain? How am I not destroyed by this?
Do you think the king will investigate? And if he does, do you think he
will uncover the truth? And if he does, will he force Lord Keighton to

make amends to me? And what amends could he make? I am ruined, Beatrice, destroyed by words spun out of air, and yet he will go on to live his life as a man of honor and pride, congratulated by all the men around him at having avoided the shame of having knitted his immortal soul to a stained and fallen woman. The one way forward for me is a life of quiet contemplation among the sisters asking God's forgiveness for sins I only ever imagined committing. How is that fair?" Her voice rose and rose, peaking in a desperate near-shriek that held tears she no longer allowed herself to shed and anger she could not vent upon its proper target.

What could I possibly say? She was right.

Aunt Ursula got up and left the room, a hand pressed to her mouth.

"I swear to you, Grace, I will find out what happened. I will not let them do this to you."

She collapsed to the floor, all the fire gone out of her. "I know you want to, Beatrice, and I love you for it. But mayhap it would be best just to let me go. Just leave it be."

I shook my head. "You know I will not."

She managed a smile. "No. You will not." She reached out to me and I picked my way through the puddles of clothing to take her hand and crouch beside her. All her violent energy seeped away and her head drooped. "What did I do?" she whispered, anguished. "What could I have done to have lost his heart so utterly?"

"You?" I burst out. "You did nothing."

She shook her head. "But there must have been something for him to doubt me thus. He must have suspected me inconstant already for him to have believed me capable of such a vile deception. Perhaps I was too willing, too eager for marriage..."

I thought of her flushed face, her tousled hair, when she would come back to our chamber after sitting up with Thomas, as I had done with Benedict. "Wait," I said, "are you suggesting that your pleasure in him —with him—is exactly what allowed him to disgrace and discard you like so much old linen when he decided you enjoyed it a little too much?"

She looked at me, her eyes dark pools of sorrow.

"Grace. This is not your fault. This is *his* fault. Every bit of it."

"But you see that matters not? Do you not? All that matters is his saying. A woman can swear her innocence and no one will believe she is aught but guilty, and a man can swear her guilt and no one ever believe her innocent. There is no way to win."

I dropped to my knees beside her, wrapped her in my embrace. "If I were a man," I whispered, fiercely, for her ears, and for God's. "If I were a man, I would eat his heart in the marketplace."

* * *

The door to my uncle's study was ajar, his voice drifting out as I approached. Aunt Ursula hesitated in the doorway, hand raised to knock but waiting, head cocked in a listening pose. I could not help but remember the day not one week past when, on my way back to dinner, I had overheard her and Grace at table, talking about Benedict's feelings for me.

Would that I could go back to that more innocent time.

I paused beside her, slipping an arm around her waist and dropping my head to her shoulder. Sighing gently, she pulled me into her embrace.

I heard my uncle say, "She leaves for the convent this day, sir."

"I understand your desire to protect your family's good name, my lord. Indeed, I do." I stiffened and pulled away from my aunt. That was Lord John Beymond. She looked as surprised as I did to hear his voice. "And neither do I blame you. The callous disregard for propriety under your own roof, the shame, the insolence, it is simply too great to be borne. And yet..." Boot heels struck stone then were muffled by carpet as he paced. "And yet, my lord, she is your only child and heir. To disown her utterly—"

I held my breath. This was the very plea I had come to make: *do not discard her*.

Aunt Ursula took advantage of the pause to insert herself into the conversation. She gave the door a cursory brush with her knuckles and swept into the room. I followed. I could not let this unfold without me.

The men looked up, startled. Lord John bowed to us and glanced under his lashes at Uncle Lionel. I suspected he was calculating just how much we might have heard. Uncle Lionel did not attempt to rise—perhaps his leg troubled him too much after the difficult morning—and nodded Aunt Ursula to the seat across from him. Lord John hastened to assist her.

"You are discussing my daughter's future, I surmise?" she said, sounding more imperious than I could ever recall.

Lord John had the wisdom to look uncomfortable, since he ought to have had no say in such matters, yet he made no attempt to exit the room. Instead, he brazened it out, raising his face and meeting Aunt Ursula's challenging gaze with his own steady one.

Uncle Lionel grunted. "As we must," he replied. Aunt Ursula opened her mouth to protest but he continued, "She knew. She knew all too well what would become of her if she fell." The wood of his chair squeaked in protest as he surged to his feet, leaning heavily on one of its carved arms, tipping it and sending it thudding to the floor as he strode away, heedless. "How could she? How could she cavort thus in lust, knowing what would come of it?"

I opened my mouth to object, but Lord John took a step forward to rest a hand on his shoulder. "Steady now, my lord," he said. "Women are weak of will and easily tempted to fall."

Fury ignited in my belly. I thought I might strike him—me, a woman, who had no training, might weave my fingers into a fist and punch his elegant jaw... Was it not enough that he had participated in her slander? No, now this man would further demean her as weak? As though she couldn't help herself because, after all, she was merely a woman? As if Thomas were not equally to blame, if indeed there were any blame to cast, though I knew in the depths of my bones that she was innocent. I could not seem to draw a proper breath. Instead, my lungs grasped and dragged at the air.

Then Aunt Ursula spoke. "For certes, Lord Beymond," she said, using his full title almost as a slur, "if a woman falls prey to an opportunistic man, as you suggest, then the blame ought to fall more upon him, and less upon her." Her mouth was tight as she spoke, and I could sense her scarce controlled outrage, as strong as my own. "Surely the predator who senses and preys upon weakness is more to blame."

Lord John's jaw clenched and his desire to snap back at her with a biting reply was evident, but this was the lady of the manor and he had to restrain himself. Instead, he turned to Uncle Lionel and said, "But mayhap you do not have to set her aside, my lord."

Uncle Lionel groaned. "No, no, I cannot think on it. Do not tempt me to forgive her. I am determined in my course. She enters the convent and I will live without son, without daughter, without child."

Aunt Ursula gasped and clutched at her breast. I rushed to her chair and stood behind it, my hands on her shoulders.

"Oh, heaven forbid it," my aunt gasped. "Lionel, what madness has o'ertaken you?"

"You would consign her to a convent forever?" My voice had no more force in it than my aunt's.

Uncle Lionel would not answer me, only stared into the fire that sputtered fitfully in the hearth.

Lord John observed us all in silence for a long moment, then cleared his throat and said, "But what then of your estate, my lord?"

I wanted to bristle with offense. I wanted to feel that surge of emotion I had felt just moments before when I had contemplated striking him. I wanted to demand of him how he dared insert himself into these family affairs. But now, having heard my uncle cast this judgment on my cousin, having heard him declare that he had no faith in her, that he would never forgive her, that he was willing never to see her again, it seemed I could not muster up outrage at Lord John. Instead, I swallowed tears and looked to my uncle to see what his reply would be.

Sounding more defeated than I had ever heard him, my uncle said, "I will settle a good dowry on both of my brother's girls, but the estate and title will pass, with the king's permission, to my sister's child." He looked at me. "To Beatrice. Only she is worthy."

Had I thought I was numb before? I was frozen, ice racing through my body, rooting me to the spot. *What did he just say? Me, his heir? Instead of Grace?*

We had begun to descend into hell when Lord Thomas refused Grace, and the day just kept twisting down, down, deeper into the abyss. The chaos unleashed by Thomas' accusation grew more unbearable by the minute.

"Beatrice?" Lord John said, his voice rising in surprise. He took a half step in my direction. "Indeed, she is worthy. But—forgive me for being so blunt, my lady—but will Lady Beatrice accept the responsibility of being your heir?"

"What do you mean?"

He looked me over, his dark eyes deeper than usual, pensive, searching. He paused, seeming to hunt for the right words. "Again, forgive me if I offend, my lady, for I do not mean to. But she seems ever to resist the obligations of her rank. She speaks in a most impertinent manner, for instance, which you yourself have been seen to encourage, my lord. And she has been most outspoken against marriage, a quite inappropriate opinion in a woman of her rank and age."

Again, I made to speak, but my uncle growled, sounding for all the world like one of his hunting hounds. With a wave of his hand, he silenced me. I bristled but let him respond, thinking he would defend me against this outsider. How disappointed I was when he looked at me through narrowed eyes and said, "She will amend her ways. She will have no choice."

No choice. Would my affable uncle now force me into silence, require me to marry a man of his choosing, all because my cousin's marriage had failed so publicly, so spectacularly?

I understood, now, that he would not listen if I pled for Grace to be restored to his favor. Neither would Lord John investigate the matter with any kind of diligence. Rather, he would leave Grace to her fate and turn his attentions elsewhere. To succeed where, once, he had failed.

Me. I was his target now.

With a final squeeze of Aunt Ursula's shoulders, I fled.

* * *

I left my uncle's study intending to retreat to my bedchamber, longing to be alone with my thoughts, but the moment I opened the door I saw them: women, members of the princess' court, lurking in the corridor, waiting to see who would come out and, more importantly, to find out what had gone on in my uncle's study. I could not—I would not—speak to them. Would not reveal the true changes to my life that had just unfolded.

Holding up my hands to ward them off, I hurried from the study. Some cast concerned glances my way, others converged upon me to obstruct my path, and even Lady Viola, whom I counted a friend, approached me with concern in her eyes and words, but I waved them all away. "Please," I begged, scarce recognizing the voice emerging from my own mouth. "Too much has occurred today. I need to be alone for a time." Diverting from my original plan, I turned instead into the hall that led to the chapel, realizing that they would not dare follow me within that sacred space.

It was much changed in the short time since we had left, back to the simple family chapel I had grown up with. Gone were the beeswax candles, gone the pure white altar cloth, gone even the carpet that warmed the aisle and softened the tread of footsteps. The benches had been removed, the windows shuttered up again. It was as if the events of the morning had never occurred.

I drifted to the altar rail and found the spot where Grace had stood, where Thomas had pushed her, where she staggered back and fell and struck her head, where I had rushed to her side, and found it hard to believe that any of it was real. Had we truly come here for a wedding, only to end in bitterness and betrayal?

I dropped to my knees and buried my face in my hands. I tried to pray, tried to force my ragged, racing thoughts into words that would rise up and make a merciful God take heed, take action, but I could not. I could not. The words tumbled, twisted, and in the end ceased to take form at all, leaving me with nothing but harsh, angry tears falling into my fisted hands.

How long I remained there, I do not know, but I became aware of the door opening and shutting, the soft shuffle of shoes trying to be silent on the stone flags of the chapel floor. I sniffled and scrubbed at my cheeks, trying to hide the evidence of my outburst and turned to face the person, whom I presumed would be my aunt.

It was not my aunt.

I wondered fleetingly, desperately, if the kneeler would fall away and let me slide away into the burial crypt under the altar.

"Beatrice," Benedict murmured, but his voice carried in the chapel. "Have you wept here all this while?"

"Nay," I replied, but of course to deny it was foolishness. "Aye. And I will weep yet a while longer."

He took a hesitant step closer, then another, as if I were a frightened dog and like to bite. "I would not desire that," he said. Compassion was writ clear on his face, pricking tears in my eyes again.

I had to look away. "I do it freely, for what else is there to be done?"

"That is not like you, to say such a thing." He sat beside me, leaning back against the altar rail. "It is not like you to give up."

I raised my hands and let them fall into my lap. "I do not know what else to do. What strength is there in a woman to protest when a man says such a thing against her?"

He reached over and took my hands in his. "I cannot tell you. I only know we cannot allow it to stand. I do believe in my heart that your fair cousin is wronged. What would you have me do?"

I stared at him. "Do? What can you do, any more than I?"

"I don't know, Beatrice, but I'm not going to just sit here and weep. Where is your anger? Where is your fire?"

I yanked my hands away from his and leapt to my feet. "Where is my anger?" I spat at him. "I have swallowed it, and it burns in my belly, turning my blood to acid, my tears to bile. Where is my anger?" My voice rose to the chapel's high ceiling and filled its encroaching walls. "My anger could tear this building stone from stone and not be slaked! Here, here, in this very spot, he let her come in her happy innocence to take his hand in marriage and what did he do? Made a public spectacle of accusing her of the basest, vile slander, then threw her body across this sacred space, dishonored and injured her—oh!" He wanted my anger? I was shaking with it, fists clenched, eyes streaming anew, shrieking like the harpy he'd once labeled me. "Oh, if I could but do my will, heaven could not stop me. If I were a man, he would not live out the night."

He stood, too, daring to place his hands on me, hip and shoulder, to still my shaking. "Beatrice," he said, his voice steady, calm. "Hear me…"

But I was in no mood to be calmed or stilled. I jerked away, my wedding finery swirling around me in a vicious mockery of how I might have looked dancing with him had the day gone differently. "If I were a man…" My fevered gaze fell upon the long dagger he had worn that day as all the men did, even to a wedding, with a fine and ornamental hilt. So beautiful, one would never imagine it was a weapon bent upon killing, needing only the slightest provocation. Too quickly for him to react, I lurched forward and yanked it from the sheath, metal squealing. It was heavier than I expected, the blade as long as my forearm and gleaming with a dull, seductive sheen. My wrist, untrained, wavered, and I fought to keep the blade level before me. Benedict startled and brought his hands up, palms toward me, warding.

"Beatrice," he said, his voice low and urgent.

I could still see Thomas standing right there before the priest, hurling my cousin from him, casting her into shame and dishonor. I could see the look of horror on the princess' face, the contempt on Lady Stanley's, the disappointment on the king's. Everyone judging, no one listening. I gripped the hilt with both hands to stop it shaking, clenched my teeth against the pain of the memories.

Benedict took a step closer to me. The point of the blade settled on his chest.

I drew a quick, startled breath and looked up into his face. His eyes were wide, as I could feel my own were—wide, worried, frightened by the wildness of my emotions—but he also trusted me. I glanced down at the dagger again, the point of it buried in the deep nap of his velvet doublet. If I leaned in, if I pressed, pushed, thrust, that was how one ended a life. If I were a man, I had said, and this is what I meant. This was the life they had lived in war. Killing. Ending lives.

Slowly, achingly slowly, Benedict brought his hands together over mine, steadying my grip on the hilt. He waited, watching me still with those deep, warm eyes. I drew in a slow, shuddering breath. Though the point of the dagger still pressed against his chest, though it must be causing him some discomfort, he did not back away, and he did not seek to take the blade from me. With his hands on the blade with mine, I could almost believe that if I began to thrust but could not carry through, he would finish it for me.

He waited.

With a ghost of a sigh, I loosened my grip under his fingers, and he took the dagger from me. Keeping hold of both my hands in one of his, he set the dagger aside on the altar beside us, just beyond my reach.

Shaking my head, I whispered, "She is wronged. I know it, sure as I have an immortal soul." I looked up at the golden cross over the altar, symbol of a benevolent god I had been taught would care for us if we followed his commandments. Perhaps only in the afterlife, not in this one, for few women were as conscientious as Grace, and yet she had been very ill-served by the men intended to protect her. "I wish I were a man for her sake..."

"To take my dagger? To kill Thomas? How would that help her?"

I sank to my knees once more, leaning back against the altar rail. "It would not. Verily, I know it. But when a man can swear untruths and be believed, and a woman swear truth and be thought foresworn, surely words mean nothing."

He sighed and sat beside me. "By this hand, Beatrice, I—"

I cut him off, suddenly weary of talk. "Use your hand to some other end than swearing."

He caught the hand I had waved in the air in a cutting gesture. Smiling, he laced our fingers together. "She will come through this happy," he said. "And even if she does not, you will."

I almost opened my mouth to tell him what Uncle Lionel intended, which would ensure that he was wrong, but that was a complication that I did not want to share, and besides, he would learn of it soon enough. Instead, I nodded and smiled. He drew my hand to his mouth and kissed it.

"You came here for privacy, and silence, and I have snatched them from you." He rose and bowed, releasing my hand. "I leave you to it."

He had made it halfway down the aisle before I called after him, "You were right."

He turned. "About what?"

"About my uncle. What I saw today..." I shook my head. "Was like nothing I have ever seen in him before. He never would have agreed to—to us. And if you and I had defied him, if we had married against his will..." I shook my head again.

He nodded, turned, and left.

I sat facing the altar, leaning against the altar rail, listening to the doors swing shut behind him with a grim, echoing thud. I did not cry again, but I sat there for a long time, wondering what to do, or worse, what I would be made to do.

When at last the sky faded to purple behind the windows and the priest's boy came in to light a few candles, I stood and left, feeling as old as my aunt Ursula. I emerged from the chapel to a world that had tilted anew towards chaos.

CHAPTER 13

I made my way back to my bedchamber at last—mine alone now, every sign of Grace wiped away because this was meant to be her wedding night, and tomorrow she was meant to depart with her husband. I sat on the bed, clutching a pillow to my chest, and looked around the room, feeling bereft.

My other cousins trooped in moments later, not bothering to knock or to ask permission. I glared at them. "Indeed, Mary, do come in, and welcome," I said, allowing my irritation to creep into my voice.

Mary ignored my scathing tone and Eleanor, bless the simple girl, seemed not to hear it. Mary came straight to the bed and climbed up to sit with me, a liberty she rarely took. Cousins we might be, but there were gradations of comfort in our family, and she and I were not Grace and me. I looked her over. Her eyes were bright, her breath coming in rapid gasps, whether from running up the stairs or from excitement at her news I could not tell. "Well? What is it?"

"Have you not heard?" She took my silence for denial and continued. "Nay, how could you know and yet sit here so quietly?" She wanted me to ask her the news, wanted me to beg. Instead I stared at her, wishing she would save her dramatic performance and heaving breasts for the gentlemen downstairs.

"Grace is banished to the convent," she said. "She left just as the sun went down, escorted by five of our uncle's men and two of the king's."

Though my heart broke yet again to hear it, I was not surprised. Uncle Lionel had wanted her gone, and so she was gone. I sighed and clutched my pillow a bit tighter. "If that is all you have to tell me, Mary, pray leave me in peace."

"Nay, it is not all," she said, shifting closer to me.

"Look," Eleanor announced, waving something at us. She was standing by the small table that had served double duty as a writing desk and dressing table for myself and Grace. In her hand was what appeared to be a sealed, folded parchment. "It looks like Grace left you a letter, Beatrice, or rather a whole page of letters!" She giggled at her joke and waved the parchment again.

I motioned to her to bring it to me, but Mary made a disapproving noise and pulled my hand down. "Forget that. Listen to me!" She shifted so that her face was in my line of sight, disrupting my view of Eleanor and the letter. "Benedict threw his gage before Thomas. They will fight on the morrow for Grace's honor."

Her words were ice water spilled down my spine. "He what?"

She grinned, nodding, and leaned toward me, happy to have garnered my attention at last. "Indeed, it is so! He came upon Lord Thomas and the Duke of Surrey in the great hall and they did try to jest with him, saying they were melancholy and needed him to divert them. He took Lord Thomas by the arm and jerked him aside, called him a villain to his very face and said he must make good the challenge or he would declare him a coward in the sight of all."

I could not swallow or even draw breath. "What did Lord Thomas say?"

"He laughed in his face, thinking he was in jest, so Benedict drew out one of his gloves from his belt and slapped him with it and called him boy and lack-beard and braggard. Then he turned to the duke and begged leave to depart his company until the challenge was resolved."

"Why?" I whispered, but my question was not for her. But I could hear my own bitter voice: *Use your hand to some other end than swearing.*

Oh, Beatrice, what have you done?

I launched myself off the bed, dropping the pillow at my feet. "I must put a stop to this."

"What?" Mary asked. "How?"

I did not answer her but marched down the stairs and along the corridor to my uncle's rooms, where the king was in residence. I hammered on the door, never stopping to consider the hour, or whether he might be engaged with his men or his secretary in discussions of some import to the kingdom or that his mother might find my intrusion upon his solitude rude and impertinent, yet another sign of my sinful nature. The only thought I could frame, twisting over and over in my mind, was that Benedict was going to fight Thomas. They were going to fight in the lists, horses pounding the turf at top speed until the thunderous clash of lance on shield, the heavy crash of an armored body on the turf, the agonizingly slow movements of armored men hacking at one another with swords that were heavy and deadly as clubs. I could see it in my mind's eye. It would happen on the morrow. One of them—mayhap both—would die if the king did not stop it before that vicious end. Over Grace. Because of me. Because of what I had said.

A page in green and white opened the door to me, his eyebrows raised just enough to convey displeasure at my rudeness. When I gave my name and my request to see the king, he looked dubious but withdrew to ask whether the king would see me, which I took to be a good sign. In a moment, he returned and opened the door for me, allowing me into the sitting room that adjoined my aunt and uncle's bedchambers where the king and his mother were staying for the duration of their visit. The room had been arranged for the king's work. A large table had been brought in and covered with a rich red cloth. Clusters of candlesticks— gleaming silver and dull pewter, slender and squat—provided illumination, and piles and scrolls of parchment waited to be addressed. The king leaned on the arm of a high-backed chair behind the table, chin in hand, and his scribe hunched over a parchment beside him scribbling with a quill.

Moving in front of the table, I sank into a deep curtsy and held it, so long and so low my knees ached. The king frowned at me. "Lady Beatrice," he said, and there was nothing friendly or kindly in his demeanor. "Why are you here?"

"Your majesty," I said, my voice shaking in time with my tormented legs, "I have just heard news of the gravest nature, and I have come to ask —nay, to beg—you to intervene."

The scribe ceased his scribbling and eased back, shifting his hands under the table so that he could stretch his fingers. He looked at me, blinking his close-focused eyes, clearly happy for the respite I had provided him.

"To intervene in what?" The king's voice was sharp-edged and thin, a knife in the air.

"Sir Edmund Benedict and Thomas Lord Keighton are going to fight on the morrow. A challenge of honor. My king, I beg you to stop them."

He dropped his hand and sat up straighter. His eyes, lit by the many candles before him on the table, gleamed. If I allowed myself to imagine it, I could say they glittered from within, like a cat's at night, or mayhap a demon's. "Why would I interfere with a challenge made and accepted between two honorable men of my company?"

I could not prevent the gasp that burst from my lips, though I knew it was wrong to make such a sound in his presence, to imply criticism of his words, his decisions. But...how could he say so?

"Henry."

A soft voice from behind me chided him and he looked up, over my head.

"Allow the poor girl to rise, at the very least, if you are going to break her heart over again."

A rustle of delicate fabrics told me that Princess Elizabeth had entered and was approaching me. I kept my pose, though my thighs were, by now, screaming in pain from holding it. When she placed a gentle hand on my shoulder, the king relented and waved a hand at me, and I staggered to my feet. As I rose, she allowed her hand to slide down my back to my waist, a surprising familiarity. I soon realized it had nothing to do with me.

"Henry, my dear betrothed lord," she said, "I would also like to understand why you will not intercede in this quarrel between Sir Edmund and Lord Thomas. Surely you do not want to see your friends at odds in this way..."

"This challenge," he replied, deliberately altering her word, "is the province of men, Elizabeth, and your sensibility, while touching, has no place in it. I will not prevent Lord Thomas from defending his own honor any more than I will prevent Sir Edmund from defending Lady Grace's." He shifted his gaze to me. "Isn't that as it should be, Lady Beatrice? Or would you prefer that she cower in the convent, her guilt assumed and unproven?"

"If I may say so, your majesty, I have my doubts as to whether Lord Thomas' death in the lists will prove my cousin's innocence. Finding out who falsely swore against her, and why, would do the job with less blood and more surety."

I felt the princess repress a chuckle beside me, and she tilted her head at the king as we awaited his response. His lips, however, did not twitch, and his eyes did not blink. All he said was, "Personal combat has long been a means to determine the truth of such matters. Both gentlemen have the right to choose it for themselves. I will not stop them."

The princess pressed her lips together for a moment before speaking. "Will you at least stop them in the fight before they kill each other? Must they die for this folly?"

Now King Henry looked angry. "Honor is not folly. Judgment is not folly. What they are doing is their right. We—their sovereign lord and lady —will not stop them."

Beside me, the princess drew in a short, sharp breath. I could tell she was debating with herself and while I did not want to be the cause of a rift between them, I hoped that she would continue to oppose him. "Yet," she said at last, "you have other means of finding out what occurred."

He glared at her, tilting his head at the scribe and at me in turn. "If we discover aught, we will act. Until then, we will say nothing."

The door to the room flew open, and the page scurried in a mere step ahead of the king's mother, who remained wrapped in righteous outrage. "Henry," she barked, "we would be wise to put this place well behind us." She held up a hand as though to wave aside a foul odor. "Lest you and Elizabeth be stained with the scandal that has marked this family." Only then did she pause and seem to notice me standing with the princess, but that did not shame her into silence, or even to retract her statement. Instead, she continued, "I say we must leave this very night. Even now."

"Mother," the king said, "events are unfolding. Men who have supported me through my exile are now engaged in a battle of honor. I cannot simply walk away. I must, as their lord and sovereign, be here to witness it."

"Their foolishness has nothing to do—"

"Mother," he repeated, no louder, but there it was again, that knife-sharp edge to his tone. She fell instantly silent. He dropped his head in acknowledgement. "We will remain through the morrow, at the least. Beyond that..." He glanced at me. "We shall see."

I judged it best to withdraw from the royal presence in that moment, so I curtsied again on protesting legs and backed toward the door. The page pulled the door open for me, and I was so focused on escaping that I almost did not notice—I did not perceive until I was already outside in the corridor—that Lord John Beymond had been in the room the entire time, standing like a shadow between the windows at the back of the room.

* * *

As I stumbled in the direction of the stairs to my bedchamber, a whispered, "Milady," tugged at my awareness and I stopped. At first, I saw no one, but then Margaret emerged from a darkened doorway. She looked miserable, her eyes downcast, her shoulders slumped, even her hair unkempt. She bit her lower lip and would not look me in the eye even though she had been the one to call out to me.

"What is it?" I asked. "Are you ill?"

She shook her head. "Nay, lady, but I can no longer bear my silence. I must confess."

I tried to laugh, but after the day we'd endured the sound was false, forced. "I am no priest, Margaret."

"I need no priest for this," she said, pulling at my hand. "Come away, please."

She dragged me, half unwilling, half curious. "Where—?" I began to ask but then realized, despite saying she needed no priest, she was taking me back, yet again, to the chapel. Groaning inwardly, I allowed her to lead me within and pull me into the chapel of Our Lady near the back. She kept hold of my hand, squeezing my fingers tightly in hers.

"Margaret," I whispered, out of respect to our surroundings, "whatever is the matter?"

Silent tears dripped down her cheeks. "Oh, milady, I have done wrong and I know not how to make it right."

Her distress was palpable, and I felt my throat tighten with tears in response. "Tell me, oh, tell me and let me help you make it right."

"That is the problem," she said, choking on her sorrow. "I fear it is too late."

Her words chilled me, and I resisted the urge to pull my hands free from hers. "What do you mean?"

She glanced up at me with her eyes full of tears. "Lady Grace," she whispered. "It is my fault she was accused as she was."

Forgetting where I was, I cried out, "What?" My body wanted action, to run for the guard, to call my uncle, the king, even without knowing what more she would say, for here was the proof I sought.

She reached for me, pulling at my hands and arms. I resisted, limbs stiff, pushing her away. "Please, please, milady, abide and listen. Please believe I had no idea this would happen." Staring a long time into her face, her overflowing eyes, at last I yielded, sinking onto my knees beside her, the statue of the Virgin watching over us.

She sighed and swiped at her eyes with the cuff of her sleeve. "Thank you, milady."

"Do not thank me yet," I replied. "You may yet find that your position here is forfeit."

She nodded. "I would understand if you felt that was proper. But please listen to my story first and see what you shall make of it."

I dropped my head to give her leave to speak, and she sighed again as she began. "You do not know, milady, that I am betrothed?"

"Betrothed? Why, no, I did not." But her words stirred a memory of a happier day, when we had teased her about a love, and she had blushed at it.

"His name is Hugh. Hugh Borrage, and he is one of Lord Lionel's retainers. We have long wished to marry but have been unable to for we have not had enough gold to establish a home together and provide for a family." Her eyes shadowed as she continued, "Also, Hugh's mother is aged and ill, and we must provide for her as well."

"But, what has this to do with Grace?"

She drew in a shivery breath. "I come to that now. Someone offered Hugh gold, enough for us to marry, if only he would do some things or ask me to do some things, all concerning the Lady Grace."

"And did he not think to refuse?"

"Of course he did! But in the end, the money was too dear to turn down. And the things asked seemed simple things, harmless things. To tear the sleeve of Lady Grace's sleeping gown, or take her lavender scent and give it to Hugh for an hour."

I remembered the torn gown. We had noted it when Margaret was moving Grace's belongings into her bower. And Lord Thomas had spoken of lavender, had he not, when he condemned Grace?

"Oh no," I burst out. "Margaret! Was that you, in Grace's gown, going into your young man's room? Is that what Lord Thomas saw?"

She burst into fresh tears and buried her face in her hands. "I had no idea," she said, her voice muffled. "None. I was visiting Hugh, as I admit I have done on occasion, which I know is sinful, but we are betrothed, my lady, I swear it..."

I held up my hand to stop her flow of words. Someone had staged Grace's destruction. Someone had found a weak spot and pressed upon it, had paid for access to her maid to manufacture evidence of secret lust, had created a moment like a scene in a stage play and made sure that the desired audience was there to see it... But who? Why?

"Milady?"

I sprang to my feet. "I must go," I told her. "Stay here and pray for your immortal soul. I cannot provide absolution but surely God will forgive you in your ignorance. I must..." What? What must I do? What could I do?

I knew not, but I must try.

As the door of the chapel boomed shut behind me, I nearly collided with my cousin Eleanor. Was the entire household seeking solace with God this night? Mayhap that was not so strange. "Was that Margaret in there with you?" she asked. When I told her yes, she said, "Oh, it is well for I must needs speak with her."

"Why?"

She leaned in closer to me, looking about the corridor as though we might be overheard, though we were quite alone. Then she leaned in closer yet, and "I have been to see her 'trothed love. Hugh. I have spoken with him."

"Have you? Where is he? What did he have to say for himself?"

I ought to have minded my tone, for Eleanor flinched, thinking its sharpness was aimed at her, not at him. "He is in irons, in the guardroom. They say the king himself will examination him this night."

"The king!"

She nodded vigorously. "Aye!"

"If he is being held for questioning by the king, how did you get in to speak with him?"

"The men holding him are our uncle's men, and they know he is Margaret's special friend. Though they are vigi—vigitant in their charge, they would not prevail one of us from bringing food and ale to the fellow, would they?"

As always with Eleanor, it took a moment to parse the meaning of her misused words. "No, I suppose they would not prevent one of us. That was very kind of you, Eleanor, to go and visit him. What did he say to you? Did he tell you aught of what he did?"

"He feels that Grace was treated tolerably, very badly, and that Lord Thomas has behaved in an odiferrous fashion. He explored to me that Lord Thomas and the duke have falsely excused Grace. Can you believe it?"

"Yes, I can believe it. Margaret has just now explained to me the same. What more did he say? Did he give you any details?"

She drew her brows together and touched the spot with the tip of her right forefinger, a sure sign that she was working hard to recall something. Poor Eleanor. We all loved her dearly, but her limitations were frustrating when, at times like these, one needed information from her.

"He said that he and Margaret were offered money to make it seem like Grace was respoiled—I think that was the word he used."

"Despoiled," I murmured, but she continued on without correcting herself.

"Margaret was to tear a gown and wear a gown—oh, I like that, it rhymes!" Her whole face brightened, and I smiled to encourage her to keep going. "And his part was to invite her to his rooms, and to spray Grace's scent in the gentlemen's wing. Near Thomas' chambers."

"Did he say aught of who asked them to do this?"

She tipped her head down again, pressing harder on the spot between her brows. "He did not speak a name. I think not. And I do not want to be the one who makes such an exclamation against another person. It would make me unhappy."

I touched her hand. "Fear not, love. It would not be you making the accusation. I will take care of everything. But I cannot do it if you do not help me. What did he say? Anything? Did he name anyone, or describe someone?" I fair shook with impatience, but I knew I must tread lightly with Eleanor.

"He said a man gave him gold."

I clenched my teeth against snappish words. Of course it was a man, who else? "What man, love? What does he look like, or sound like? Anything would help."

"All right, let me think. He said it was one of the men come with the king. A rich man. A dark man, a man of shadows."

A chill ran over my skin and nestled at the base of my spine. "A man of shadows? Is that what Hugh said?"

She pulled her hand away from her face. "That's how I think of him, always. I never can quite see him proper. He's always glum to me, like there is a veil over him."

It took a moment for my throat to unfreeze enough to swallow, to speak. "Do you mean Lord John? Lord Beymond? King Henry's secretary?"

She did not lose her pinched look but some of her tension eased. "Oh, aye, that be his name. Beatrice," she said, shifting closer to me again, "I do not like him."

I slipped my arm around her waist to hold her close. "I do not like him either, love." I drew a deep breath and asked, "Did Hugh Borrage say Lord John by name as the man who gave him the money to destroy Grace's reputation?"

She nodded, her head tucked under my chin. I could feel her melting into me, seeking comfort. She was done being brave, done talking. That was all right. She had done enough. I could do the rest.

"One more thing, Eleanor. Did Hugh still have the money? Is it hidden somewhere, or is it gone?"

"Nay," she whispered. "He said Margaret had the money for sure-keeping."

I kissed the top of her head. "You are a good, brave girl, Eleanor. Get you to bed. I will tell Margaret that you have seen Hugh and that he is well." Still she clung to me, so that I had to remove her arms from about my waist and press her toward the stairs that led to the family rooms. I watched her go, smiling and waving each time she glanced over her shoulder at me, and when I was certain she would not return, I grabbed hold of the chapel doors and hauled them open. Margaret leapt up from her knees, blinking back at me, wiping at her tear-streaked cheeks.

"Margaret," I demanded, "where is the gold?"

CHAPTER 14

It might have been the most foolish thing I had ever done in my life
—it was, without doubt—but with the pouch of gold in my fist and
the information giving me courage, I rapped my knuckles on Lord
John Beymond's quarters. He had a room near the king's, one that usually
housed my uncle's manservants during the night so they could be near him
if he needed aught. That was how trusted this man was. But if he had been
the one to disrupt Grace's wedding, he was not the trustworthy servant he
appeared. Who was he, in fact, and what desires was he concealing?

He opened the door a slight crack and peered out. "Lady Beatrice," he
said, his eyebrows rising in surprise. "What do you here?"

"I must needs speak with you."

"Indeed," he said. "Well, then, do come in."

He swung the door wide to admit me and I hesitated. *What are you
doing, Beatrice?* If Grace was accused on a shadow of nothing, what could
you be accused of for going into a man's room? But this was the king's
personal secretary, and I was Beatrice, known to be wise and sensible and
uninterested in men and marriage, and no one would believe anything
untoward of either of us.

I stepped across the threshold.

The room was tiny, but because of Lord John's role as secretary, a large
desk had been wedged across the middle, forcing the narrow bed into the
farthest corner and leaving space for little else. As if seeing the place

through my eyes, he seemed faintly embarrassed and moved a pile of dispatches off a stool for me.

"I apologize, my lady," he began, but I waved away his words. I did not want to feel bad for him. I did not want to feel anything for him.

I perched on the stool, teetering and vulnerable. He settled in the large carved chair behind the desk, leaning back and gripping the arms almost as though he were the king on a throne.

"How does your cousin, if I may enquire?" he asked.

"Very ill, my lord, as may be expected," I replied. I neglected to mention her departure for the convent. He might be aware of that in his role as the king's clerk or he might not, but he need not hear it from me.

"Truly, a sad state of affairs," he said, tutting his tongue. "The poor child. Even if the tale is true..." His voice trailed off and he raised his dark eyes to meet mine. I realized with a feeling like a blow to my stomach that he was seeking verification. I stared back at him in stony silence. He raised a shoulder, as if he cared not. "Whether or not it is true, the young man's behavior is inexcusable. He should never have treated her so. To so publicly humiliate her, it is shameful to him as much as her. It is not the act of a gentleman but of a coward."

I found myself nodding. "And yet he suffers naught by it." I could not keep the bitterness from my voice.

"Well, I would not say so. He does undergo Sir Edmund's challenge, and I would not feel confident of the outcome were I Lord Thomas." At his words, my heart squeezed so tightly in my chest that I stopped breathing. His narrow mouth stretched in a smirk, as though my reaction was exactly what he had hoped for. One hand reached out to the desk and without looking, he picked up a writing quill, twirling it in his long fingers. "You know," he said, extending each of the words past their natural length, "I went to your uncle earlier to urge that he be merciful to his daughter. Before you and your aunt arrived to argue the same. I suggested that he might be able to find a man less fastidious than Thomas. A man who would take Grace as she is, one who would look away from her flaws." He leaned forward, pinning me with his gaze. I had heard men say that a snake would do this to its prey, stare at it until it is unable to move. That was how I felt, listening to Lord John. "That man, I said to your uncle, might have the ear of the king. He could protect your cousin from rumors and slanders by his proximity to the royal house." He sat back again, certain he had my full attention. "But your uncle was unmovable. He had made up his mind to pass the title and inheritance to you, Beatrice. And so, Grace is ruined and will be a nun." He waved a hand and released me from his spell. "What do you want of me, my lady?"

"I—" For a moment, I could not remember why I had come. Then I spied the pouch still clutched in my left hand. "What do you know of a man named Hugh Borrage, one of my uncle's guards?"

He tapped a forefinger to his lips, making a show of thinking. "Borrage, you say? I don't know your uncle's men very well, having only been here a few days, my lady."

He was lying, I could feel it. But how to make him admit it?

"He is in irons in the guardroom, I am told, awaiting the king's interrogation. I would think you, as the king's secretary, have heard of him."

His lips twitched. "Oh, that fellow. The one who defiled your cousin."

I gave him his false smile back. "Nay, he did not. Grace is innocent, as you well know, my lord. If Hugh Borrage is guilty of anything, it is of trusting you."

He cocked his head. "My lady Beatrice, I hardly know what you mean."

"What I mean, my lord…" I weighed the honorific with as much scorn as I could. "What I mean is that Hugh Borrage has never even met Lady Grace. Never set his eyes upon her, much less his hands. But he is betrothed to our maid, Margaret, and they wish to marry but do not have the money to do so. That weakness, sir, you did exploit." I slammed the pouch down on the edge of the desk, and the coins slithered and rattled inside. "You paid them to destroy Grace, although of course they had no comprehension that that was what you asked of them or they'd never have done so."

He narrowed his eyes. "I am sorry, but your story makes no sense at all. For one thing, you must be aware that I wished to marry your cousin. Indeed, I had discussed it with your uncle. You know this, do you not?" He looked away as if the subject made him uncomfortable or embarrassed. "But the duke intervened on Lord Thomas' behalf and your cousin was besotted with him, and so…" He shrugged his shoulders. "What man has not been disappointed in courtship? I bear no ill will toward your cousin or Lord Thomas. Why would I?

"And as for mistaking Lady Grace's maid for the lady herself? I find the idea preposterous, as would the Duke of Surrey and Lord Thomas, who, you should remember, were also there that night. For certes there is a passing resemblance between them from a distance—they are of a height, and both have rich, dark hair—but no one would mistake one for the other."

I smiled. "Indeed, there is a resemblance between them, my lord, as we who live here well know. But as you say, you have only been here a few days and could not possibly know my uncle's men one from the other, let alone the lady's maids. Unless you had some illegitimate reason to know Margaret so well."

He smiled as well, lips stretching over teeth like some predator. "Very well, Lady Beatrice. But to what end would I be so intimately connected to a ladies' maid?"

My skin crawled at the way he said "intimately connected." He was not even speaking of me, and had not been "intimate" with Margaret at all, and yet, somehow he made me feel like he had improper knowledge of both of us nevertheless. Even his eyes on me felt inappropriate. I forced my body not to squirm under his scrutiny, though I longed to wipe the invisible touch of his eyes off me. Instead, I focused on the tale I was weaving. "You brought about Grace's destruction by having Margaret provide evidence that you could present to Lord Thomas. The torn gown, the scent of lavender, the midnight visit to the guard's room that you gentlemen just happened to discover... You created the entire fiction. You were the playwright and the properties master, you hired the actors and told them where their entrances were, and you made sure the audience were in their places when the show began."

Lord John's smile had broadened as I spoke. "O villainy!" he whispered.

I leapt up off the stool. "I do not consider this to be at all humorous, my lord. I intend to go straight to the king with this." I brought my hand down to sweep up the pouch of coins but he leaned forward and grabbed my wrist. I gasped, startled, and protested, but he did not let go. On the contrary, he tightened his grip, bearing down until I released the pouch from white, nerveless fingers.

He scooped up the little sack, hefting it in his hand. "You will do no such thing," he said. "You will not waste his majesty's time with such trivialities." Suddenly his voice shifted from cold iron to warm sun. "What you have is the word of a knave being held in irons against that of a lord. The king's most trusted servant." He stood and walked around the desk, turning to squeeze between the desk and the wall. "What you have is a nondescript pouch of coins that could have come from anywhere, from anyone. Could have been stolen. In fact—" His eyes widened. "In fact, I do believe I mentioned to someone not long ago that I was missing some coins. What are there, twelve gold coins in that purse? That is exactly the number that went missing. I must ensure that this Borrage fellow receives the punishment he deserves for his villainy.

"Now. That's been resolved in a very tidy manner, I think." Though he stood very close, he took one step closer, and with the stool behind me and the desk beyond that dominating the room, there was nowhere I could retreat to. He reached out to touch my face, sliding his fingertips down my cheek.

I shuddered. The blood rose in my face, turning it hot red. I brought a hand up to slap him away but again he grabbed my wrist, already sore from the pouch. I hissed as he squeezed. He grinned as I yielded, dropping my hand. "Do not touch me," I snapped, and he barked a harsh laugh.

"Oh, my lady Beatrice, it is far too late for that," he said. "You have been here, in my chambers, with no one but me, for quite a while now. You came here of your own volition. No one forced you. If anything, you forced your way in. I must say, I rather agree with Lady Stanley. The morals in this place are far from what would be expected from any decent family." He brought his hand back up to my face again, and I turned my face away. His fingers slid along my cheek, down my neck and along my collarbones. I shuddered, wishing myself away. Suddenly, he put both hands on my shoulders and yanked hard on the bodice of my kirtle, tearing at the lace framing the neckline and straining the ribbons that attached the right sleeve.

I cried out and pushed back, stumbling for the door. He did not pursue, though, and I realized that he had done enough harm. Just as the appearance of wrongdoing had destroyed Grace, it would be enough to destroy me as well.

He clucked with his tongue. "Well now, what's to be done? If you leave here in this state, your reputation will be destroyed, and you will end no better than your cousin Grace. For you must be assured, everyone will hear of your transgression." His voice hardened and he approached me, to lift my chin with fingers that felt like iron. "Believe me, they will." When I finally met his gaze, he relented, dropping his hand. I pressed my back flat against the door, wishing I could slide through it and disappear. "You heard your uncle," he went on, his tone lighter, satisfied with my apparent fear. "He does love his brother's daughters but he'll not leave the title or the fortune to them. There's only one way to save your reputation, would you not say, Lady Beatrice?"

My mind raced, grasping for a way out of this tangle. There had to be one, if I could but devise it...but he was so clever, I could not seem to think around him. For now, the best course was to seem to acquiesce and to find another way. Tomorrow. When I was not so tired and confused.

"Very well, my lord. Speak to my uncle. I will not say aught against you."

His eyes sparked with victory and greed. I yanked on the door handle and fled, my heart pounding but my eyes dry. I had no more tears left to cry.

* * *

The moon was clawing its way across my window, as reluctant as I to see the morning arrive. I knew I should close the shutters against the night air and its ill spirits and foul humors, but I could not bring myself to care. How much worse could this night be? Grace sent off to a convent, mayhap for the rest of her life; myself, manipulated into agreeing to marry the man who had orchestrated her downfall; and Benedict preparing to fight, perhaps to the death, against Grace's beloved in a futile effort to prove her innocence. How had my life come to this?

I leaned back against the pillows of my bed and felt something out of place, a small square of parchment. Grace's letter! In all that had happened, I had forgotten it. I cracked the seal, tiny fragments of wax pelting my lap like rain, and unfolded the letter. Grace had a particular way of folding her writings, ever since she was a child, and I nearly lost myself to tears once more, opening the folds of soft parchment to see her words.

My dearest Beatrice, she began.

Before I depart, I must beg your forgiveness, although you know not that you have been wronged. Or mayhap not wronged, but deceived in troth, though we saw no harm that could arise from it at the time. Let me be clear, lest you think I run mad. It is my fault, mine and my parents' as well, that you believe Benedict loves you, and in that you were deceived.

At the party, after my father and Thomas had agreed that we would marry in a few days' time, the duke proposed a plot to bring about another marriage, a marriage between two people who were determined never to marry. It began as a jest for, as my father said, if you were but a week married, you'd talk each other mad. Yet, truly, all can see how well suited you are to one another, save the two of you of course. You do see it now, do you not, dear Beatrice? That you can love him, mayhap even marry him? I have only ever wished to see you happy, and I wanted you to be happy as I had been with Thomas. Thus, I did not demur when the duke asked me to let you overhear me talking with my mother about Benedict's love for you, for I believed it would lead you to a good marriage and great happiness. The men—my father, the duke, and Thomas—would do the same for Benedict. "If we can do this," the duke said, "Cupid is no longer an archer. His glory shall be ours, for we are the only love gods." We all laughed. I will never forget how we laughed, how innocent a thing it seemed at the time when we were all overflowing with joy and looking forward to the future with hope. Now I see that deception and trickery are no path to love, and I am ashamed of my part in it. I beg you will forgive me. Forgive all of us.

Finally, if you must share this story with him, I beg you be gentle, and remember that he has ever been your friend.

The letter fell into my lap with the bits of wax. I should feel fury, resentment, annoyance—any number of emotions. Instead, I felt nothing. Could feel nothing. Nothing but the relentless sense of waste. How had all the lightheartedness of the early days of the king and the princess' visit, the flirtation and the fun, come to this?

Well, if I were to be honest, Benedict and I had not been having fun in the beginning. That had not begun until—until my family and his friends made us believe we were in love.

But we were in love. Always had been. It was not pretend for us. What a trick to play on them, if only they knew.

I rose from the bed, wax and parchment falling like a flower and its blown petals, and went to the little table. I pulled parchment and ink to me and began to write, scribbling in my haste.

Grace, dearest, there is nothing to forgive. I have been a fool though I could not admit it to you, nor to myself. I have loved Benedict for years, since long before he went away. I am sorry I never told you.

Let me start at the beginning...

* * *

A light tap on my bedchamber door stopped the flow of my words. I leaned back in the chair and stretched my fingers, calling out, "Come in." My uncle Lionel entered, leaning heavily on his cane. He seemed to have aged ten years in the past few hours, his eyes shot with red, his mouth pulling down over sagging jowls, his hair flying like floss around his ears. I rose to offer him the chair, but he made his slow and painful way to the window first, to drag it closed.

"Do you not know enough to keep a window shuttered at night?"

"Of course I do. I just... I wanted..." I could not say what I wanted.

He nodded and sank onto the bed. "Beatrice," he said. "What are you thinking?"

I sat on the chair, shifting so I could face him. "What do you mean, uncle?" I was evading his question, and he knew it.

"For years you have avoided even the mention of marriage. You have made a show of mocking the estate, maintaining your preposterous claims against it, whatever jest carries you through the latest argument against taking your proper place in the world. I admit I have coddled you and indulged you for I enjoy your wit and your will." He assayed a smile, but the effort of stretching his lips, his cheeks, seemed to cause him great pain. "I adore your refusal to accept your lot in life. You are the son this family never had."

I opened my mouth to object. I was manifestly not a son. I was not a man at all, which fact had been emphasized by my mother's complaints, tears, and disappointment until her death, but of course it was not my physical state he was describing. I blinked rapidly to stop my emotions from spilling out my eyes yet again. Would there be an end to tears this day? Or only an end to the day?

"But my indulgence has, perhaps, encouraged you to be unwomanly. Or to think yourself more like a man than you are." He peered at my disarray. I still wore the kirtle I had been wearing earlier, and the signs of Lord John's mauling were clear upon it. "You take liberties, or permit liberties to be taken, and you risk ending like your cousin." He bit down on his lips before he said Grace's name. "Did you know that Lord John sought to marry your cousin first? And now he has obtained your hand? He seeks only this manor, this title, this inheritance." He smacked the heel of his cane on the floor, and the sound echoed in my small room. "How could you allow him to take advantage of you in this way, and permit him to obtain his object?"

Rather than answer the question, I posed one of my own. "Are you not pleased to have your family attached to a man so closely placed to the king?"

"I do not trust him!" He smacked his cane on the floor again.

"Then deny him what he wants!" I leapt up from my chair, spreading my hands wide. "Do not accept his story, and do not allow him to gain your niece, your title, and your lands."

He shook his head slowly. "But I must, in order to protect you."

I covered my face with my hands. "Princes and kings. Lords and dukes.

How easy it is but to swear a thing and have others believe it when you are a man, especially one with the ear of a king. How may a woman stand against that?"

My uncle stood, wavering until he caught his balance with his cane. "She may not. She cannot. And we all must live with the consequences of that, Beatrice."

CHAPTER 15

The morning of the challenge had dawned cold and grey. I knew because I had been awake to see it, still sitting on my bed, waiting for sleep to overtake me. As a pale sun broke the horizon, I sat on a low stone wall behind the manor house watching the bustle of servants setting up for the morning's activities. A veil of mist hung low over the grass, obscuring their feet as they went to and from the house carrying bundles and boxes. I watched as they erected two tall, broad pavilions, the sort we would use for hunting parties in the fall or luncheons on long summer afternoons out berrying. But these tents were set in opposition to each other, one at each end of a long, flat expanse where, in a few hours, Benedict and Thomas would play out their deadly game. Other workers set up a long tilt barrier, rather like a single-railed fence, down the middle of the field to mark where the horses would race toward each other, one on either side. I could already see them in my mind's eye, two massive warhorses charging at full speed, their thunderous footfalls shaking the earth, their riders in full harness with the sun glinting off steel, lances pointed straight for each other's shields, each hoping to strike the other off...

I could scarce swallow for the thick lump in my throat.

The mist settled its chilly fingers on my face and froze on the thick wool of my cloak. I knew I should go inside to warm up and eat something, but the thought of food was sickening and for some reason it felt right that I should suffer the cold. Why should I have comfort when Grace was in a convent and Benedict was about to endure this? And after years of refusing to even entertain the idea of marriage, I had managed to walk myself into a betrothal last night instead of getting Lord John to confess to his wickedness. Sheer foolishness, that had been. What had I been thinking, going to him by myself? I had been too upset, too foolishly certain that after all that had gone wrong, I could force events back into a shape of my own devising. There was a way out of my betrothal—I would find a way out of it—but for the moment, I could not think beyond this tiltyard being constructed in front of me.

Men in livery began to walk past me from the house, carrying boxes and armfuls of armor. Helms, greaves, gauntlets, shirts of chain mail, gleaming breast plates. It appeared that my uncles had opened the armory for Benedict, as he was defending Grace's honor. Mayhap the Duke of Surrey had done the same for Lord Thomas. One man brought out a shield that was painted a deep red with a pattern of four pale gold crescent moons in a circle. Across the pattern was the mark of a bastard—the bar sinister—and on this shield, the bar was painted black with three gold crosses on it. This, then was Benedict's shield. I could not divine the meaning of the colors and shapes without asking him or perhaps my uncle who had more knowledge of the language of heraldry, but I watched as the man carried it to a stand in front of the eastern pavilion. So that was where he would be getting ready for the joust.

I stood up and wiped my frigid, shaking hands down my skirts as I tried to gather my courage to cross the field. I wanted—nay, I needed to talk to him.

"I believe I am to congratulate you."

I wheeled about. Benedict stood behind me on the steps, clad in the thick, padded garments I realized one wore underneath a suit of armor. His tone was colder than the mist that froze on my cloak and did nothing to still my trembling.

"Please," I said, "don't."

"Don't what? Don't congratulate you?" He took a step down, then another, until he was beside me. "Don't criticize you? Of all people, Beatrice, why him?" The scorn, the hurt, in his voice were palpable.

My hands curled into fists, nails driving into my palms. "For reasons of my own."

"There can be no reason to support marriage to him."

"Oh indeed, just as there is no reason to support your throwing your life away in a brawl with Thomas!"

"That is not—that is entirely different."

"Oh yes? How so?"

"This is a matter of honor."

"A matter of honor." I scoffed. "Ought you not beat your chest with your sword when you say that? And vow to kill yourself like a good Roman if you fail to die in combat? What century are we living in, Benedict? Whose honor are you truly defending?"

I was arguing with him. Why was I arguing with him? Why did my tongue run away like a vicious horse? I wanted to plead with him, kiss him, beg him not to do this...and yet, here we were again, fighting. And I could not stop.

Why could I never be like Grace and say nothing, just once?

He sucked in a deep breath and collected himself rather than striking back at me with more words. "I think I will take my leave," he said.

He stepped down onto the field, the frosted grass crunching beneath his boots. My heart squeezed in my chest until I could no longer bear it. "Wait!" I cried. "Benedict, wait!"

He stopped and turned on his heel, but he did not come back. I flew down the steps to close the space between us, reaching for him. He looked startled, his eyes burning, flinching as though I might hit him but no, I had already hurt him more than a mere physical blow. "I am sorry. Edmund," I whispered, laying my palm against his cheek. "I am sorry. Please do not do this. Please."

Sighing, he closed his eyes and leaned into my hand, but only for a moment. Opening his eyes again, he put his hand against mine, twined our fingers, and slowly pulled my hand away. "You know I must."

Miserable, I nodded. "Stay alive. Please. Just do that for me."

His eyes flared again, with pain, with betrayal, with the knowledge that despite everything, I had agreed to marry another man. "Even if..." In response, my own eyes stung with sudden tears. I had no right to ask anything of him. I had betrayed him, even if I had not intended to. And if I could not find a way out of it, I would have to marry Lord John.

"Yes," I whispered, my voice breaking. "Even if."

He nodded and released my hand. "I would do anything you ask of me, Beatrice." He started to turn away again, then looked back at me, a bleak, broken smile on his lips. "I do love nothing in the world so much as you. Is that not strange?"

My breath escaped in a sound that was half a sob, half a laugh. "No stranger than what I meant to tell you when you walked out here this morning. That I love no one else but you."

He shook his head, ran a hand through his already unruly curls, and walked away.

* * *

With a click and a groan, the heavy door to the chapel opened and shut behind me. I twisted on my already sore knees to see who else had thought to come and pray before the challenge and watched my uncle Lionel make his slow, limping way down the aisle. In obvious discomfort, he lowered himself onto the kneeler beside me, his joints protesting in pops and snaps, and set his cane down on the floor between us. He clasped his hands as if to pray but instead rubbed them together for warmth, blowing on them.

"Don't know who decided that the Lord would object to a fire in His house of worship on a cold morning," he grumbled. I smiled and leaned my head on his burly shoulder, stretching my arm around him to share my cloak. He muttered appreciation and patted my cold hand with his.

"My dear girl," he said at last, gazing up at the icons of the holy family painted beside the altar, "how did it come to this?"

"If I blame it on male pride, will that satisfy you?"

He shot me a sidelong glance. "It is not only male pride that has caused this trouble."

I sighed. "I know. I want to explain…"

"Explanations will not save you. I told you that last night."

I sighed again. It seemed to be the only way to keep from crying again. "I should have protected Grace better, Uncle. I should have seen what was happening. I should have stayed with her that night."

He slid an arm around my waist, pulling me close. "Beatrice, dear one. There was nothing you should have done, and likely nothing you could have done. I know you say she is innocent—"

I pulled away, turning to face him. "She is!"

He nodded, but I could see he still did not quite believe me. "But whether she is innocent or no, your word added to hers would have changed nothing. As you acknowledged last night."

I sank back onto my heels. "If nothing else, I should have stopped the men from this folly."

"That, too, is naught to do with you. The men will have their moment, and God will judge."

"That is the foremost of my fears."

He leaned forward and squeezed my knee. "And mine as well." Taking up his cane once more, he leaned on it and the altar rail to heave himself back to standing. "Do not linger too long, Beatrice. We need you. He needs you."

I stared down at the altar rail. "Yes, Uncle." I listened to him shuffle away, heard the door swing open and shut behind him, then listened to the silence settle around me once again.

Not long after, I left, for God had no answers for me either.

* * *

Leaving the chapel, I noted one of my uncle's guardsmen heading for the rear of the manor. I did not know his name—I made a silent vow to make the acquaintance of every guard in the future—and stopped him with a hand on his shoulder. He whirled, hand on dagger, and relented when he saw me. What a state we had reached, when the guards were on high alert even within our home.

"Milady," he said, bowing. "How may I be of service?"

"Tell me, sirrah, if you know, has the king questioned the guard who was taken for improper conduct?" I searched my exhausted brain for the name Margaret had given me. "Borrage. Hugh Borrage."

The fellow looked puzzled. "The king, milady? Nay, for Borrage was taken away this morning under guard to Westminster. To the Tower."

"The Tower—" My breath caught in my throat. It could not be. Taken away before the king questioned him? "By whose order?"

He shrugged. "I suppose by order of the king, milady. For they were the king's men in green and white that did take him hence."

I scarce managed to choke out my thanks and let him continue on his way. I was rooted in place, my mind spinning in circles. If only I had managed some sleep the night before, mayhap I could wrest some control over my thoughts. Borrage taken away by the king's men, sent to the Tower...to what end?

"Beatrice, my dear."

My skin twitched as if a thousand crawling insects roved over my body. I forced myself to turn and face him. "Lord Beymond."

He lifted my hand to his lips, lingering. "Such formality. Do call me John."

I stared down at him, leaning over my hand, looking up at me with fathomless, unknowable dark eyes. I knew the response that was expected of me, and I would not give it.

He released my hand and straightened, his smile tight. "You look troubled."

"I have just learned that the man who was accused of seducing my cousin has been removed to Westminster, to the Tower, before the king has had a chance to question him." He nodded, feigning interest. "Do you not find that odd, as the king had said he would question the man himself?"

"Perhaps he changed his mind. He is, after all, a king." He turned so that he was beside me, placed a hand on my elbow, and began to guide me toward the front of the manor. For the moment, I allowed myself to be led.

"Why send him there?"

Lord John scoffed. "Why do you think? He will be put to further questioning. The kind of questioning they cannot—or will not—do here."

I pulled my arm from his and faced him. "It will not go well for you if he speaks the truth, whether on the rack or to the king or even to his jailers on the way to Westminster."

"Indeed," he mused. "It would be most unfortunate if he were to meet with an accident along the way. Or if the first thing the torturer takes is his tongue."

Guards in green and white. "You," I gasped. "You ordered him taken hence. You did not want the king to speak to him, so you sent him away before... And now you have me bound as well... I will not! I will not keep silent!"

My voice was rising, and his face darkened. Looking around, he pulled me through the closest open door. It was my uncle's study. He pushed me down into a chair, holding me by my shoulders, his face inches from mine. "Calm yourself, my dear," he said through gritted teeth. "You will pull the whole manor down stone by stone with your screeching."

When I stilled, he went to the sideboard and poured two goblets of wine, walking back to hold one out to me. "Here. It will help calm your nerves." I stared at it for a long moment. Once I accepted it, he settled in the chair across from me—my uncle's chair, I could not help thinking. I took a sip of the wine and considered him there, all dark, arrogant confidence.

"You like that chair? This room?" I said. "They will all be yours one day, when you are Baron Welles and the Earl of Ashley, when we are married and Uncle Lionel is dead." My heart clenched to say it so bluntly, but I had to.

He smiled, just a little. "Well, yes. I suppose you are right."

"Do not dissemble. At the least, be honest with me if I am to be your wife." Again, my heart spasmed. Wife. "You have thought of nothing else since you arrived in this place."

"If you wish my honesty, *wife*, I will say that I did not immediately imagine being Baron Welles, although I did, yes, hope to be the Earl of Ashley. But your cousin would not cooperate and so I had to...improvise."

I held my breath. Would he speak of it? Could I get an admission out of him?

But even if I could, what help would it be?

I forced myself to raise the cup to my lips, to sip, to swallow. "Who do you suppose will win at the tilt?" I asked, trying to keep my voice light. "Lord Thomas or Sir Edmund?"

He smiled again, and I was astonished at how false that simple gesture could be. He lifted his hands, then his eyes, heavenward. "Providence will determine the outcome to instruct us in the ways of righteousness."

Now it was my turn to scoff. "Do not say you believe that God Himself takes an interest in the tiny disputes of men."

"Do you not?"

"All right," I said. "If He does, what will the outcome be? Is Grace innocent or not?"

"Why are you so certain that I know the answer?"

"Because you do. Because you are the one who set out to ruin her."

He steepled his fingers and regarded me for a long moment. "Beatrice," he said at last, "you are most outspoken for a woman. The princess herself, I believe, has chided you for this. If you are to come to court with me, if you are to be my wife, you must learn restraint."

If I were to be his wife... I repressed a shudder, looking at him through narrowed lids.

He lowered his hands, elbows on his knees, so that his laced fingers pointed at me. "If I tell you the truth, if I share this with you, you must agree to marry me at once. Today." He leaned forward, now touching my knees with his open hands. "Because your vows will compel your faithful duty to me." He leaned ever closer as he spoke, and I watched him, motionless, transfixed. "Your obedience. Your silence." He touched a light finger to my lips and I willed myself not to flinch. "Can you do that, Beatrice?"

I did not want to move my lips against his finger. I did not want to give him the slightest sensation of pleasure from touching me. I nodded.

"Good," he said, curving his lips again in that false smile. "This is promising." He tapped my lips twice, then my chin. Was that meant to be endearing? And then, to my relief, he leaned back in his chair once more.

There was an odd little noise outside in the corridor, a strange skittering sound like rocks being tossed down on the flags. *Skitter-skitter-skitter...* I pushed the distraction away, focusing on Lord John's voice, on the confession he was about to make.

"You have divined most of it," he said at last. "I was unhappy when Grace chose Thomas. Her father and I had an agreement, or at least so I thought. I was going to speak to her that night, the night of the masque ball, you remember?"

I nodded again, but he was no longer looking at me. Unable to sit still, he pushed out of the chair and began to pace, his heels thudding on the carpet and then striking loud on the stone flags. "But when I arrived, I found her dancing with the duke first, and by the time he had finished with her, it was too late. She was flushed pink as the first rose of spring, and I could see I had lost her." He turned, running his hand along the back of the chair. "To the duke, I could have yielded gracefully. But to that nobody, that young imp—" He bit down on his words.

"That jumped-up bit of dust?" I offered. He raised his gaze from the chair to meet mine, and something I could not name sparked in its depths. I drove my thumbnail deep into the flesh of the opposite palm and smiled at him.

His intensity diminished by my jest, he continued. "It was unthinkable, to lose her in that way. Intolerable. I had to act."

"Could you not have targeted Thomas, then, and not Grace?" I demanded.

He made a derisive sound. "You yourself know how easy it is to bring down a woman. How could I tear down perfect Thomas, friend to the king, in a few days? But Grace? A hint of scent in the air in the men's wing, a torn gown, a woman who resembles her seen in a man's room..." He gestured like a painter with a brush. "It is the thing of a moment to destroy a woman's reputation. Men will believe the worst of women, for they fear the worst in themselves."

"And so women take the blame for men's weakness," I bristled, and he agreed.

"It has always been thus."

"But how did you learn of Margaret and Hugh? Margaret has been my maid for years and she kept it from me, yet you arrived here days ago and you discovered their secret?"

One side of his mouth twitched. "Do you not know why I am high in the king's favor? Why I am his secretary and kept close by his side?"

"I assumed you wrote a good hand," I said, only half in jest.

He was not amused. "The king is a man in need of information," he said. "Accurate, current information. I supply it to him."

Tired as I was, and with the stony striking noises from without the room pulling at my thoughts, I struggled to make sense of him, to consider him anew. This man who supplied information to the king had not been with the king in France or Brittany, like Benedict or Lord Thomas, had not fought with him on the battlefield at Bosworth. Where —how—had he come to the king's notice?

I made the leap. "You were in King Richard's court. You were his spy."

His nose wrinkled. "We do not use that word."

I spoke past him, over him. "You sent him information from England before he returned. And this, all this—" I swept my hand around my uncle's study. "This is your reward."

He watched me with his dark, level gaze, long fingers cradling his chin.

"You were a traitor."

His eyes narrowed. "Henry was always my king."

"Does he believe that?"

"Of course, he does. He knows it. A king always needs men like me, men who discover information and reveal it."

"Does he know that you manipulate events to your own benefit, using his influence in your favor?"

His tongue flicked out to lick his lips, the first sign I had ever seen in him of discomposure. So he was not certain that the king would not be angry he had used Tudor yeomen to remove Borrage from the manor. He was not certain that the king would forgive him for removing the opportunity to examine Borrage himself.

He was not entirely sanguine after all.

At that, I relaxed back against my chair. Mayhap, a chink in his armor. Mayhap, a chance for me to break free of his influence.

Somewhere, out in the corridor, someone was yelling. "Get that thing out—" The skittering rock sound approached quickly then passed by. "I should have shut that door," Lord John muttered.

"So," I blurted, to pull his attention back to me, "you ruined Grace so that Thomas could not have her. In the process, you destroyed Margaret and Hugh as well, but you will say that they are nothing, they do not matter." He nodded, and I continued, "Was it really so difficult to see her happy?"

"I did not..." He trailed off and considered his words. "I had not expected Thomas to be quite so cruel, and I never anticipated your uncle's reaction. Events got quickly out of hand." I scoffed, and he seated himself in the chair again, leaning forward, eager to convince me. "Indeed, I did not want or expect Thomas' behavior in the chapel. I assumed he would take your uncle aside before the ceremony, as I urged him to, and break the betrothal in private. Then, I would step in and provide your uncle with a respectable alternative to public shame."

"How kind of you."

He ignored the sarcasm in my tone and continued. "But Thomas, for some reason, decided it was not enough to set her aside, he must publicly ruin her. And then your uncle, he piled shame on shame, beating her in front of everyone and then sending her away before anyone could speak for her." He sat back, letting his hands drop in a helpless gesture. "What was there to be done?"

"And then you urged my uncle to name me his heir in her stead, so you would not lose all."

"He did not need much urging. You made the choice easy for him."

I rose and paced toward the hearth, letting him see that I was taking it all in, pondering all he had said. Letting him believe I was accepting it.

I put one hand on the mantle and turned to face him. "If you are, as you say, indispensable to the king, if you and your information are so important to him, you must have a great deal of influence over him."

He tilted his head, a self-deprecating gesture I had not anticipated. I almost smiled. "Well, then, it should be an easy thing for you to ask him to call off today's tilt."

"Call off—but why?" His thin brows pulled into a sharp line. "Are you suffering a softness of heart, Beatrice?"

I did not twitch, did not blink. *Reveal nothing, Beatrice.* "Not at all, not for myself. But Sir Edmund spent much of his boyhood here, and I worry that my uncle's heart could not bear the strain if he should come to harm so soon after Grace's fall."

"Your uncle," he mused. "You are kind to think of the old man."

I gritted my teeth at his callous words.

He stood. "If I do this—if—you will marry me before midday." He stalked to the hearth, standing beside me and leaning so close I could see every long lash on his fathomless eyes, could feel his breath on my cheek. He brought one hand up and traced the line of my jaw with one finger. I struggled not to flinch or pull away, to keep my gaze fixed upon him. "We will seek out the priest and marry in private before the joust occurs." In a quick, sharp move, he shifted his hand to grip my chin, squeezing tightly. "And I will have my full rights before the sun sets. There will be no question of who Baron Welles is, and who will be Lord Ashley. Do you understand?"

I swallowed hard. "Why not await the outcome of the joust?" I asked, my voice small and shaking despite my will. "If Sir Edmund wins and Grace is proved innocent, then my uncle will welcome her back and I will lose my sudden inheritance. For certes you would want Grace in those circumstances?"

He scoffed and released my chin, stepping away from me. "If I was not such a fool as to leave Grace's wedding to chance, do you think I will leave the outcome of this afternoon's challenge to chance? I have you now, and all that comes with you. Would I gamble that on the possibility of your uncle's taking his daughter back and restoring her to his favor, only to watch him hand her back over to Thomas?" He shook his head. "No, I think you and I will make the best of things as they stand."

My heart stuttered in my chest and my legs trembled beneath me. "And so? Will you? Speak to the king? Convince him to stop the challenge?"

He pointed a finger at me, waving it in a gentle, teasing scold. As if we were lovers enjoying a private jest. "Ah, but you have not yet agreed to my terms. Why should I exert my influence on your behalf with no guarantee of your acquiescence?"

"Why indeed, Lord Beymond?"

I was thankful for my grip on the solid mantle because I jumped at the sound of the king's voice. Lord John lurched around, knocking into my uncle's chair and oversetting a small table. King Henry stood framed in the doorway to the study, clad in deep green, holding his cap in one hand

and leaning on the door with the other. His gaze swept from John to me and back again, and his expression was impossible to read.

Recovering from my shock, I attempted a curtsey. Unable to hold it, I simply fell to my knees. Lord John moved away from the tumbled furniture and bent low at the waist. "Your majesty," he began, his voice smooth and measured, the perfect courtier.

The king shook his head. "No," he said, his voice a knife cutting across John's. He took a slow step and then another into the room, gripping his cap in both hands. "You see, John, I am not sure what most concerned me about what I have heard here this morning."

Lord John cast a glance back toward me, and I saw a glint of fear in his eyes as he tried to calculate exactly how much the king might have heard. Behind the king, Princess Elizabeth appeared in the doorway, and from the look on her face, I guessed that she, too, had heard everything the king had. "I am not one to listen at doorways, but the occasion does present itself from time to time. As you should be aware." The king flung his hat, now twisted out of shape, onto the chair in front of Lord John, who flinched. "Having engaged in this less than desirable activity, I find that I better understand the work that you have undertaken on my behalf. I also better understand the nature of the man I have chosen to do such work for me. I am not sure if the work has driven you to such ends, or if you would have behaved in this way regardless and your position merely gave you the power with which to accomplish them. In the end, it matters not."

Princess Elizabeth had, by now, walked into the room and stood beside the king, slipping her hand through his arm. Lord John looked from one to the other and though his face remained stoic, his voice trembled as he pled, "Your majesty..."

The princess' voice interrupted his like a shattering glass. "You know, my dear, I think the worst affront of this entire affair might just have been his presumption that he could simply instruct you in what to do and you would do it. As though he, not you, were the sovereign."

Good God, this woman had been born to power. Lord John had miscalculated badly to forget it. I bowed my head, grateful to be on my knees.

"I cannot fault your conclusion, my lady," the king replied. "In that alone, he has offended beyond forgiveness." The princess released his arm and took a step forward, skirting the chair to approach me. "Lady Beatrice, do not think we have forgotten you," he said, softening his tone. "Rise, please."

Surprised, I stumbled to my feet and forced myself to look up at them. "Your majesty. Your highness."

"My dear lady," the princess said, "your concern for your cousin is commendable. And your willingness to unite yourself to this—opportunist —for the sake of uncovering the truth of what occurred shows more love and faith than any battle for her honor." She took my hand. "Allow me to assure you that the king has not only heard Lord John's confession to you here this morning, he has spoken with Hugh Borrage—"

"Impossible!" Lord John blurted, and immediately clapped a hand over his lips in recognition of his blunder.

The king turned to confront him. "Impossible? Why should that be so?"

He looked up from his abject posture, and his face was pale. For the first time, he recognized that he was trapped. "Impossible, your gracious majesty, because I had sought to protect the princess and the other ladies here from such a vile, offending knave by sending him away, back to the Tower, where he could be properly dealt with."

"I like your turn of phrase, Beymond. 'Properly dealt with.' Do you not mean 'put to death'? So he could not speak against you? Is that not a harsh way to deal with a man in your service?"

Lord John made a brave show, at the last. "The man is a knave, your majesty, and an inveterate liar. He would say anything to please your majesty."

"And you would not?"

John began to protest but must have seen something in the king's face that decided him against it.

I gripped the princess' hand. My throat was so tight I could scarce force the words out, but I must speak. "Your highness, please, I must know. Will the men still tilt today?"

She smiled, and as always, it was as if the sun had emerged from behind clouds. Laying her other hand over mine, she said, "Oh, no, my dear. We have already sent word to them to return to the great hall. The king and I will address them as soon as we are done in here."

My knees buckled and I went down again. The princess joined me on the floor and held my hands in hers as I wept.

CHAPTER 16

A short time later, after Lord John was led away by two stout yeomen, the princess sent me to wash and change before joining them in the great hall for the king's audience with Lord Thomas and Benedict. I raced to my bedchamber, where Eleanor and Mary regaled me with tales of a goat running loose in the house, which explained the noises outside the study, and helped me change into a clean kirtle. Stunned into silence by all that had just happened, I let their words flow over me like cleansing water, smiling at their good-natured chatter.

My cousins had never been so dear to me.

My face and teeth clean, my hair tidied—although, as Mary lamented, it never will stay in its pins, will it?—and my dress a becoming red to heighten my complexion, I descended to find the great hall converted into a royal audience chamber. Two large chairs sat on the large dais that had been created for the masque, but now a drape of cloth-of-gold hung behind it, framing the chairs. The room glowed golden as sunlight streamed in through the windows while every torch and candle had been lit as well. The room was full of well-dressed, chattering, curious people— family, courtiers, servants—who had gathered to hear why the challenge had been called off and learn what was to happen next. I stood with my family to the left of the dais.

Trumpets sounded as the wide doors opened and the king and princess entered. They, too, had changed into finery befitting the occasion, and the king wore the circlet of gold I had not seen since he first arrived.

As the king and princess settled into their chairs, a commotion erupted at the doors. Two yeomen in Tudor livery were attempting to close them, but someone had burst through in a clatter of steel. It was Benedict, only half his armor on, his sword clanking against his steel-clad leg, his hair wild and his face flushed and sweaty from running with so much weight on his body. My heart swelled so large and light, I thought it might float up and out of my chest.

He was safe.

He skidded to a halt just inside the door. "Where is she?" he demanded of the room at large, paying no heed to the fact that the king and princess were sitting on the dais.

As one, my aunt and my cousins each took a step back, exposing me amidst the crowd at the front of the hall.

He took a few halting steps forward. I thought he would embrace me, and I moved forward, reaching for him, but then I realized where we were and what we were doing...and he did too. He pivoted mid-step and bowed low. "Your majesty," he said, "your highness."

Trying to hide his amusement, the king said, "Please, join us, Sir Edmund. We all await Lord Thomas Keighton to put everything to rights." He gestured with one hand, as though it mattered not at all where Benedict stood, but he clearly indicated my direction.

Bowing again, Benedict came and stood beside me, casting a sidelong glance my way. "You...look well," he whispered.

"As do you," I whispered back. "Although perhaps a bit less...knightly... than I imagined you would look this morning."

The corner of his mouth quirked. "I was interrupted. I assume I am to find out why?"

"Yes," I said. "When Thomas arrives."

As though my words summoned him, he strode into the hall. He had completed his arming, and his every step was both slowed and made loud by his shining suit of armor. All he lacked was his helm, which his squire, following, carried in the crook of his arm. So suited, he could not do much beyond a stiff bend at the waist.

"Thank you for joining us, Lord Keighton," the princess said, making a similar gesture to the one that the king had made. "I am going to explain why the both of you are being denied the satisfaction of your challenge this morning."

"I do appreciate that, your highness, for I am much confused."

"The king has called off the tilt over the matter of the lady Grace's innocence because that issue has already been established. You were deceived, Lord Keighton, and deliberately so."

Lord Thomas' face drained of all color, and an audible gasp went up from the watching court. "By whom, your highness?" he managed to ask. "If I may enquire?"

"My secretary, Lord John Beymond, was the villain," the king replied, yielding another gasp and following murmurs from the assembled crowd.

"Hold a moment," my uncle Lionel exclaimed. He pressed forward, still leaning hard on his cane as he came to stand in front of the royal couple. "Lord John, a villain?" he repeated. He looked around until he found me. "Did you know this?"

"I knew it well, Uncle."

"Yet you would have married him," Benedict muttered, bitterness painting his tone.

My aunt, overhearing, touched his shoulder. "There are many kinds of courage," she said.

He looked so hurt and confused, and I tried to show him so much of the last hours with my eyes, knowing now was not the time or place to speak.

"Let me assure you, one and all," the king said, "I had no idea the depths of villainy of which he was capable. I would never have kept him near me had I believed he would treat my friends in such a way. My enemies, certes, but not my friends."

As the courtiers chuckled, Benedict turned and said to the king, "If you will permit me, your majesty, I will devise exquisite punishments for him."

"If it will give you satisfaction, Sir Edmund, the job is yours."

"And so," the princess said, "we come now to what is to be done about Lady Grace and the wrongs done to her. Lord Keighton, come forward." In the short time she had been with us, I had come to recognize the signs of her displeasure: the tiny line between her brows, the slightest dip of her mouth. I was glad that I was not, at that moment, Lord Thomas Keighton.

"You did not have faith in your betrothed, Thomas. Not the kind of faith she had in you. And it was your jealousy, your suspicion, your easy belief that she could stray that enabled Lord John to trick you into thinking she was unfaithful to you. All of us know better now. Do you?"

Thomas' mouth dropped open as though he would speak. Benedict fairly growled at him. "I will bash you senseless right now if you need that to convince you, Keighton."

"How could I have been so deceived?" he said, his voice pleading.

"Do you doubt my lady's word?" the king said, half rising from his seat, but the princess quelled him with a hand on his thigh.

"We have heard him confess all. And we have the testimony of the man who was put forward as Grace's lover, and of the woman who posed as Grace for one night, and one night only. You, sir," she finished by leaning forward for emphasis, "were deceived."

The duke of Surrey stepped forward and put his hand on Thomas' armored shoulder. "It is so," he said. "I was likewise deceived."

Thomas shook his head in stunned disbelief. "And yet if this is true, then Grace is innocent…"

"Yes," the princess snapped. "She has been falsely accused, her good name besmirched, her honor broken, and her future destroyed, all on the word of a knave. She was condemned by those who would not trust their hearts."

Thomas still resisted. "Nay, your highness, say not that she is condemned. If the story is not true, if she is yet a maid, then surely—"

The princess silenced him with a look. "Grace has been ruined, Thomas, and for this you bear a nearly equal measure of the blame with Lord John. Turn your thoughts from her. What is there for her but life in the convent?"

My heart broke to hear this, but I had to acknowledge that the princess was, like as not, correct. The princess and the king had wanted to avoid scandal in their new court, and Grace, even redeemed, would never escape the rumors and whispers. Perhaps, in time, Uncle Lionel could find some obscure knight who would marry her for her beauty and a generous dowry, but she would never come home to us the same Grace. She would never be his heir again.

Thomas staggered, and his friend the duke had to bear his cumbersome weight to keep him from falling. "Then, with your majesties' kind permission, I will withdraw from court and return to my home."

The king appeared like to agree, but the princess commanded, "No, Lord Thomas. You will not slip away to brood and wallow in your sorrows. You must atone for what you have done, and you must make good your part in it."

Stunned, Thomas blinked up at the princess. "What must I do?"

"Not only have you ruined young Grace's future, you have deprived Lord Ashley of his sole child and heir." She pinned him with a stare that would have made a snake proud. "He expected a wedding this week, sir, and a son-in-law, and children to secure his family's future. Will you go cower in your ancestral lands and deny him these comforts in his old age?"

Thomas shot a glance at me. "But...?"

A cold sweat broke out on my torso, running down between my breasts. "No," I whispered. Surely the princess would not require that. I looked at Uncle Lionel, but he was stone faced as he said, "Do you not think marriage to one of my nieces is proper payment for the harm you have done to me and my family, young sir?"

"One of your nieces?" Thomas almost squeaked. "Which one?"

"No," the princess said, "you must agree to the bargain before you know the woman."

Thomas cast his gaze down at the princess' feet and fell to one knee before her, the picture of abject defeat even in his glorious steel plate. "I will do as you require."

"Excellent." Princess Elizabeth permitted herself a tiny smile. "Tonight, you will keep vigil in the chapel and seek God's forgiveness for making false accusations against an innocent maid. For not trusting the woman you had sworn to marry. For believing the words of others over the words of one devoted to you."

The king covered her hand with his. "I think he understands, my dear," he murmured.

The princess looked as though she would have liked to continue berating Thomas for quite a bit longer, but she deferred to her betrothed. She settled for a final fierce glance at top of his miserable head and finished her instructions. "You will not rest this night, is that understood, my lord? And in the morning, you will return here to this hall prepared to marry, without protest, whichever daughter of his house Lord Ashley has chosen for you."

"I will do as you say, your highness."

Thomas bowed over his knee, rose, and exited, stiff as an old man, escorted by the Duke of Surrey. I did not envy him the long night ahead of him, but neither could I pity him. Every minute of soul-searching on the chilly stone of the chapel was earned and deserved.

* * *

I followed my aunt and cousins out of the hall after the king and princess
departed, preparing sharp words for my uncle if he thought to offer me to
the faithless Thomas in Grace's stead. My thoughts bent on that purpose,
I did not see Benedict walk up to my side until he touched my arm.
"Come away, Beatrice," he said.

I stepped aside with him in the hall, as it was empty of courtiers now
that the display of Thomas' punishment was over. I glanced over my
shoulder to make sure that my family left and did not return to seek me
out, watching as he shut the door behind them.

He grinned as he returned, holding his hands out for mine. "Well, this
is a change. Will you now come when I call you?"

I lifted my brows at him. "Oh, indeed, and depart when you bid me."

He took my hands, kissing one then the other. "Stay but till then."

I tipped my head. "'Then' is spoken, and so I must go." I pulled my
hands free of his and made as if to walk away, then, at his stricken look,
relented and went back, throwing my arms around his neck and pressing
myself against him. "I was so afraid for you," I whispered in his ear, and his
hands tightened around my waist, sliding up and down my back, pulling
me close...and then pushing me away.

"Beatrice," he said, and I could hear the hurt and anger in his voice.
"How could you agree to marry—that man?"

I placed both my hands on his chest and pushed back at him. "How
could you believe that I would agree? How can you not see that I had no
more to say about marrying him than Grace did in not marrying Thomas?
When a man uses words as weapons, women fall in battles we do not even
know we are fighting."

Sparks flared in the depths of his eyes. "What words? What did he
say?" He gripped my arms, giving me a little shake. "Beatrice, what did
he do?"

I pulled my arms free of his hands and took a handful of steps back.
"Do not make yourself into what you despise," I said. "I am unharmed by
him, and there is naught for you to do, no vengeance to be sought. I would
never have married him in any case."

"Would never..." He grinned, and my bones turned to water. "For
which of my bad parts did you first fall in love with me?"

I fought back sudden tears. I did not have to watch him fight today,
Grace was redeemed, Lord John was seen for the villain he was. I could
banter with him again. "For all of them together, of course." I kneaded an
imaginary ball of dough in my hands. "They are so closely bound up that

they will not admit any good part to intermingle with them, so, alack, what could I do?" I took a step closer, then another, and lay my palm against his cheek. "But for which of my good parts do you suffer love for me?"

"Oh, aye, 'suffer love,' a fine epithet! I do suffer love, for I love you against my will." But his eyes, gleaming, gave the lie to his words.

"In spite of your heart, I think," I said, placing my free hand against his chest. I could feel nothing through the thick padding of his suit, and I wondered if his heart was racing as fast as mine was. "Poor heart," I whispered, leaning close, letting my breath tease his lips. "If you will spite it for my sake, I will spite it for yours, for I will never love that which my friend hates."

He dropped his mouth to mine, his hand coming up to the back of my head. Fire shot through me and I pressed my body close, closer...until the bite of metal into my skin reminded me of where we were. Anyone—a servant, a guard, or, heaven forbid, my-lady-the-king's-vigilant-mother—could come upon us at any moment.

I pulled away again and staggered back. He ran a hand through his hair and collected himself. I tried to do the same.

"How do you, Beatrice? Truly?" he asked.

With all that had happened, my feelings rode impossible waves, up and down, with every moment. I was wrung out like a damp, twisted bedsheet. I needed sleep.

"I know not."

He took a step forward, reaching for me, then fisted his hand, reminding himself not to touch. I felt the same. How long could this go on? Hope rose, fluttering in my belly. Would he perhaps speak to my uncle, at last? "Have no fear," he said. "All will be well."

"Do you think so? I cannot believe it."

He nodded. "Serve God, love me, and mend. All will be well."

* * *

We agreed we should part, him to divest of his armor, me to find my uncle and find out what he intended, since he clearly knew something about the princess' plan. I did not find my family anywhere I expected to, however. Not in my uncle's study or in the rooms he had taken for his own while the king was using his, or in the rooms Aunt Ursula was staying in, or even my cousins in the old nursery.

I decided to go back to the room reserved for me and wait until someone found me.

The door was shut, which was odd, since I knew I had left it open.

I opened the door, and the room was not empty, which was also odd since it was, since Grace's departure, my room alone.

There was a person on the bed, sitting with knees drawn up, arms wrapped around legs, chin on knees, looking at the door, waiting for me.

Grace was waiting for me.

Slamming the door shut behind me, I flew across the room and embraced her.

"You're back," I said, and kept repeating it. "You're back."

"I am," she said, holding me close. "Thanks to you."

"How? Wherefore? It cannot be."

"Oh indeed! Father said that as soon as Lord John claimed your honor had been compromised and demanded your hand in marriage, he knew some evil was afoot. He went to the king with his suspicions, and it seems they spent last night endeavoring to uncover it."

I went weak with relief and dropped my head to the bed. She was here, she knew all. But... I lifted my head. "But you know that though I may not have been compromised by Lord John, I am no innocent."

"Beatrice," she said, her eyes sparkling with good humor, "do you think you are the only one?"

"Grace!" I exclaimed, and we laughed and hugged again.

Like a candle blazing to life, I realized what her presence here meant. "Grace! You are the cousin! You are the unknown woman Thomas will marry tomorrow!"

Her cheeks pinked and she grinned at me.

I leaned back against the wall and hugged a pillow to my chest. "But after all that happened? After how he treated you? Grace, how can you?"

She sobered and leaned against the wall beside me, resting her head against my shoulder. "I had time to think about it at the convent. Nothing but time. It may have been only one day, but it felt like a lifetime." She shuddered. "If I've learned anything from this, it is that I do not want to be a nun. I know that I want a life. A life with a husband and children, a life of joy and laughter and quiet moments by the fire with a family and friends."

"You could have those even if you do not accept Thomas."

I felt her smile against my shoulder. "But I love Thomas. His lack of trust in me was...unfortunate, but I do believe he has learned his lesson."

She sat up to look me in the eyes. "Beatrice, one thing the nuns make you contemplate is forgiveness. What is forgiveness, what can be forgiven and what should be forgiven? Our Lord forgives all sins, and we must strive to do the same. And when I view the situation through Thomas' eyes, I understand what he must have felt. How it must have looked to him. Thus, I don't blame him for what he felt."

I could not forgive him so easily. "But his actions were abominable!"

"Yes, he behaved badly, but he nearly paid with his life for it, and tonight he is contemplating a marriage to one of my cousins. A woman he does not know and does not love. It might even be you." She jabbed a sharp finger into my ribs, and we laughed.

"That would be a lifelong punishment for him indeed!"

"Indeed. So, you see, he is suffering too. And I know that he has suffered in my absence, for he did love me, Beatrice. He does love me."

I could not disagree with her on that score. "Indeed. That he does."

CHAPTER 17

As the bells tolled the ninth hour, I led a line of young women into the chapel where, once again, guests awaited. We were all dressed the same in pale blue dresses, like that which Grace had worn on the fateful day, with linen gloves on our hands and veils to obscure our faces. To disguise Grace's presence among us, we had dressed up some of the serving girls as well, so a crowd of a dozen of us streamed down the aisle. There were fewer guests this time, as the king and princess had decreed that their courtiers stay away, so it was just our family on one side and on the other, the royal couple, the duke and Benedict behind them. And of course, Thomas, at the altar with the royal chaplain, staring back at us in disbelief.

Thomas, watching us create a line in front of the altar, said hesitantly, "My lord, I was under the impression that you had but three nieces."

Uncle Lionel turned upon him and snapped, "Oh, you have such intimate knowledge of my family now? These are the unmarried women of my house. Do you dispute me?"

The duke stepped between them, holding up his hands in a placating gesture. "Your pardon, sir. He meant no offence, to you or to the ladies."

With a sound suspiciously like a bull's snort, my uncle stumped up the altar step to Thomas. "Are you yet determined to marry with a daughter of my house?"

Thomas looked as though he might be sick, right there in the chapel.

However, he placed his hand over his heart and bowed to Uncle Lionel. "I hold to my word. I will marry the woman you have chosen." His gaze swept over our many veiled faces as though he could peer through and see the women beneath. "Which is the lady I must seize upon?"

Goodness. *"Seize upon."* Could he not have used some gentler word?

As we had planned, we all started moving about like cards in a game of Find the Lady until at last Grace went to her father and placed her hand on his outstretched arm. Uncle Lionel said, "This is she, and I do give her to you, and as her husband, one day, all that is mine shall be yours." Taking Grace's hand in his, he extended it toward Thomas.

Thomas swallowed hard and reached for her. "Then I do accept her from you, most humbly."

Better, I thought.

Grace placed her gloved hand in his and stepped up beside him. Uncle Lionel made his way back to the family. Thomas forced a smile. "Sweet lady," he said, raising a hand toward her veil, "let me see your face."

"No!" Uncle Lionel boomed. "Not until you swear before this priest that you will marry her, no matter who she is, no matter what lies beneath."

The priest raised his voice, speaking both to my uncle and to the assembled company. "I did watch through the night while Lord Keighton kept his vigil here in this chapel. Your majesty, your highness, Lord and Lady Ashley, I do believe in his sincere contrition for his part in the suffering of this family and the lady Grace."

"Nevertheless," Uncle Lionel growled. "He will swear."

Thomas glanced at him, then at the priest, then at the princess. He knelt, taking both of Grace's hands in his. "My lady, I swear to you before this priest and in this company, I am your husband, through whate'er may come, until death do part us. And more, I swear I will never doubt you on the word of others but will trust in your good heart."

The veil moved as Grace sighed, and she raised her hand to pull the fine fabric from her head, letting it drop to the floor of the chapel. As recognition dawned, Thomas' mouth fell open and his eyes lit up.

"At last," she whispered. "For though your vow is delayed, I have never been other than your true and faithful wife."

Thomas sprang to his feet, staring at her from arm's length as if he couldn't believe she was real. "Grace," he whispered. "It is you."

"It is me," she said.

He pulled her to him, wrapping his arms around her waist and lifting her off the floor. She squealed in surprise and delight as he spun her in giddy circles, both of them laughing. She laced her fingers through his hair and slid down him as he slowed.

"I am so sorry," he whispered. "I know you were never unfaithful. I was a fool."

She gazed down at him with tears in her eyes. "Yes, you were. But I forgive you." She leaned down, her mouth close to his, until the chaplain coughed twice and they seemed to realize they were not, in fact, alone. Thomas set her down and they turned to face the altar, his arm around her waist, as though he could not bear to be separated from her for even an instant. Their joy at being reunited was almost painful to watch. It pinched my heart even as I was happy for them.

"But," the duke stammered, "I thought she was in the convent." He turned to my uncle. "I thought she had taken vows!"

"That story was only needed whilst slander stalked her," Uncle Lionel replied. His tone suggested that while Grace might have forgiven Thomas, it would be some time before he forgave the duke for his part in her shame.

The priest cleared his throat again. "Might we, mayhap, proceed with the wedding?"

"Hold, father, if you will, and wait a moment longer." Benedict's voice rang out in the chapel, echoing from the high ceiling. Everyone turned to look at him, and he flushed deep red but did not flinch. Rather, he stepped away from the bench and into the aisle. "Holy father, I must entreat your help this day, I think."

Was his voice shaking? By heaven, my hands were.

The priest looked puzzled. "To do what, Sir Edmund?"

Benedict laughed, an uneasy sound. "To bind me, or to undo me. One of them." He glanced at my uncle. "My lord Lionel, your niece regards me with an eye of favor."

I could not keep silent. The gasp burst out of me before I could stop it, and he looked in my direction but could not seem to make out which of us women had reacted.

My uncle smirked. "That eye my daughter and her mother lent her, I should say."

Benedict frowned but continued, "And I do with an eye of love requite her."

Chuckling, Uncle Lionel replied, "The sight of which you have from myself, Lord Thomas, and the duke. But what is your will in this regard?"

Benedict tilted his head. "Your answers are enigmatical, my lord, and I do not understand. Nevertheless, my will is to obtain your good will and to be joined this day..." He paused to swallow hard. "...in the honorable state of marriage with your niece Beatrice."

My knees well and truly deserted me then, and I swayed against my cousin Eleanor. She could not hold me and collapsed against the serving girl next to her. That girl, Alice, strengthened by years of hauling firewood up and down stairs, shoved us both back up. Meanwhile, at the other end of the line, my cousin Mary collapsed too, causing a commotion there to create, I suppose, the impression that she, not I, might be Beatrice.

My uncle, a smug smile on his face, pivoted on his good leg to face the line of women. He did not know which of us was which any more than Benedict did, and his gaze swept over us. "Marriage with my niece," he said, his voice full of satisfaction. He angled his head back toward Benedict. "You realize, of course, that with my daughter Grace's return, she is no longer my heir, only her father's."

Benedict's lips quirked. "Her inheritance was never what interested me, my lord."

"A just and proper answer, sir," Uncle Lionel replied. "You may have my niece's hand, if she will give it you."

Benedict bowed his head then looked at us, his gaze lingering on each veiled woman in turn. I could see him dismissing some of the women at once. Alice was too sturdy, Margaret too short, to be me, but he truly could not tell. At last he blurted out, "Which is Beatrice?"

My heart raced, my blood throbbed in my veins with the word marriage. I could not seem to move, or breathe, or think properly. I was glad for Eleanor's arms around my waist, lest I stumble again or do something equally foolish. Such as removing my veil.

The silence that greeted his question stretched and lengthened, grew painful. The other women started looking at each other and whispering, nudging with elbows and gesturing with hands. Mary hissed down the line: "Beatrice!"

Eleanor, in her usual way, said, "I think our cousin is unabashed by being so publicly reposed."

I could not help it. I laughed, and in so doing, I exposed myself. I pulled the veil from my head and bunched it in my hands. "I answer to that name." My voice was weak as a newborn kitten's mew, and I tried to swallow though my mouth was painfully dry. Eleanor gave me a gentle push forward and the other women pushed me along the line until I was standing in the aisle, a long stride away from him.

I forced myself to look at him for the first time since entering the chapel. He wore a dark green doublet, for certes his best color, and the sleeves were slashed to show deep red underneath—my best color. White lace cuffs spread over his hands where they rested on his hips, and a matching collar spread beneath his chin, still clean shaven. But all of this could have been forgotten, he could have been wearing the padding for underneath his armor for all I cared, because all I saw—all I wanted to see —were his eyes, warm cinnamon with a hint of gold. In them, I saw the friend of my youth and the love of my life, but also the fear of this public display, of asking without knowing.

I saw the fear, because I felt it too.

He held his hand out. "Come," he said, "let us marry."

I reeled back inwardly. So abrupt? No declarations? I glanced at Thomas and Grace, so full of joy and love even in company... "What? No."

Whispers, even a gasp or two. I hated the confusion and pain I caused to appear in his eyes, but he was not, after all this time, going to take my assent for granted.

His eyes upon me were dark wells of emotion. He gritted his teeth and asked, "Do you not love me?"

"No, no more than long friendship requires."

He glanced away, unreadable emotions flickering on his face. He drew and released a deep breath. Pointing with a stiff arm, he said, "In that case, your uncle Lord Ashley and my friends Lord Keighton and the Duke of Surrey were much deceived, because they did swear that you did love me." His use of their formal titles was for the others in the room. The message was clear to me. It was my words and actions that had led him to believe it.

I lifted my chin. "Do you not love me, then, to ask my uncle for permission to marry me?"

He smirked, dismissing the thought. "No, no more than friendship requires."

Like a target at a mark. I remembered he described that feeling in response to my words. Now I knew what it felt like.

"Well, in that case, my Aunt Ursula and my cousin Grace are very much deceived because they did avow that you did love me." I had Grace's letter explaining these conversations, but he did not. Even so, in that moment, it mattered not *why* they had said it, only that they had.

He took a step toward me. "They swore you were near sick with love for me!"

I took a step toward him. "They swore you were well-nigh dead for me!"

As one, we stepped closer. Another step and we would embrace. My hands were rising of their own accord, my body leaning in, my lips yearning, and he as well...

Someone pushed a bench, wood scraping on stone.

We halted.

"As you see, I am well," he said. "Then you do not love me?"

Now, with everyone watching, with what they had just seen, how could I answer? *Of course not? Don't be silly?* I hesitated for too long.

"I shall answer for her," Grace said, stepping down from the altar, her feet seeming to float above the floor in her joy. "She does love him. Here is proof in her own hand, a letter written to me but days ago confessing her love of Sir Edmund Benedict." She waved a small, folded parchment in the air above her head.

Perfidious friend!

I snatched at it and she danced away. Though I am taller and stronger than she, she whipped it out of my reach by spinning away and ducking back into the arms of Lord Thomas, who had followed her down from the altar. Laughing, he took the letter and tucked it within his doublet. "And I will swear that he loves her as well, for I have here in my possession a halting sonnet fashioned to Beatrice, which I may say was not up to the task of expressing the contents of his heart..."

"Oh, fie!" Benedict objected. "I shall call you out again, my lord!"

"In truth?" Thomas asked. "To rhyme 'lady' with 'baby'?"

Benedict subsided. "Yes, well, I was not born under a rhyming planet." Turning to me, he said, "What say you, lady? Here we stand, condemned by our own hands against our very hearts." He heaved a theatrical sigh and said, "Come, I will marry you, but by this hand, I take you only out of pity to keep you from pining away."

While everyone around us laughed and talked and enjoyed our embarrassment, Benedict took my hands in his. Fingers twined, we clung to each other. "We are too wise to woo peaceably," he murmured, his forehead but a hair's breadth from mine, "but if you will have me, I will love you so long as I have strength in my body."

I drew a shuddering breath. "I would not want a peaceful love or a witless husband." I noted that the chapel had grown quiet, and I raised my voice, squeezing his hands so he would know I was speaking more to them than to him.

"I would not deny you, but I yield upon great persuasion, for I did believe you were in a consumption and like to die."

"Indeed," he said, his eyes sparkling with humor. Leaning down, he kissed me gently. We were in a church, after all, and in front of my aunt and uncle.

Mary whooped, the princess applauded, and the priest harrumphed his displeasure. "After the wedding, if you please," Uncle Lionel said, but he was beaming, not scolding. He offered me his arm to escort me up to the altar. Dazed, I went with him and stood beside Grace. We would both marry this day!

The Duke of Surrey came forth from his bench and put his hands upon Benedict's shoulders to force him toward the altar. "I believe I shall stand beside you both, to ensure the wedding goes forth this time," he said. Steering Benedict to stand beside me, he winked at me. I blushed to think of how we had flirted at the masked ball. "How fares Sir Edmund Benedict, the married man? Have we a good horse for hire now?" he asked as Benedict took my hand.

"You may laugh if you wish, my lord," he replied, not taking his attention from me. "A college of wit-crackers and joke-makers will not flout me out of my happiness." He raised my hand to his lips, his gaze locked on mine, the touch sending a thrill down my arm and through my body. "Since I do intend to marry, I care not what the world may say against it, nor do not repeat to me what I may have said against it, for man is a giddy thing, and this is my conclusion."

The duke nodded, smiling, and stepped back to stand by the altar rail. Thomas leaned in to murmur in Benedict's ear, "Glad I am that we have come to this, rather than come to blows on the field yesterday."

Benedict grinned at him. "And I too, for I had thought to have beaten you. But since we are now to be kinsmen, live unbruised and love my cousin."

The priest fixed us all with a stern look. "Is there to be a wedding today or no?"

I glanced at Benedict, and he at me. Now that we were sure of each other, must we hurry? Did I want to marry in my cousin's dress on her day in the selfsame moment?

Red was a more becoming color for me, to match and complement the green my betrothed wore...

"Let us dance," I said.

"We shall have dancing after," Uncle Lionel protested.

"Nay, now," I said, and Benedict said, "My lady wants to dance!"

The priest shook his head. "This is most improper."

I tugged at Benedict's hand. "Come, we shall step aside and let Lord Thomas and Lady Grace have their wedding, then we shall dance after, as my uncle says." I kissed Benedict's cheek, mindful of priest and chapel. "I have all I want in the world, and I may wait until another day for my wedding."

"Another day? Another wedding?" Aunt Ursula sounded delighted by the prospect.

I grinned at her. "Mayhap tomorrow?"

THE END

Thank you for reading! Did you enjoy?

Please Add Your Review! And don't miss more of Shakespeare's Women Speak from Maryanne Fantalis coming soon!

Until then, turn the page for a sneak peek of EVERYTHING BUT THE EARL by City Owl Author, Willa Ramsey.

SNEAK PEEK OF EVERYTHING BUT THE EARL

Was there any greater satisfaction than the satisfaction of a party gone wonderfully well?

Miss Caroline Crispin didn't think so. Or if there was, she hadn't found it just yet.

She lifted her foot from the cool tile of the entry hall, curling her toes discreetly. She'd been on her feet nearly a whole day by then, and her soles were telling the tale. But as she recalled the sea of ruddy cheeks rolling across her parents' grand ballroom, the echoes of wildly stomping feet, and the sweet, summertime heaviness in the air, she smiled. The sleepy, achy, sated ending to a ball was always her favorite part.

It was nearing dawn, but rest could wait.

Lords Strayeth and Chumsley were next in the queue to make their goodbyes to her, each of them puffing out their chests as if they'd just discovered a new continent in the retiring room.

"My lords," she began in a low voice, returning their smirks. "Did everything meet with your approval this evening? Was the conversation stimulating? Were the ladies' bodices...stimulating?"

"Indeed," Chumsley replied, his mouth a tight line. He was short but sturdy-looking, with white-blond hair and striking blue eyes that some had compared to the waters of the West Indies. "Lovely evening, Miss Crispin."

She shifted from one sore foot to the other. *When had these gentlemen become so...straitlaced?* Certainly, it was racy to talk this way. But she'd danced and flirted with them at countless social events since her seventeenth birthday, four years earlier. She had even kissed Strayeth once, at a public ball, behind what was perhaps the largest potted ficus in all of England.

"The conversation and the bodices were just to our liking," Strayeth added, his eyes fixed elsewhere in the crowd. He was the lankier and more fashionable of the pair, with a floppy brown forelock he had to constantly shake back from his eyes.

"Both were rather deep then, I imagine?" she asked, trying to egg them on.

She no longer sought attention from men their age, really. They were beginning to look for wives, and the very thought of marrying sent a shiver all through her. She'd watched her mother toil silently beside her father her whole life; had seen her design the grand home in which they now gathered but give Papa all the credit; had heard her cry quietly in the studio when she thought everyone had gone to bed. Caro knew a husband of her own would expect her to leave her ideas unsaid, too; to give up her charitable schemes. And her ideas and schemes were like wildflowers: They were exuberant, plentiful, and deeply resistant to the forces of domestication.

But she *so* enjoyed a bit of good repartee! Couldn't she jest with these gentlemen anymore? They had been friends of a sort, once.

"Thank you, Miss Crispin," Strayeth replied, bowing and nudging Chumsley toward the door. "Your abilities as a hostess are...most remarkable."

They hadn't stepped more than a few feet away, however, when Chumsley leaned over and murmured something in his friend's ear. She wasn't certain, but it sounded a bit like, "*Even my pointer has learned to shake hands.*"

Now she was confused. And a little bit unsettled. But just as she was resolving to speak less of bosoms and bodices, a loud *clang* sounded from the ballroom followed by several whoops and whistles.

"*Lud,*" Caro said to herself, looking at the ceiling. "I asked Mr. McNabbins not to juggle the serving bowls anymore. His new assistant is hardly a proficient."

Grinning now, Strayeth and Chumsley made a quick bow and trotted off toward the ballroom, in the direction of the clattering dishware (and in all likelihood, her guests from the Sadler's Wells theater). She was confronted at once by another departing guest, a stooped older man in an unfashionable powdered wig.

"Where is your father?" Lord Tilbeth demanded, his mottled complexion growing pinker by the second. "I had but one moment's conversation with him all evening."

"He's in the studio, my lord." She rubbed her temple, glancing behind him at the long queue of guests that still extended through the spacious entry hall and into the ballroom beyond, all waiting to speak with her. "You know how it is."

He looked at her blankly.

"You see, when a person is in trade, he often has to *work*. Rather hard. Sometimes even at night."

"But your father is the Prince Regent's favorite architect! Look at all of these...these *people*!" he fumed, gesturing at the assortment of aristocrats and merchants, entertainers and artists, professors and cabinet ministers, all drooping sleepily behind him. "Half of London wants him to build their next home or some such! The least he could do is make himself available."

"They're like fighters, my lord."

"I beg your pardon?"

"Champions must stay in top form, Lord Tilbeth! Other architects are waiting just outside the ropes, so to speak, eager to take my parents' place."

He scrunched up his face—possibly upon hearing the word "parents" when most people would expect to hear "father"—but just then his wife emerged from a group of ladies standing nearby. She gave Caro a curt nod, the feathers in her turban bobbing haughtily behind her. Then she tugged her husband forward with a lurch, through the open door, and into the earliest glimmers of dawn.

Caro turned back to her guests and was delighted to find her dearest friend awaiting her next.

"It always amuses me," Edie whispered as they shared a firm embrace, "to watch the Tilbeths pretend to have fun at your balls."

"They fear they'll break into hives if they accidentally rub elbows with a shopkeeper," she replied, her laugh fluttering Edie's straw-colored hair. "Heaven help them if they ever bump into my butcher. He never misses my parties."

She stepped back and watched as Edie bent down to pick up an enormous basket at her feet, its contents obscured by a piece of white linen.

"Dearest! What are you doing?" Caro asked.

"It's your apples. I thought I'd bring them to the orphanage for you. Well done, Caro. Wherever did you get the idea to ask everyone to harvest the ornamental trees in their gardens? This might be your cleverest scheme yet."

Just one basket? From three hundred guests? This was a disappointing result, indeed. "I suspect all the credit goes to a half-dozen servants," she replied over a sigh, "as they were the ones who did the harvesting."

"Actually, my brother picked all our apples," Edie replied, looking into her basket. "Although he had to steal them, I believe—"

"Edie!" Caro exclaimed, cuffing her lightly on the shoulder. "Your own brother is here, and you haven't introduced me?"

Edie cuffed her back, bobbling her basket a little. They'd spent many a year together at Mrs. Hellkirk's Seminary for Wayward and Willful Girls, and had taken rather well to the unusual set of manners taught there. Like fish to water.

"I'm not his keeper," Edie replied as she adjusted her heavy load. She nodded toward the ballroom. "He's the big one."

Caro whipped her head around and looked.

And then she looked some more.

That was Edie's brother?

"Thank you for a lovely time," Edie told her.

Caro had long been curious about Edie's mysterious older sibling. He wasn't a recluse, she'd explained, just a determined homebody with a preference for the country. Caro strained on her tiptoes, angling for a better look.

"I'm putting on my bonnet now," Edie added, waving a hand in front of her face. "And my cape. And sword."

Caro knew that Edie's brother—Adam Wexley, the Earl of Ryland—had some notoriety as a fighter. Everyone did. But in school Edie had described him as "oafish" and "insufferable." Caro had been left to imagine a lumbering, pasty sort of man. Weak-chinned, and prone to sneering at independent-minded ladies.

"And I'm taking your apples, Caro. I'm going to throw them into the River Thames, and dance a jig along the bank."

But Lord Ryland appeared to defy Caro's low expectations. He was standing rather far away from her, but she could see that he was indeed exceptionally tall and broad-shouldered. His hair was very dark—was it black?—and seemed shorter than most men were wont to wear it. Caro couldn't make out any other details, but one thing was certain: Lord Ryland was striking. Even from the next room.

And his chin seemed perfectly fine.

Caro settled back on her heels and pulled her friend close.

"Edie."

"She speaks."

"*Edie!*"

A gentleman farther back in the queue cleared his throat, and Caro knew she must hurry things along.

"Yes?"

"Nothing. Nothing of any consequence," Caro replied as she leaned in for a one-armed embrace. "Give my regards to your mother. I do hope she feels better soon! And put down that basket, Lady Edith Wexley! It looks heavy. I can manage it."

"Honestly, Caro," Edie replied, smiling as three or four apples tumbled from the basket as Caro took it. "If you're going to conduct all these schemes of yours, you're going to have to accept a hand every now and again."

* * *

Adam was struggling.

Struggling against the urge to let out a cracking-good laugh.

He was standing with one of the foremost Italian opera singers, and the poor soul was enduring a small torture of his own: that of having to pick apple peel from his lower front teeth.

"Does an Englishman always bring such gifts to a party?" the baritone asked, giving up on the remains of his first pilfered apple and moving on to a second, greener one.

Adam was accustomed to being the deepest-voiced person in a room, but he could swear he'd seen the candelabras tremble in the presence of the bushy-bearded performer's low and sonorous authority.

"No," he replied. "We're not often asked to bring a hostess something we've found on the ground."

The singer bowed and headed to the refreshments, so Adam was free to step into the loose queue of people waiting to leave the party. He wondered where his sister Edie had gotten off to, and lamented being torn away from the novel he'd begun earlier that day.

He glanced around the ballroom. *Criminy!* The view into Crispins' back garden was unbelievable. The ceiling soared, and the windows were positively enormous. The room must be bathed in sunlight all day long. Now he understood why the crème of society had lined up to kiss the hand of Mr. Crispin's only daughter and hostess: the architect's talents were extraordinary, and his home showed it. No wonder everyone admired him.

What would Father say, if he could see the state of his own beloved townhouse?

He rubbed hard at his forehead, trying to banish the unflattering thought.

Father wouldn't have neglected the place. And he wouldn't have allowed Edie to run about without an escort. And Mother wouldn't be recovering from a terrible injury.

The couple in front of him stepped forward a few paces, giving him a better view into the entrance hall. And for the first time Miss Caroline Crispin was in his view, too. He'd never seen the hostess before, but he could tell it was her by the way all of the heads in the vicinity oriented themselves toward her—watching her, hoping for a moment of her notice.

He could hardly blame them.

Edie had mentioned that her friend was confident and outspoken. Brash, even. She'd told him that she admired the architect's daughter for the quickness of her mind and tongue, her bottomless generosity; her relentless pursuit of the things she wanted to accomplish.

What his sister wouldn't have known, of course, was that such levels of confidence, when combined with an already-pretty countenance, tended to render a woman stunning. Unforgettable, even.

And Miss Caroline Crispin already had a pretty countenance.

Her hair was a dark brown—that was all Adam could tell of it, from a distance—and perhaps it was strange, but the next thing that struck him was her posture. She was of average height, but she carried herself more naturally than was fashionable. She gestured expressively with long, gloved arms, nodding and swaying, deep in debate with the gentleman standing before her.

The lucky devil.

Whomp—a man's hand landed hard between his shoulder blades, sending him forward a full step.

"Ryland, old man! When did you get here? Been hiding out in the hinterlands again, pruning those pretty little flowers of yours?"

Adam swallowed a frown and made a quick bow. "Strayeth, Chumsley. I arrived in town last week, actually." *I'm just very good at avoiding you.*

They hadn't changed a bit. Clearly. He'd met them at his club some years earlier, when they'd been drinking hard and wagering over something awful—an upcoming cock fight, perhaps? He hadn't wanted to know the details.

Strayeth grabbed and squeezed his shoulder, then gave him a light shake. "We need to get you brawling again, Ryland. Don't we, Chum?"

Adam's heart began tapping a little harder at his ribs. Father had often squeezed him on the shoulder, whenever Adam asked to stop sparring; when he craved the serenity of his small garden—the roses he could never get enough of, the shaded bench he could read on for hours. Father had been firm with him as a boy, but never rough; as if by placing a big, still hand on his shoulder he could infuse in him the drive not only to fight, but to win, and the mental fortitude to train for it. It never worked, though. Adam could not find the first of those traits within himself, though he could—and did—force himself to continue doing whatever Father had asked of him.

Adam both missed and dreaded that hand on his shoulder—and the memory of it—all at once.

"I have no plans to return to the ring," he replied as he wiped a bead of sweat from his brow.

"What, now? You wouldn't want to break the Ryland tradition, would you? Your father was a fine man, they say."

"The very best," Adam replied.

"Then why not honor him?" Strayeth continued, letting go of his shoulder and poking him instead, deep in the recess of his collarbone. "Besides, you can't break the Duke of Portson's arm and nose then retire to a life in the country, Ryland. Tell him, Chum."

Adam took a deep breath as the heat in his skin ticked up still further. He *so* hated to be poked and prodded. "Right now, gentlemen," he replied finally, turning back toward the entry hall for another look at Miss Crispin. "I'd just like to shake hands with our fair hostess and get back to the comforts of my own home."

"Who?" Strayeth asked. "Caro?"

Adam winced at the use of the young woman's given name.

"You know the lady?" he asked.

"Is that what we're calling the opinionated young miss from Marylebone these days?" Chumsley asked, looking at Strayeth with a snort. "That honor is conferred a bit too broadly, is it not?"

Now Adam had had enough. He could only assume that they disdained Miss Crispin on account of her birth, and his patience for their arrogance had been worn to a husk. "Do watch yourself, both of you!" he growled, snapping back to them. "You are guests in this home!"

Strayeth took a step back, his chuckle bloating rapidly into a full-throated laugh. "Oh ho ho, Ryland! Didn't realize you were such a friend of the lower orders! Want to take it outside, then? Is this how we finally get you brawling again?" He put up his fists and took a fighting stance, biting his lip and punching the air in front of Adam's face.

Adam closed his eyes and leaned away from the jabs, regretting his angry outburst. He opened his eyes and bid them farewell, exited the ballroom, and gestured to a footman for his hat and cane.

He knew it was terrible manners to leave without a proper farewell, but he'd become rather adept at withdrawing from the world, at avoiding obligations whenever it was convenient for him. So with his accoutrements in hand, he strode briskly down a darkened corridor toward the rear of the house, where he expected there would be a servants' staircase of some kind.

But as the voices faded behind him, he stopped. *No. Not this time.* He rapped his cane on the floor and recalled Father's dying words: *Be a gentleman, Adam. A true man. Always.*

He'd been just fifteen years old when he'd heard them, and they'd gone with him everywhere, ever since.

He might never forgive himself for abandoning the family's boxing legacy, but he could begin fulfilling other duties: He could fix the townhouse. He could better protect his family. He could step up his efforts to find a wife and get an heir. And he could stop avoiding people. Or at least, do so a little less often.

He was about to turn back when a familiar voice called out, "Ryland? A word?"

He turned to find an old schoolmate, Lord Quillen, approaching with Miss Crispin on his arm.

How does a person laugh without really laughing? Because that's what Miss Crispin seemed to be doing, her eyes the color of tea left out in the afternoon sun. And then she smiled at him, those strong-brew eyes growing wide—unnaturally wide, he thought—as if they could absorb all the light from the nearly extinguished candles along the walls.

It was an expression that seemed to say: *Finally, something exciting is going to happen.*

"Our hostess just informed me that if I didn't introduce her to the gentleman sneaking away from her party," Quillen began, "that I'd find myself seated between two Tilbeths at all future card parties." He gave an exaggerated grimace and performed the introductions.

"I beg your pardon, Miss Crispin," Adam began, pulling at the bottom edge of his coat. Why did his throat feel so dry? *Say your piece, Ryland. Look stern. Exit through door.* "But my mother is quite—"

"You cannot blame this on your mother," she interrupted.

He stilled. "I beg your pardon?"

"Your mother's injury *cannot* be the reason you're skulking through our portrait gallery, my lord! I saw Lady Ryland just yesterday, and she felt *so* well that she sang me the latest from Schubert. Loudly, and with feeling." Her lips twisted into a wry sort of expression, raising the hair on his forearms in tandem.

You were in my house just yesterday, and I missed it? Clearly, I haven't worked nearly hard enough at being a homebody.

Quillen glanced back and forth between them, a bemused expression stretching slowly across his face. Then he bid them farewell and headed back toward the entry hall. Adam was now quite alone with Miss Crispin, about a hundred feet from the nearest guests and servants.

"Do not vex yourself, Lord Ryland. I'm not going to check your pockets for silver," she continued, adjusting the tops of her gloves. "Your sister warned me about these peculiar manners of yours."

"She warned me about you, as well," he replied in a rush, straightening and re-straightening his shoulders.

"Did she, now?" Miss Crispin opened her fan with an exaggerated *crack*, fanning herself theatrically. "And what did my dear Edie say about me, my lord? I'm all anticipation."

"She said that you are—what was the word?" He stepped closer. He wasn't sure what had come over him, but all thoughts of leaving seemed to have evaporated.

"*Brash*, I believe. Edie said you were brash."

"Ah, yes. An American word. A good word."

"An apt word?"

"Most certainly."

He found himself eager to impress Miss Crispin, to keep her eyes on him, to keep her talking. He scratched at the hair above his ear. "She also told me you had a quick mind," he said softly, leaning down. He was now only a foot or so away from her.

"Oh, *stop*," she replied. "I'm blushing now."

"And a quick tongue."

And with that, the loquacious Miss Crispin went quiet, her loose posture suddenly quite still.

He stepped back. *Too bold, Ryland. Too bold by half!* He feared he'd offended her, though she continued to smile and look him straight in the eye. "And you clearly have little sympathy for gentlemen who feel entitled to sneak away from your party," he continued, more warily now. "Rightfully so, I might add. I must apologize."

"Ah, yes," she responded, her limbs suddenly fluid and easy again. She fanned herself some more. "What *is* it with you modern gentlemen, and your prodigious sense of entitlement? If only I could make a fuel from it, no one in London would so much as shiver, all winter long."

He laughed aloud—he couldn't help it—but she spoke again before he could think of a riposte.

"You are free to go, Lord Ryland. In return for your rather generous donation of apples this evening, I give you leave. *Sneak away.*" Then she curtsied and turned, heading back to her guests in the entry hall.

As he bowed and watched her go, he felt utterly strange. On the one hand, their exchange had been a burst of pleasure he hadn't realized he'd been needing. Disappointment at the brevity of it coursed through him.

But he also knew that parting ways with Miss Crispin was for the best. He might not be well-practiced at moving in society, but even he knew better than to flirt unguardedly with a lady unless he intended to court her.

But then, what if he *did* intend to court Miss Crispin? He wanted to marry. His family wasn't concerned about her birth, and seemed to admire her for more than her impressive position in society. And couldn't everyone benefit from a few more bursts of pleasure in their lives?

Perhaps finding a wife would be one duty he could attempt with some ease.

* * *

"Toby, you're a true prince! Just don't tell ol' Prinny that I said it," Caro told the dog as they descended the stairs to the ground floor. She wanted to take him on a sunrise constitutional now that the last of her guests had departed, but they needed to see the housekeeper first. So she brought the beloved mongrel—half-bulldog, half-terrier—to a secluded nook off the entry hall where she could drop into a small chair and wait. Toby sank obediently to the floor, his foot landing hard on her slipper.

"You've a head like a small anvil," she cooed, leaning down and massaging his velvety ears. He yawned back at her. "And a mouth like a small lion."

A soft knock sounded on the wall. The tiny space was little more than a wrinkle at the edge of the room—the snuggest of snuggeries—and had a narrow opening that wasn't visible when looked at straight-on. "Miss Crispin, you wanted to see me?" asked Mrs. Meary in her familiar lilt.

"Yes!" Caro replied, holding out a sack of coins. "May I give you this now?"

"For splittin' amongst everyone, Miss?"

"That would be lovely, thank you. The evening went off so beautifully. And would you ask Stinson to take this beast on his walk?" Caro handed her the dog's leash. "I thought I could manage it, but I'm not sure I could keep pace this morning, after all."

As Mrs. Meary led Toby away, Caro leaned back and lifted her skirts, giving her feet a much-needed rubbing. She smiled at an assortment of pleasant memories from the ball: The pungent smell of the garden when the windows were opened at midnight. The shouting of witty parries over jubilant music. The refreshing tang of the lemonade after an especially brisk waltz.

And what about that exchange with Lord Ryland? *Lud!* Where was the oaf Edie had promised? The mythic fighter? He'd been positively timid with her—apologetic, even.

Perhaps he was simply good at play-acting. His words had eventually turned salacious, after all, and when her pulse had begun jumping and dancing in her veins she'd figured it must be her conscience, reminding her not to flirt with men of marrying age. She resolved, now, to make conversation that was a bit less personal—and not about bosoms or bodices—in future.

The sound of heavy boots clomping on the entry-hall tile roused her from her reverie. *Who could possibly still be in the house?* She stood up and brushed at her skirts but didn't move fast enough; she was still out of sight when two gentlemen started speaking.

"All right, then. I will see you later on."

Chumsley.

"Right, Chum. At White's, per usual."

And Strayeth, of course. Perhaps they expected Barclay to come forward with their hats and canes? They wouldn't know that the butler was already busy with the myriad extra tasks that awaited him after a ball. It was just like them to linger after giving their farewells, to claim the last of Cook's delicacies and have a laugh about the nude portraits and sculptures throughout the home.

"I don't understand it," Chumsley sighed.

"What is it, man?"

"I *do* understand that everyone is quite desperate to put Crispin to work for them. But there's got to be another way, without having to bow down to his whore daughter all of the time."

She felt as if she'd been kicked in the chest by a horse. She exploded with pain and dropped into her chair with a *shoosh*.

Strayeth cackled in response, a loud *crack* suggesting that he also slapped himself rather hard on the thigh.

"I cannot be the only gentleman who finds it tedious to have to keep pretending that she's respectable!" Chumsley went on. "Who on Earth does she think she is, with all that talk of bodices?"

"I don't know," Strayeth replied through his laughter. "Someone who hasn't realized that a lady doesn't speak of bare bosoms? But she's always been quite the coquette, Chum. You know that."

"True enough," Chumsley said, sounding exasperated. "It's as if a common whore has all of society wrapped around her little finger. I saw her with a bishop earlier, Stray. Do you suppose she spoke to *him* of stockings and petticoats?"

More laughter.

Caro burned behind the eyes, her chest still throbbing.

"She claims she doesn't want to marry, but it's just another one of her jokes, I'm sure," Chumsley went on. "Anyone can see she's set on marrying well. Can you imagine, Stray? Honestly, it's embarrassing."

The other lord snorted his agreement. "I make it a rule that once a woman's been compromised by three of the men in my circle, I no longer dance with her."

Compromised? Caro sat up again, suppressing a snort of her own. *What in Heaven's name are they referring to? That I've kissed a few men over the years?*

And three? She looked down at her fingers and did some quick accounting.

Fair enough. Three it was. Possibly four, depending on how one looked at things.

"Pish!" Chumsley continued. "I wouldn't hand that woman into a carriage!"

More laughter.

"She might not be suitable for proper courting," he went on. "But she might be useful for other...purposes."

His voice softened, and seemed to be moving closer to the nook. Caro stopped moving. Every bone, breath, and sinew, every hair and nail and thought and fiber—all of her stood as still and cool as a new headstone, gone fresh into the ground.

"I've long suspected she was mine for the taking," Strayeth whispered, his voice a low rasp. "She flutters over to me whenever I enter a room. And she sometimes puts a hand on my sleeve!"

"Pish! *You?* You've a gift when it comes to the debutantes, Strayeth. But while you've been worshiping at the finer doorsteps in town, I've entered into many an enjoyable apprenticeship with the daughters of shopkeepers and newspapermen."

"And what about the daughters of builders?"

"They might as well be next in my education."

More laughter.

Really, it was the snickering that sickened Caro most of all.

"Well then, Strayeth. We seem to be at odds on the issue. Perhaps we can make it a wager?"

"Always! What did you have in mind?"

"Let's do it this way: whichever of us gets under Miss Crispin's petticoats by the end of the season, wins."

"And what coin are you willing to put on it?"

Chumsley paused a moment. "The losing gentleman shall pay the other one hundred pounds."

Caro heard the hollow *clap* of two hands coming together, and knew they were shaking on it. The dull *click* of the front door soon followed, together with the familiar rattling of frames against the walls. At these sounds, she slid from her chair—and into a large urn—before hitting the floor, a pile of limbs and fabrics and shards of fine porcelain. Tears of mortification plummeted down her cheeks.

* * *

Don't stop now. Keep reading with your copy of EVERYTHING BUT THE EARL by City Owl Author, Willa Ramsey available now.

Don't miss more of Shakespeare's Women Speak from Maryanne Fantalis coming soon! Until then, try EVERYTHING BUT THE EARL by City Owl Author, Willa Ramsey.

* * *

Miss Caroline Crispin is on top of the world. But she's about to take a painful fall.

As the daughter of London's most in-demand architect, Caro has laughed and danced and pursued her interests with gusto—free from Society's censure. So when she overhears two lords calling her vulgar names and wagering on whose lover she'll become, she's shocked and stung—and determined to teach them a lesson. Though it pains her to ask for help from another brutish lord...

Lord Ryland isn't the man his father wanted him to be. But he's about to make an excellent catch.

Adam, Earl Ryland, just wants to get married and tend his country garden, away from the bucks, fops, and gossips who pester him to box like his late father. When this gentle giant meets his sister's friend Caro—who parries his flirtations with double entendre that would make a barman blush—he's smitten. But there's a problem: she's looking to him for a different sort of partnership. And it's a risky one.

* * *

Please sign up for the City Owl Press newsletter for chances to win special subscriber-only contests and giveaways as well as receiving information on upcoming releases and special excerpts.

All reviews are **welcome** and **appreciated**. Please consider leaving one on your favorite social media and book buying sites.

For books in the world of romance and speculative fiction that embody Innovation, Creativity, and Affordability, check out City Owl Press at www.cityowlpress.com.

AUTHOR'S NOTE

This book is a work of fiction. Most of the characters were invented by William Shakespeare in the late 1500s for his play *Much Ado About Nothing*, which he set in southern Italy. I took his characters and further altered them. Lady Beatrice Welles, Sir Edmund Benedict, the Duke of Surrey, Lord Lionel Ashley and his family: none of these people existed.

However.

King Henry VII was a real person and became the king of England by conquest when his army defeated King Richard III's at the Battle of Bosworth in August of 1485. Prior to that battle, Henry had spent most of his life in exile from England, living in France and Brittany. Elizabeth Plantagenet, the princess who would become his wife, was also real, the daughter of King Richard's older brother, King Edward IV. King Henry's mother, now commonly known by her birth name Lady Margaret Beaufort, was also a real person, who did, in fact, insist that everyone call her "my lady the king's mother."

I couldn't resist adding them to this novel for several reasons.

First, there was the question of Henry and Elizabeth's relationship. Henry swore that he would marry her, without having met her, on Christmas Day of 1483, long before he and his army defeated King Richard. After the battle, Elizabeth went to live with his mother while he settled in as king for several months. He wanted to establish his reign without people saying he was only king because he'd married her, the daughter of a "rightful" king, not a conquering foreigner.

The Wars of the Roses didn't just end when Henry VII took the throne. If you have questions, there are lots of books you can read to decide who the "rightful" king was at any point in time from like 1400 to 1500.

Anyway.

Henry and Elizabeth were married on January 18, 1486. Their first child, Arthur, was born in September, apparently a healthy, full term infant although he was reported to have been born (surprise!) a month early. Based on Arthur's early arrival, many historians speculate that Henry and Elizabeth were sexually active prior to their wedding day.

As I considered how to adapt *Much Ado About Nothing*, which contains at its heart the destruction of a woman's reputation based on an unfounded accusation of a premarital affair, the idea that Henry and Elizabeth were sleeping together before marriage took root early on. That their behavior might have set an example for the men and women around them, creating an atmosphere in which others might be tempted to stray... with devastating consequences. I combined that compelling idea with the fact that Henry traveled to his mother's estate in Woking at the beginning of September 1485. It took only a little invention to create a fictional stop-off to visit supporters at Ashley House, and the perfect – purely speculative – environment for Grace's betrayal was set.

Also, Lady Margaret Beaufort seems like she must have been a miserable person to be around – controlling, in-your-face pious, ambitious to a fault. For example, she insisted on choosing everything for Prince Arthur's nursery, when everyone knows a big part of a mother's joy is getting ready for her new baby. The thought of Beatrice's disrespectful mockery of "my lady the king's mother," if only behind her hand, amused me. And, I think, it would have endeared her to Princess Elizabeth, who must have been one of the most tolerant and even-tempered women who ever lived to put up with that woman.

If you are interested in learning more about King Henry and Princess Elizabeth, who are the parents of King Henry VIII and grandparents of Queen Elizabeth I, I would suggest starting with the following books: *Winter King: the Dawn of Tudor England* by Thomas Penn and *Elizabeth of York* by Alison Weir. Welcome to my obsession.

ACKNOWLEDGMENTS

This book was dragged out of me kicking and screaming. They talk about the sophomore slump, and I can assure you, it is a real thing. I could not have finished this novel without my writing group: without the knowledge that, at least once a week, I had to show up and write something, dammit. Trudy, Jack, Kenji (and Lisa, in spirit), you were this book's babysitters. You provided the care-taking, the support, the encouragement without which I could not have weathered the challenges of writing in the shadow of publication.

Thank you to Jack Dreyer, Jessie Gussman, and Courtney McKinney-Whitaker for being my first readers. Jack, your careful reading pushes me to think carefully about what I'm trying to accomplish with every one of my words. Jessie, thank you for reminding me that this is Benedict's story as well as Beatrice's. Courtney, you told me what I needed to hear when I needed to hear it; you embodied the niggling voice in my head and forced me to make the big change I already knew needed to be made.

Thank you to the City Owl author family. I love how this crew has always got each other's backs. This journey would not be nearly as much fun without you as my traveling companions. Meeting so many of you at RWA in New York this year and spending time with you at the retreat was priceless, and I will cherish those memories always. Special thanks to brilliant, compassionate Willa for always supporting me and being there when I'm angry, frustrated, or lost. And Negeen, I never imagined that when we met, I'd find a true soul sister. Your generosity, vivacity, and determination astound me.

The City Owl publishing team were, as always, amazing to work with. Tina and Yelena, your tireless work made City Owl a presence at RWA 2019, and then you gave us the gift of time and togetherness at the retreat. You understand what we need because you are writers and creators too. Also, to my new editor, Tee, thank you for your wonderful insights and assistance in polishing this difficult manuscript. I couldn't ask for a more supportive, professional publisher than City Owl Press.

Thank you to the young person in Cindy Matthews' Language Arts class who asked me what the title of my next book was and offered her suggestion – *Loving Beatrice* – which was exactly what I had been toying with for months. So, young woman, thank you for giving me the push to follow my instinct. I wish I had thought to ask your name. I hope someday you'll see *Loving Beatrice* and recognize your contribution.

Finally, my family. Special thanks are owed to my kids this time around.

First, to Newt, who chose to do their Study Abroad semester in London last year, which meant that I had a perfect excuse to go back to England. In addition to our adventures in town, we spent an unforgettable, if rainy, day in Shakespeare's hometown of Stratford-Upon-Avon. The emotions I felt upon being in the same places as he had, 400 years later, were overwhelming. Thank you, Newt, for sharing that pilgrimage with me.

Second, Jake. I am so proud of the courage you've displayed in the last year and the way you've grown. I am envious of your adventures in the world and I know they will be a great foundation for all that comes next. Also, thank you for the ice cream. I don't know how I would have survived your senior year – or this manuscript – without Sweet Cow.

Finally, and always, gratitude and love to my husband Jeff, whose spirit breathes in all my heroes (and who gave Benedict his coppery beard). I couldn't do any of this without you.

ABOUT THE AUTHOR

MARYANNE FANTALIS lives in the foothills of the Rocky Mountains with her husband and two kids, and it's the only place outside of England she'd ever want to live. Her fiction combines her two favorite subjects – medieval England and Shakespeare's plays – and she'll talk your ear off about either of them if given the opportunity. In addition to writing novels, Maryanne teaches writing at the University of Colorado at Boulder. Look for her in one of her favorite spots: playing in a racing mountain stream, browsing at the local public library, or getting inspired at the Colorado Shakespeare Festival.

© Cedric Pereira Photography

mfantaliswrites.wordpress.com

facebook.com/mfantaliswrites

twitter.com/mfantaliswrites

ABOUT THE PUBLISHER

City Owl Press is a cutting edge indie publishing company, bringing the world of romance and speculative fiction to discerning readers.

www.cityowlpress.com